AMERICAN HUMORISTS SERIES

LIFE AND SAYINGS

OF MRS. PARTINGTON

BENJAMIN P. SHILLABER

LITERATURE HOUSE / GREGG PRESS

Republished in 1969 by

LITERATURE HOUSE

an imprint of The Gregg Press

121 Pleasant Avenue

Upper Saddle River, N. J. 07458

97471

Standard Book Number—8398-1858-0

Library of Congress Card—79-91092

Printed in United States of America

FRANKLIN COUNTY LIBRARY

THE AMERICAN HUMORISTS

Art Buchwald, Bob Hope, Red Skelton, S. J. Perelman, and their like may serve as reminders that the "cheerful irreverence" which W. D. Howells, two generations ago, noted as a dominant characteristic of the American people has not been smothered in the passage of time. In 1960 a prominent Russian literary journal called our comic books "an infectious disease." Both in Russia and at home, Mark Twain is still the best-loved American writer; and Mickey Mouse continues to be adored in areas as remote as the hinterland of Taiwan. But there was a time when the mirthmakers of the United States were a more important element in the gross national product of entertainment than they are today. In 1888, the British critic Grant Allen gravely informed the readers of the *Fortnightly*: "Embryo Mark Twains grow in Illinois on every bush, and the raw material of *Innocents Abroad* resounds nightly, like the voice of the derringer, through every saloon in Iowa and Montana." And a half-century earlier the English reviewers of our books of humor had confidently asserted them to be "the one distinctly original product of the American mind"—"an indigenous home growth." Scholars are today in agreement that humor was one of the first vital forces in making American literature an original entity rather than a colonial adjunct of European culture.

The American Humorists Series represents an effort to display both the intrinsic qualities of the national heritage of native prose humor and the course of its development. The books are facsimile reproductions of original editions hard to come by—some of them expensive collector's items. The series includes examples of the early infiltration of the autochthonous into the stream of jocosity and satire inherited from Europe but concentrates on representative products of the outstanding practitioners. Of these the earliest in point of time are the exemplars of the Yankee "Down East" school, which began to flourish in the 1830's—and, later, provided the cartoonist Thomas Nast with the idea for Uncle Sam, the national personality in striped pants. The series follows with the chief humorists who first used the Old Southwest as setting. They were the founders of the so-called frontier humor.

The remarkable burgeoning of the genre during the Civil War period is well illustrated in the books by David R. Locke, "Bill Arp," and others who accompanied Mark Twain on the way to fame in the jesters' bandwagon. There is a volume devoted to Abraham Lincoln as jokesmith and spinner of tall tales. The wits and satirists of the Gilded Age, the Gay Nineties, and the first years of the present century round out the sequence. Included also are several works which mark the rise of Negro humor, the sort that made the minstrel show the first original contribution of the United States to the world's show business.

The value of the series to library collections in the field of American literature is obvious. And since the subjects treated in these books, often with surprising realism, are intimately involved with the political and social scene, and the Civil War, and above all possess sectional characteristics, the series is also of immense value to the historian. Moreover, quite a few of the volumes carry illustrations by the ablest cartoonists of their day, a matter of interest to the student of the graphic arts. And, finally, it should not be overlooked that the specimens of Negro humor offer more tangible evidence of the fixed stereotyping of the Afro-American mentality than do the slave narratives or the abolitionist and sociological treatises.

The American Humorists Series shows clearly that a hundred years ago the jesters had pretty well settled upon the topics that their countrymen were going to laugh at in the future—from the Washington merry-go-round to the pranks of local hillbillies. And as for the tactics of provoking the laugh, these old masters long since have demonstrated the art of titillating the risibilities. There is at times mirth of the highbrow variety in their pages: neat repartee, literary parody, Attic salt, and devastating irony. High seriousness of purpose often underlies their fun, for many of them wrote with the conviction that a column of humor was more effective than a page of editorials in bringing about reform or combating entrenched prejudices. All of the time-honored devices of the lowbrow comedians also abound: not only the sober-faced exaggeration of the tall tale, outrageous punning, and grotesque spelling, but a boisterous Homeric joy in the rough-and-tumble. There may be more beneath the surface, however, for as one of their number, J. K. Bangs, once remarked, these old humorists developed "the exuberance of feeling and a resentment of restraint that have helped to make us the free and independent people that we are." The native humor is indubitably American, for it is infused with the customs, associations, convictions, and tastes of the American people.

PROFESSOR CLARENCE GOHDES
Duke University
Durham, North Carolina

January, 1969

BENJAMIN PENHALLOW SHILLABER

Benjamin Shillaber ("Mrs. Partington"), poet, newspaperman, and humorist, was born in Portsmouth, New Hampshire, in 1814. After elementary school, he was apprenticed to a printer. Then followed a position with Tuttle & Weeks, publishers of the "Peter Parley" sketches and Whittier's anti-slavery poems. Next he was a journeyman printer, a trade which he was forced to abandon because of poor health. After a trip to the tropics to recuperate, he went to Boston, married Ann Tappan de Rochemont, and was hired by the Boston *Post*. In 1847, Shillaber began to contribute "Mrs. Partington" anecdotes to this paper. To his astonishment, he soon found himself famous, and the obscure and ill-paid journalist was able to devote his full energies to "reporting" the comical adventures, awful malapropisms, and folksy wisdom of his Yankee widow. In 1850 Shillaber became Editor of the *Pathfinder and Railway Guide*, but resigned the next year to found the *Carpet Bag*, a humorous weekly. This short-lived publication counted "Artemus Ward," "John Phoenix," John T. Trowbridge, and Elizabeth Akers among its contributors. Samuel Clemens anonymously published his first piece, "The Dandy Frightening the Squatter," in the May 1, 1852, issue. After the demise of the *Carpet Bag*, Shillaber went back to the *Post*, then worked for the *Saturday Evening Gazette* for ten years. Shortly before his retirement, he made the obligatory lecture tour. He died in 1890.

The first edition of *The Life and Sayings of Mrs. Partington* sold about 30,000 copies shortly after its publication in 1854. The second sold about 10,000. "Mrs. Partington" is probably the foremost female character in the history of early American humor. It is believed that Mark Twain used her as the model for "Aunt Polly" in *Tom Sawyer*, which was published two years after Shillaber's work. Mrs. Partington has a benevolent, occasionally picturesque comment ready for subjects as diverse as "our relations with Mexico" ("The Mexicans had better not trouble any of our relations, I can tell 'em!"), mistreatment of slaves in the South ("I know a poor old colored man here in Boston that they treat jest like a nigger."), Dickens' novels, "Swedenvirgins," and babies. Her clever country nephew, who tortures cats and drops lighted firecrackers in people's pockets, also brought laughter to thousands, and an endless list of malapropisms such as "Vociferous" for Vesuvius and "denouncement" for denouement add to the general hilarity. *The Life and Sayings* was followed by more of the same in *Partington Patchwork* (1872). Shillaber also wrote comic verse.

Upper Saddle River, N. J.   F. C. S.
May, 1969

RUTH PARTINGTON

LIFE AND SAYINGS

OF

MRS. PARTINGTON,

AND

OTHERS OF THE FAMILY.

EDITED BY

B. P. SHILLABER,

OF THE BOSTON POST.

"I did fynde her a woman of manye words, yet of a verie pleasaunte fancie withal, and havynge much good counselle." — DOCT. DIGG HIS WORKS: Lib. cxl.; Art. — "*Mistresse Unis Hyte.*"

NEW YORK:
J. C. DERBY, 8 PARK PLACE.
BOSTON:
PHILLIPS, SAMPSON AND COMPANY.
CINCINNATI: H. W. DERBY.
1854.

STEREOTYPED BY
HOBART & ROBBINS,
NEW ENGLAND TYPE AND STEREOTYPE FOUNDERY,
BOSTON.

PRINTED BY
JOHN A ·GRAY,
95 & 97 Cliff St.

TO THE

FRIENDS OF MRS. PARTINGTON,

WHOSE FAVOR HAS ENCOURAGED

THE OLD LADY

IN HER ECCENTRIC SAYINGS,

THIS VOLUME

IS "RESPECTIVELY" DEDICATED.

PREFATORY.

Mrs. Partington once declined an introduction to a party, because she did not wish to be introduced to any one she was not acquainted with. She needs no introduction now. In all parts of our own land, and over the sea, her name is familiar as a household word; and "as Mrs. Partington would say" forms a tributary clause to many a good story, or an apology for many a bad one; a smile attending the utterance of the name in evidence of its appreciation. But a preface, of course, is expected; and so, in the most gentle manner in the world, we will tell to you, reader, a little story about the origin of the Partington sayings, and why they were said, and why they are here collected. Perhaps you have guessed it all; but it is well to be certain.

In the first place, they were written, as the canine quadruped is said to have gone to church,

1*

for fun, — for the author's own amusement, —
with a latent hope, however, half indulged,
that the big world, which the author very much
loves and wishes to please, might see something
in them at which to smile. He was modest in
his hope, and hid himself behind an incognito,
impenetrable he thought, where he could see the
effect of his mild squibs upon the public. The
result pleased him, and he kept vigorously blazing away, unseen ! — as much so as the simple
bird that thrusts its head under a leaf and fancies
itself unobserved ! — until they have arisen to a
magnitude that some people might deem respectable.

The origin and object of the Partington " sayings " being thus described, the motive for their
collection shall be confessed. It is the hope that
their author may make a little money on them.
He is not so squeamish or pretending as to talk
of public good, and public amusement, as his
leading motives in the matter; but if these can be
obtained through the publication, he will be most
happy. The author confesses to certain pressing
contingencies — by no means peculiar to him,
however, among authors — that would be relieved
by a generous return for his outlay of time ; and
that his pouch may take a more silvery hue from

the circulation of his book, is a consummation devoutly, by him, to be wished.

This motive, so entirely original, for the publication of a book, the author has secured under the guarantee of his copy-right. There might be no necessity for this, where all the rest of the author tribe are writing and printing from higher motives; but he pleads selfishness, and, like the old lady in her variance with St. Paul, there is where he and they differ.

Some wiseacre has recently made a discovery, of what we have proclaimed from the outset, that the name of Mrs. Partington was not original with us — that Sydney Smith first gave it to the world. Most profound discoverer! But the *character* we claim as ours; and whether it had been embodied in Mrs. Smith, or Brown, instead of Mrs. Partington, would have been immaterial. Those sayings are *ours*, and we venture to affirm that Sydney Smith would not lay claim to them from the fact that they were uttered by one of the same name as his heroine of the mop. Because, forsooth, he had spoken of Mrs. Partington's sweeping back the Atlantic with her broom, would he claim the illustrious PAUL, and the roguish ISAAC, and the jocose ROGER, and the great PHI-LANTHROPOS, and the poetical WIDESWARTH, as his progeny ? We trow not, even though others might be found ready to do it for him.

The reputation of Mrs. Partington belongs to the Boston Post, as much as if Sydney Smith had never uttered the name in his great speech in Parliament.

The character has been drawn from life. The Mrs. Partington we have depicted is no fancy sketch, and no Malaprop imitation, as some have thought who saw in it naught but distorted words and queer sentences. We need no appeal to establish this fact. Mrs. Partington is seen everywhere, and as often without the specs and cap as with them.

There are many matters placed within the covers of this book that the sponsor of Mrs. Partington has written beneath the inspiration of her geniality, to the influence of which alone their merit, if they possess any, is to be attributed. Her portrait looks down upon him now as he writes, and her pleasant voice seems inwoven with the souchong smile it sheds, and seems to say,

"PRINT A BOOK."

CONTENTS.

X CONTENTS.

BIOGRAPHY

OF

MRS. PARTINGTON,

RELICT OF P. P., CORPORAL.

AUL PARTINGTON, whose name is immortalized by its association with that
of the universal MRS. PARTINGTON, a
portion of whose oracular sayings our
book comprises, was a lineal descend-
ant of Seek-the-Kingdom-continually
Partyngetonne, who came from the old
country, by water probably, somewhere
in the early days of our then not very extensive civilization. At that time, people were not in the habit of
putting everything into the papers, as they do now, when
the painting of a front door, or the setting of a pane of
glass, or the laying of an egg, is deemed of sufficient
consequence for a paragraph; much, therefore, of interest

2

concerning the early history of his family is merely
known by the faint light which tradition has thrown
upon it.

A story has come down to us from remote time,
through the oracular lips of the oldest inhabitants, that
" Seek-the-Kingdom-continually Partyngetonne " — ab-
breviated to Seek — was troubled in the old country by
certain unpleasant and often-occurring reminders of
indebtedness, yclept " bills," which were always, like a
summer night, falling due, and certain urgently-pressing
importunities, the which, added to a faith that was not
too popular, by any means, at last induced him to warily
scrape together such small means as he could, and
incontinently retire from metropolitan embarrassment to
the comparative quiet of an emigrant's life, where he
might encounter nothing more annoying than the howl-
ing of wolves, or the yelling of savages, — sweet music
both when contrasted with the horror comprised in the
words " PAY THAT BILL ! " which had long distressed
him.   Here the voice of the dunner was done, and Seek,
under his own vine and pine-tree, worshipped God and
cheated the Indians according to the dictates of his own
conscience and the custom of the times.

But little, however, can be gleaned of the early sup-
porters of the family name, save what we procure from
the ancient family record, a Dudley Leavitt's Almanac,
on which agricultural memoranda had been kept, and from

the memory of such members of a foregone generation as remembered the Partington mansion in Beanville, — of course before it was torn down to make way for the new Branch Railroad.

The "*new house*," as the mansion has been called for a century — (see the accompanying sketch, drawn on a piece of birch bark by a native artist) — to distinguish it from some *old* house that had at some previous time existed somewhere, was erected about the year ——, as is supposed, from the discovery of a receipted bill from Godffrey Pratt, for "Ayde in Rayse'g ye Nue Eddiffyce," which bears date as above, and likewise from the fact that a child was born to the erector of the new house the same year, which was duly chronicled in the ancient Bible, with other blessings, and the word "Howse" is distinctly to be traced among them.

It is supposed by some that the old house was upon a slight hill opposite the gentle acclivity upon which the new house stood, and fancied outlines of an ancient cellar are there discernible by those whose faith is large enough. But a younger class have set up another hypothesis : that what they suppose must have been a cellar, was in reality an apple-bin ; and there is no knowing when or how the point will be determined.

The new house was a stanch piece of work, erected at a time when men were honest, and infused much of their own character into the work they put together ; the beams of oak so sturdy, that Time, failing to make an impression upon them, gives up at last in despair. The interior of the mansion, in the latter day of its existence, contrasted gloomily with the modern houses, that sprang like mushrooms around it ; its oak panelling and thick doors imparted an idea of strength, and the huge beam overhead, beneath which a tall man could not stand erect in the low-studded room, showed no more signs of decay than if placed there a hundred years later. It was not destitute of ornament, for around the fireplace were perpetuated, in the everlastingness of Dutch crockery, numerous scriptural scenes, more creditable to the devotional spirit that conceived, than to the art (or artlessness) that executed, them. The house was intended as a garrison, and where the clapboards had chafed off were revealed the scarfed logs, denoting where the loop-holes

were, and the leaden bullets, still left there, which Paul
was wont to dig out with his knife, when a boy, and
make sinkers of for his fishing-lines. Many a story that
venerable house could tell of ancient warfare, of the
midnight attack and gallant defence; but it never told a
thing.

It was in this house that Paul Partington was born
and grew, amid all the luxuries that the town of Beanville afforded,—said town at that time consisting of five
houses and a barn.

In this house he was married,—the most momentous
act of his life, as through the hymeneal gate came upon
the world the dame whose name we are delighted to
honor. We find upon the fly-leaf of a treatise on
calcareous manures, yet sacredly treasured, the following
memorandum, in the corporal's own writing, significant
of the methodical habits of the man who shed, in after
life, as far as a corporal's warrant could do it, undying
glory upon his country :—Married this day, January
the 3, 1808, to Ruth Trotter, by Rev. Mr. Job Snarl.
Forty bushels of potatoes to Widow Green."

There is a blending of bliss and business in this entry
that strikes one at the first glance. The record of the
sale of the potatoes in the same paragraph announcing
his marriage to Ruth might signify to some that they
were held in equal regard. But we see the matter
differently. The purchase of Ruth and the sale of the
2*

potatoes were the two great events of that important 3d of January, and they naturally associated themselves. So you, madam, might associate the birth of your first-born — the most blissful moment of your life — with the miserable matter of the death of a lame duck, or the blowing down of a pig-sty.

Of the courtship that preceded that marriage we can say nothing, except what we have gleaned by accident from the old lady herself. In rebuking the want of sincerity of devotion now-a-days, on the part of lovers, she once spoke of a time when *some one* would ride a hard-trotting horse ten miles every night, and back, for the sake of sitting up with her. But no name was mentioned. When it is remembered that the ancient borough of Dog's Bondage was just ten miles from Beanville, it is easy enough to guess who the individual was.

Ruth Partington — born Trotter — came amid sub-lunar scenes several years before the nineteenth century commenced; consequently, she is older than 1800. She was a child, by law, for eighteen years before she became a woman, and performed the duties " incumbered " upon her, as we have been informed by her, with great fidelity. We have often endeavored, in fancy, to picture the Ruth of Dog's Bondage, in the check apron and homespun gown, by the brook engaged in washing; or, basket in hand, feeding the yellow corn to hungry ducks, emblematic of that throwing forth of gems that have since been scrambled for by admiring crowds; or seeking berries in the woods, crowned with wintergreen, as the meed of popular approbation surrounds her brow in the latter day of her existence ; or engaged in incipient benevolences — as binding up the broken limbs of barn-yard favorites, or protecting the songsters of the marsh from predatory boyhood — fitting fore-heralds of that matured benevolence which embraces the world in its scope : here speaking the consoling word, and there dispensing comfort, mingled with catnip tea. In fancy, we say; the check apron, homespun gown and all, are but the stuff that dreams are made of.

There are vague reminiscences of things that have past which we catch occasionally, when souchong has released the memory of Mrs. Partington from the overriding care for the world's welfare that would fain keep it home, and we roam back through scenes of her early life that breathe of rurality like a hay-field in June, or a barn-yard in the month of March. We have tales of apple-parings, and attendant scenes and suppers ; of huskings full of incident and red ears, and resonant with notes the sweet import of which Mrs. Partington can well tell; and jolly quiltings, great with tattle and tea, and moonlight walks home, with the laughter of mirth mingling with the song of the cricket in the hedge, or that of the monarch of the swamp singing his younglings to sleep in the distance, or the whippoorwill upon the bough ; and

stupendous candy pullings, with their customary consequences to broad shirt-collars and cheeks sweeter than
molasses; and slides down-hill on the ox-sled runners,
in winter, that the boys hauled up to the summit, disastrous at times to propriety and health, but full of a fun
that looked at no result but its own enjoyment — the
means a secondary consideration. And there gleams
through this a ray that reveals early loves and dreams
that had an existence for a time, to be swallowed up
eventually in admiration for that embodiment of war and
peace, Paul Partington, whose flaming eye and sword,
upon an ensanguined muster-field, won a regard that
only ended in Beanville, when the name of Trotter
became merged in that of Partington.

Tradition — which, in this instance, may be partly
right — tells of rivalry for the possession of the belle of
Dog's Bondage. We can conceive of rivalry among the
men, and envy among the women; of struggles on the
one part to gain her favor, on the other part the struggle to lose it by provoking her hostility. Hostility?
Herein might arise a question as to whether so gentle a
being ever entertained hostility to anything. We should
be false to our object — that of writing a true biography
of Mrs. Partington — did we pretend that she was perfect. We would take this pen and inkstand, as well as
they have served us in our need, and throw them in the
grate, before we would make any such assertion. But

we must say that we never heard she had an enemy, and Tradition — that grim old chap, that has so many bad things to say about people, and so few that are good — never said a word about it.   Doubtless many a rustic heart beat warm beneath a homespun coat of numberless years, and sighs redolent of feeling poured from beneath the rim of many an old bell-crowned hat of felt.   But the meteor came, — Paul swept the field, — the heart of Ruth surrendered with discretion, — and other people stood back.

Great was this for Dog's Bondage !   The sun rose on the brightest day of the year when it happened; the brook, that had frozen up previously, immediately thawed out; two robins were seen looking round for places to build their nests, thinking it was spring, so mild was it; the lilac buds almost "bursted" in their anxiety to notice the occasion; and old farmers, as they talked to one another across dividing fences, spoke most sagaciously about the extr'or'nary spell of weather.   As old Roger, Mrs. P.'s cousin, remarked, when he heard the circumstance, it was a wether very like a lamb.   But, as we were saying, —

Schools were not so common at that time as now, and as there was none nearer the Trotters than Huckleberry Lane, in the Upper Parish, and as there was a quarrel between the Upper and the Lower parishes, old Trotter, who belonged with the Lower, felt bound to stand by that section, — though he knew nothing about the quarrel, — and hence Ruth was kept at home to receive by the fireside the domestic accomplishments nowhere else to be learned, and drink in the oracular wisdom of the venerable Trotter, as it fell from his lips through the aroma of pigtail tobacco and hard cider.

Alas for Trotter! His day is done, his pipe is out, his cider has gone, and even Dog's Bondage has become a name obsolete among the places of the earth, that town rejoicing now in the more euphonious title of Clover Hill, probably from the fact of there not being a leaf of clover within seven miles of it.

And thou, Dame Trotter! — famous for pastry and poultry, beneath whose ready skill Thanksgiving became a carnival of fat things, whose memory yet lingers about the olden home, now in stranger hands, with the fragrance of innumerable virtues, like the spicy odor of many Christmas dinners, — thou, too, art gone, and Dog's Bondage may know thee no more forever! The Rev. Adoniram Smith, who preached her funeral sermon, drew largely upon the book of Proverbs for illustrations of her character, and said that better pumpkin pies, or a better exhibition of grace, he had never known any woman to make before.

A kind heart has characterized Mrs. Partington from her childhood up, displayed in many ways. Her benevolence got far in advance of her grammar in her early days, and in her sayings at times are detected certain inaccuracies that some people are inclined to laugh at; but if they will stop a little and see the yellow kernels of wisdom gleaming out through the thickly-surrounding verbiage, they will raise their hats in grateful respect for the bounty afforded.

The domestic history of Mrs. Partington requires a nice pen to portray it, so full was it of delicate beauty and delightful incident. Marriage meant something in old times. It was no holiday affair, donned like a garment, to be regarded as worthless when the fashion changed. It grew out of no sickly sentiment that had its existence in the yellow fever of a wretched romance, as unlike true life as a cabbage is to a rose; or the sere of autumn, — a more fitting simile, — to the vernal spring. It was a healthy, hearty, happy old institution in those days, was matrimony, and people jogged along together in the harness of its duties, as harmoniously as the right hand and the left, that help each other and yet don't seem to know it, so natural is the service rendered, — as if they were born to it. And as the right hand or the right eye sympathizes with the left, so did the twain thus united sympathize. Duty and affection leaned upon each other, and inseparably strove to make the home hearth cheerful. It became pleasure to carry the sweet drink to the thirsty man, in the field a-mowing; or to bear the basket of luncheon to the woods where the red-browed man was chopping wood for winter; or to patiently hold the light in the long winter evenings when the yokes were to be mended or the harness repaired. And it became pleasure when the goodman went to town to stow his pockets with something nice for the wife at home, — a new dress or a new apron, — the remembrance of whose face would come to him when away and hasten his departure back. It was that remembrance which prompted the mare into an urgent trot on the last mile home, — though *she* couldn't see the necessity for it, — and his eye looked brighter when he saw the cheerful face at the window, looking down the road, and shook his whip at it as it smiled at him, as much as to say, let me get near you, and —— and what? Ask the walls, and the bureau in the corner, and the buffet where the china was, or the milk-pans upon the dresser, what.

No jars occurred in a home that owned such a pair. Can the right hand quarrel with the left? Can the left eye cast severe glances upon the right? The home where a true marriage exists is blest, and the man who finds his domesticity cast in a mould such as we have described, may be called happy in the fullest sense of the blissful word.

It would have done all of us good to peep in upon fireside scenes at the Partington mansion. The fireplace, with its wide and hospitable arms extended, looked

like an incentive to population, having family capacity
revealed in its huge dimensions.   It was a brave idea
of Seek Partyngetonne, and when he laid the corner-
stone of the Beanville structure he had visions of a
posterity as numerous as the leaves of the sweet-briar
bush that waved by his door.   Alas ! how were those
visions verified, as a few generations saw the line of Seek
diminishing, to find its end, at last, like the snap of a
whip-lash, in one little knot.

But those scenes !   It was the custom of the corporal,
in the long nights of winter, to seat himself in the right
corner of the old fire-place, while the dame occupied the
other, and read, by the light of a mutton tallow candle,
such literature as the house afforded.   This was comprised in the family Bible, an old and massive volume
that adorned the black bureau under the glass ; a copy
of army tactics, presented to Paul by a revolutionary
soldier ; and a copy of Dudley Leavitt's Almanac.
These were read, by the light of mutton fat, aloud, while
Mrs. Partington pursued her knitting in the corner,
nodding at times, perhaps, as the theme was dull or
familiar ; but the smile always rewarded Paul's effort to
amuse her, as much as if he had n't read the same things
over and over a thousand times.   The small, covered
earthen pitcher kept time to his reading often, and sung
and sputtered upon the coals between the old-fashioned
dog andirons, as if a spirit were within struggling to
3

throw off the cover that restrained it and escape. Regularly, as the hand of the old bull's-eye watch on the nail over the mantel-piece denoted the hour of nine, was the book laid by, and the mug taken from the fire and its steaming contents poured into the white earthen bowl upon the table, which sent up a vapor that rolled upon the dark walls like a fragrant cloud, and made the room redolent with the fume of the "mulled cider" that smoothed the pillow of Paul.

It was pleasant, too, to have a neighbor come in at times and spend an evening, when the big dish of apples would be brought on, and the sparkling cider, that snapped and foamed, in an ambition to be drank, crowned the board. And then such stories as would be told of " breakings out," and "great trainings," and " immense gunnings," in which exploits were achieved that my veracious pen would hardly dare recall! And the old Indian wars would be fought again by the light of tradition and the above-named tallow candle ; and the tales be retold of revolutionary valor that signalized itself in '76. Perhaps a song would be sung commemorating old times, in the quaint melody that knew no artistic skill beyond nature's teaching.

Mrs. Partington, as the presiding genius of these scenes, shed the radiance of her presence over the circle, as the sunflower claims eminence in a garden of marigolds. Her sage voice was heard in wise counsel; and in giving the news of who was sick, or dead, or about to be married, or was n't about to be married, but ought to be, she was at home.

The time we speak of was near the close of Paul's career, before the sad military reverse took place which broke his heart. It would be impossible, in the small space allotted us, to describe all the virtues of Mrs. Partington. It were best to make an aggregate of good, and call it all hers. The herbs that adorned the garret walls in innumerable paper bags, were not gathered for herself; the balm-of-gilead buds and rum, that occupied their position in the buffet, were not prepared for her; but at the first note of distress from a neighbor her aid was ever ready. She was the first who was sent for on important occasions, when goodwives must be wakened from their beds at midnight; and to this day half the population at Beanville speak of the benevolent face that bent over them in the first moments of their struggle with existence, and gave them a better impression of life than after-experience verified; and catnip tea and saffron became palatable when commended by a spoon held by her. She knew the age of every one in the village, and, had politicians not rendered the word hackneyed, we would say she had the "antecedents" of every one at her fingers' ends. She was as good as an almanac for chronological dates; and in the matter of historical incidents

Dudley Leavitt and Mrs. P. generally came out neck-and-neck.

She had a great reverence for this same almanac, and we cannot refrain from speaking of an incident in connection with it. She put implicit faith in its predictions, and the weather-table stood like a guide-board to direct her on her meteorological march through the year. One year, however, everything went wrong. Storms took place that were not mentioned, and those mentioned never occurred. The moon's phases were all out of joint, and the good dame sat up all one cold night to watch for an advertised eclipse that did n't come off. For a long time she tried to vindicate her favorite, but at last, when a "windy day" predicted proved as mild a one as ever the sun shone on, her faith wavered, to be entirely over-thrown by a cold north-easterly storm that had been set down for "pleasant." A timely discovery, that Ike had put a last year's almanac instead of the true one, alone saved the credit of that mathematical standard of natural law.

Her domestic virtues were of the most exalted kind. Cleanliness was with her a habit, and every windy day was sure to see Paul's regimentals upon a clothes-line, in the yard, dancing away with a levity altogether at variance with the rules of military propriety. A spider never dared to obtrude his presence upon the homestead ; a moth never corrupted the sanctuary of woollen that her care and a little camphor had touched.   The white floor of the Partingtonian kitchen was as full of knots as a map of New Hampshire is of hills, from frequent scourings, and, though she never scoured through and fell into the cellar, like the Dutch damsel we read of, it did not seem at all improbable that such an event might happen.

But her benevolence was the crowning characteristic of her life, developing itself in a thousand and more ways.   It sought to make every one around her happy. She commenced taking snuff with an eye solely to its social tendencies, and her box was a continual offering to friendship.   When the " last war " broke out, she headed a volunteer list of patriotic women to make shirts for the soldiers, and gave them encouragement and souchong tea to work for the brave men that were exposing themselves to peril; and she scraped Paul's only linen shirt — an heir-loom, by the way, in the family — up into lint for the wounded soldiers.   A fitting spouse was she for Corporal Paul.   Her reputation for benevolence was spread all over the land, like butter upon a hot Johnnycake of her own baking, and her currant-wine for the sick got a premium for three successive years in the cattle fair.

Alas that we have not room to pursue the theme further!   We must take a flying leap over many incidents and hasten on.

3*

When Paul's younger brother, Peter — the Peter that
went "out West," in his youth, whose wife joined the
Mormons — died, he sent his little Isaac to the care of

the widow of Paul, and from his earliest infancy he has
been her care. She never had any children of her own,
and her solicitude is earnestly engaged for him. He is
as merry a boy as you will find any day, and, though a
little tricky and mischievous, the first beginning of malice
does n't abide with him. His tricks do not flow from
any *premeditation* of fun even; they spring spontane-
ously and naturally, as the lambs skip or the birds sing

Whether he takes the bellows' nose for a cannon, or saws off the acorn on the tall, old-fashioned chair for a top, it is all a matter of course, and his bright face knows no cloud when rebuked for what he has done, but he turns to new mischiefs with new zest. Such is Ike. He is now eleven years, just upon the dividing line between accountability and indulgence, — beyond which boyish mischief becomes malice, to be trained by the magic of a leather strap.

Professor Wideswarth, a member of the Partington family — like a "remarkable case" in the paper — of long standing, has associated the two in a poem, which for sublimity is surpassed by Coleridge's Hymn in the Valley of Chamouni; but then they are nothing alike, and parties may divide on their respective merits. One thing about the song, — it is authentic in its details, as we have heard averred by the old lady herself. The music, set to a rocking-chair movement, was very popular when it was first issued, and the editor of the Blaze, in a complimentary notice of it, said no musical library could be perfect without it. The poem we give below : —

MRS. PARTINGTON AT TEA.

Good Mistress P.

Sat sipping her tea,

Sipping it, sipping it, Isaac and she ;

What though the wind blew fiercely around,
And the rain on the pane gave a comfortless sound ;
    Little cared she,
    Kind Mistress P.,
As Isaac and she sat sipping their tea.

    And in memory
    What sights did she see,
As Isaac and she sat sipping their tea !
She turned her gaze to the opposite wall,
Where hung the portrait of Corporal Paul ;
    And fancies free,
    To Mistress P.,
Arose in her mind like the steam of the tea.

    And little saw she,
    Blind Mistress P.,
As silently she sat sipping her tea,
With her eyes on the wall and her mind away,
That Isaac was taking that time to play ;
    And wicked was he
    To Mistress P.,
As dreamily she sat sipping her tea.

    For Isaac he,
    In diablerie,
Emptied her rappee into her tea ;
And the old dame tasted and tasted on,
Till she thought, good soul, that her taste was gone,
    For the souchong tea
    And the strong rappee
Sorely puzzled the palate of Mistress P.

> This moral, you see,
>
> Is drawn from the tea
>
> That Isaac had ruined for Mistress P
>
> Forever will mix in the cup of our joy
>
> The dark rappee of sorrow's alloy,
>
> And none are free,
>
> Any more than she,
>
> From annoying alloys that mix with their tea.

We have spoken before of the Partington mansion having been removed to make way for the Beanville railroad. It was taken after Paul's demise. He never would have parted with it thus. He would have fortified it and defended it while a charge of powder remained in the old powder-horn that hung above the mantel-piece, or a billet of wood was left to hurl at assailants! But, alas! Paul was not there; and his amiable relict opposed but feeble resistance to the encroachment of the new power. As she herself forcibly expressed it, "What was the use of her trying to go agin a railroad?"

It was hard for her to give up the old mansion, endeared by so many recollections, — not a thousand, merely, the number usually given as the poetical limit, but infinite in number, for they embraced all of the days of her wedded happiness, and the companionship of the corporal.

This sketch of the life of Mrs. Partington would be imperfect were we to omit giving a brief notice of the

picture of the inestimable lady that stands as our frontispiece. We have long felt that an admiring public
deserved a more definitive expression of her than could be
gained from the mere words, however wise, that fell from
her oracular lips. A sense of justice to her innumerable
merits has impelled us to redeem her from the uncer-
tainty of mere verbal delineation, and here we have produced her, the fair ideal of wise simplicity.

It was with great difficulty that we secured this boon
for the world. A modest diffidence, that fifty-seven
winters have not weakened, made her unwilling that her
likeness should be thus submitted to the unsparing gaze
of thousands. In vain we urged many illustrious examples of like martyrdom, — of men, who, from pure philanthropy, had sacrificed themselves in the everlasting
reproach of stereotype, from the never-souring " Old
Jacob " to the meek " Elder-Berry," blessing the world
with disinterested benevolence at a dollar a quart bottle,
six bottles for five dollars. She was not to be moved by
any argument we could offer, and we were about to
abandon the idea in despair, when the strategy of Isaac
effected what diplomacy had failed to accomplish. Snugly
ensconced in an old clothes-press, by Isaac, for three
days, our artist was enabled through the key-hole to
watch the varied expression that flitted across her time-
worn face, and his genius achieved its high triumph at
the moment when Paine's gas had become the concen-

trated object of her thought, and, oblivious to all external scene and circumstance, her mind was grappling that huge problem, in a vain effort to get a little light upon the subject.

This is the precise moment at which the artist has taken her — impaled her, so to speak, in view of its correctness, on his pencil point, and transferred her, still quick with life, to the breathing — paper.

The faithfulness of this picture cannot be too much admired. We have, at a glance, the whole character of the old lady, in her blessed " liniments," with a benignity, like a cup of Sleeper's best ningyong, irradiating every feature. The cap-border crowns like a halo the brow, upon whose lofty height benevolence sits enthroned ; the lock of gray vibrates tremulously in the wintry air ; the specs repose tranquilly in the abstractedness of meditation ; the pinned kerchief, in modest plaits, enfolds a breast whose every throb is kindly ; the knitting-work, the close attendant upon her loneliness, has its position, and the busy fingers, in diligent competition, ply the gleaming wires ; the ancient chair, " sacred to memory," the one that came over in the Mayflower, is presented in its puritanic uprightness, and at its back hangs the " ridicule," in whose mysterious depths dwelleth many a rare antique, that the light of day hath not seen since the memorable '14 ; upon the little pine table, white as snow, from frequent inflictions of soap and sand, are seen *that*

snuff-box, and *that* teapot, the little black one, in the
respective solaces of which the ills of life have found mitigation, and grief has been allayed of half its bitterness;
the amelioration of maccaboy relieving the woes of widowhood, and sorrow finding cessation 'neath the softening
influence of souchong.   Above, upon the wall, hangs
Paul's ancient profile, in dark rigidity, like a soldier on
parade, staring straight forward at nothing, the unbend-
ing integrity of whose dickey stands in marked contrast
with the charcoal of his complexion.   And long and often
has that profile been scanned by fond eyes in vain effort
to detect one line of the olden affection that warmed the
original, or dwelt in the hard-spelt character of Paul's
epistles, that, well-worn and well-saved, are yet treasured
in the old black bureau-desk in the corner.   And carefully the sprig of sweet fern is renewed above the picture,
every year, when the berries lure Ike to the woods, and
he comes back laden with pine, and fern, and hemlock,
to garnish the fire-place and mantel-piece withal.   That
handkerchief has been preserved as a sacred relic since
the corporal's battle days, when in young devotion he
laid it, blazoned with the glory of the Constitution and
Guerriere, upon her lap, and, standing by her, with his
artillery sword gleaming in his hand, vowed by its edge
that his love for her should divide with that for his
country !   The story has not been written of his deeds
of arms, of his " moving accidents by flood and field,"

and dangers in the imminent deadly breaches, of his pa-
rades in the artillery, and his campaign-dinner once a
year. These remain to be written, and the biographer
of Paul Partington shall set the world aglow with the
recital of deeds that have been hid, like the diamond in
the ashes, but have lost no ray of brilliancy.

It may, however, be well to give a few of these exploits, as illustrative of the character of the person in
whose heroism we may detect an influence that dates from
Dog's Bondage; and nice discriminators may, by close
scrutiny, see therein the fusion of the fiery blood
of Seek-the-Kingdom-continually Partyngetonne — the
trumpeter of Oliver Cromwell — and the gentle outside
current that met, mingled, and softened — the *veni, vidi,
vici,* of conjugal triumph — and formed no merely
bloody warrior, but a hero, whose sword would be stained
by nothing worse than the mark of cheese that crowned
the board of war.

When the news came, in the " last war," that the
British had landed on the coast, although nine miles
from Beanville, his voice waked the people from their
slumbers, calling them to arms; it was his plume that
was seen gleaming in the light of the stars, as he dashed
through the town on horseback, urging his steed on
through the mud at the rate of five miles an hour; it
was his warlike skill that arranged the eleven men of
Beanville into a phalanx of attack; and it was his elo-

4

quence that called upon them, as husbands, fathers, patriots, and Christians, to fight and die like men. When afterwards it was discovered that all the alarm arose from seeing two men in their boats drawing lobster nets, the merit of valor did not depart from Paul Partington, and, though he never got the brevet as sergeant, promised him by the general of division, yet the people honored him, and the battle of the " Bloody 'Leven," as they were called, formed a theme for gossip in the tavern at Beanville for many a day.

When the call came for volunteers to throw up fortifications in Boston harbor, he was the first man to enrol his name; his pickaxe struck the first blow for his country in this service. His use of the spade rendered his advice invaluable to the commanding officer, and he could tell, to a fraction, how many shovels full to take from one portion, and how many wheelbarrow loads to put in another. His overalls were in the front of the fight; his arm was fearlessly bared in the encounter. " But, alas for his country!" he got a grain of gravel in his eye, and had to go home, after exhorting his comrades in arms to dig on, and giving his overalls to one who needed them. He was afterwards pensioned for his injury, having been very favorably mentioned in the orders of the day.

But in the muster-field was his greatest triumph. The smell of gunpowder he snuffed like the war-steed from afar.

In the intricacies of sham-fight he was at home. He was always selected to lead the forlorn hope in an attack, and his compressed lips and flashing eyes were precursors of victory. It became a standing rule that he must beat; but when the mad sergeant from the city, who commanded the point to be attacked, wouldn't give in, and charged home upon the corporal, driving him back at the point of the bayonet, whereby he lost three of his men and his credit in a bog through which they were compelled to pass, the star of the corporal waned. His martial spirit departed from that hour. Even though a court-martial was ordered at once, and the sergeant ordered to be shot, — which fate was only avoided by his speedy departure from Beanville, — it was of no avail. The careful nursing of Ruth availed nothing. He took to his bed, had his artillery sword and cap hung upon a nail where he could see them, and lay down to die. The skill of the country doctor, with a pair of saddlebags filled with medicine, and the whole pharmacopœia of Mrs. P., couldn't save him, and, after making his will, like a prudent citizen and a good soldier, he bade the world good-night, and —— Paul was not.

"No sound can awake him to glory again."

He was buried with military honors by the Beanville Artillery, who for twenty years voted annually to erect a monument to his memory, and then gave it up. The poet of the village, in anticipation of the monument, had prepared an epitaph, which we subjoin : —

" Here lies, beneath this heap of earth,
A hero of extensive worth,
A whole-souled man, full six feet tall,
Surnamed Partington, christened Paul."

The parish burying-ground in Beanville, — a sketch of which is here subjoined, — is situated in the bend of

the turnpike leading from Clover Hill, — and it is a shrine much visited in the summer months by tarriers at the village ; for all that was Paul Partington rests beneath the turf, with naught but a tall sweet-briar to mark the spot, standing like a sentinel on duty, armed at all points, and watching the slumber of the hero of the Bloody 'Leven. The picture was taken by a travelling artist while riding over the turnpike on the stage-coach, who was so struck with the picturesque beauty of the scene that he made an eight-miles-an-hour sketch of it in his portfolio.

It is to this spot, on each returning season, that Mrs. Partington comes, — by virtue of a free pass allowed her by the Beanville Branch Railroad, — and brings Isaac, and praises the ancient corporal's virtues, and tries to incite the boy's ambition to be like him; and he likes to come, for, while he is drinking in the words which Mrs. Partington imparts, he can watch the chip-munks on the decaying wall, and slily shy stones at birds whose confidence leads them to approach the spot and twitter upon the mullein-stalks that grow rankly by the gate.

We say naught but a sweet-briar tree marks the spot. The old gravestone, with its hard-faced remembrance of Paul, has been carried off in relics by modern Vandals. Chip by chip has the ancient monument disappeared, that affection paid for to the city stone-cutter and placed here, until not a scrap of it is left. The ancient stone of blue slate, with its jolly death's-head, that appeared as if quick with mirth; the winged, chubby cherubs in the corners, that looked like babies living in uncomfortable fat, like doughnuts; the simple inscription, in Roman characters, commemorative of the Roman virtues of Paul, and the quaint epitaph that told in equivocal English of a future hope, all have been chipped off.

But, thanks to art, that can restore the lost and create that which never existed, that monument is before us for our admiration. How many shocks of elemental war has that an-

4*

tiquated block of monumental sculpture withstood suc-
cessfully — standing despite the snow and frost of winter,
or the tornadoes of summer, to be carried off piece by
piece in the pockets of encroaching pilgrims! But there
is a glory in the idea of a gravestone's being used up in
breast-pins, to be more choicely cherished than the richest
rubies.

There were melancholy days in the Partingtonian
mansion when Paul stepped out. The old chair stood
by the right side of the fire-place, as if waiting to be
occupied ; the mug simmered in the winter evenings
between the andirons, with a mournful measure, as if
responsive to the wind that made a muss and hurly-burly
about the chimney-top, but only one now partook of its
contents; the regimentals were aired upon the clothes-
line, and, inflated with wind, seemed at times like the
corporal himself, cut up in parcels, who was, alas! to fill
them no more. The settling of the estate broke in upon
this dull and monotonous existence, and, in the excitement of the law, she forgot the sorrow that, as she said,
made her nothing but flesh, skin, and bones. The remark she made concerning probate offices is recorded as
a living evidence of her sagacity. Some one spoke to
her about the probate proceedings regarding the estate.
" Yes," said she, " it is probe it, probe it, all the time ;
and if the poor, widowless body gets the whole she don't
get half enough." The remark, likewise, about doing

things by attorney will be remembered until it is forgotten: —"Don't do anything by power of eternity," said she, "for, if you do, you will never see the end of it." What profundity!

But the estate was settled, after much delay, and the farm carried on at the halves by a neighbor, whose honesty was no security against the temptation of plethoric crops and opportunity. The hay fell off in the accounts, the recorded corn denoted a speedy famine, and a more disastrous havoc of potato rot has never since transpired than assailed her crops. But this state of things came to an end, instead of the farm as was threatened.

The march of improvement led to the need of a railroad through Beanville, and the Partingtonian mansion became a sacrifice to the ruthless spirit of progress, that, all-grasping, stops not at anything in its path, whether it be a homestead or a hemisphere. Mrs. Partington left Beanville reluctantly. As she herself has said, it was useless to try to stand against a railroad; and the city offering inducements in the way of education for Isaac, the legacy left her by the brother of Paul, she anchored her bark in the municipal haven, where her benevolence of act, intention, and sentiment, has been spread broad-cast, and many a smile has grown out of her " lines " that " have been cast in pleasant places."

There is a mystery thrown about the brother of Paul that we cannot unravel. All that is known of him is, that he was a pioneer in western civilization; was wounded in the Black Hawk war, and died on his way to Bean-ville, forwarding Isaac and a black silk handkerchief of boy's clothes by stage to their destination. But in Isaac is centred the affection that shed its rays about her early years, and in him she sees the nucleus of a Partingtonian progeny that shall appease the spirit of Seek-the-King-dom Partyngetonne, if it be knocking round amid sub-lunar scenes. She takes every occasion to describe his exalted origin. On a recent occasion, while in the street with Isaac, a citizen soldier in all the pride of regulation-uniform passed them. " See ! " said the boy with anima-tion, " does that look like uncle Paul ? " She looked at him, half offended. " No," said she, with pride in her expression, " he is no more like your uncle than Hy-perion fluid is like a satire ! " There was Shakspeare and dignity in the remark, and Isaac turned with emotion to look at the picture of a monkey, in a window, tempting a chained dog by holding his tail within an inch of the canine nose.

Speaking of the monkey's tail reminds us that we are nearly to the end of our tale about Mrs. Partington. We at the first thought of getting an autobiography of the old lady, which would have greatly enhanced the interest of the book, and had asked her to give us something of this kind. But one afternoon, as we were revolving some stupendous idea, — the Nebraska bill, may be, or the

Gadsden treaty, or Mr. Marcy's letter, — with our feet in slippers a foot or two above our head, and puffing one of those choice Habanos that the importer had sent in, we felt a finger on our shoulder.   " Get out, woman ! " we cried, somewhat tartly, " there 's nothing for you." Heaven help us ! we thought it was the woman with the rummy breath that had haunted us for days.   The touch was repeated, and, looking around to frown down the intruder, the mild gaze of Mrs. Partington was bent upon us.   The chair from the other room was brought in.

" So you thought it was the beggar woman, did you ? " said she.   " Well, suppose it had have been ?   Could n't you have given her a soft word, if you had n't any money ? Was there anything harmonious in her asking you for a penny ? "

We felt rebuked.

" But," continued she, smilingly, " I have come to say, about that writing matter, that it will do just as well if you write it for me.   Generally, I s'pose, a naughty biography is better if it is writ by one's self, but I can trust you to do me justice."

What a privilege !   Macaulay says somewhere that Boswell was the only true biographer that ever wrote. " By the star that is now before us ! " we ejaculated, looking at Mrs. Partington, " he shall yet confess that another has been found, and Bozzy's glories be shared with us."

Mrs. Partington smiled at our enthusiasm, and passed out of the door, and down the stairs, and waved an adieu to us a moment afterwards from the steps of an omnibus that was to take her home.

We have thus given the LIFE OF MRS. PARTINGTON, with her antecedents and coässociates. It is a desultory story, unlike, perhaps, anything you have seen before, dear reader. Try to fancy its oddity a reason for praise. Remember the dull and hackneyed path of common biographers, and remember, too, that this is the biography of no common person, but that of MRS. PARTING-TON — a name not born to die. Perhaps you may recognize in the oddity of the sketch a gleam of the eccentricity that has marked her sayings. In the hope that he has pleased you, the biographer places his hand on his heart and bows, as the curtain descends to slow music.

MILD WEATHER.

His is grand weather, mem, for poor people," said Mr. Tigh, the rich neighbor of Mrs. Partington, on a very warm day of winter, and indulged in a half-chuckle about it as he rubbed his hands together. It is a remark that almost everybody would make, and mean it, too, — at a time when coal, by the rapacity of man, was eight or nine dollars a ton, and cold weather, by the blessing of Heaven, that tempers the wind to the shorn lambs and ragged children, was withheld, — but not Mrs. Partington.

"Yes," said she, gently laying her hand at the same time on the sleeve of Mr. Tigh's coat, and looking him in the face. "Yes, and don't folks use this good weather too much as an excuse for not helping the indignant widows and orphanless children? Depend upon it, cold weather is the best for the poor, for then the rich feel the cold, and think more of 'em, and feel more exposed to give 'em consolation and coal. Cold weather comes down from heaven o' purpose to make men feel their duty, and it touches the heart, as the frost touches the milk-pitcher and breaks it, and the milk of humane kindness runs out, and the poor are made better for it. Cold weather is a blessing to the poor, depend upon it."

She stopped here, and Mr. Tigh cast his eyes down and struck his cane several times against a brick at his feet; then, bidding the old lady good-morning, he moved away. There was a large " Dr. to Sundries" on his book that night, which the book-keeper will find it difficult to explain; but Heaven knows all about it, and the secret gift, in charity, and the prayer of the poor recipient, invoking blessings on the unknown benefactor, were great records that night in the angel's book.

THE CHINA QUESTION.

"You never see sich chaney no ware now, as this,' said Mrs. Partington, as she took from an obscure corner of the old cupboard a teapot of antique appearance, noseless and handleless, and cracked here and there, and stayed with putty where Time's mischievous fingers had threatened a dissolution of the union. "That teapot was my grandmother's afore she was married; I remember it just as well as it was yesterday."

"Remember when your grandmother was married?" queried Ike.

"No, no, the teapot," responded she; "and it was a perfect beauty, with the Garden of Eden on it, and the flowers and Adam and Eve on it, so natural that you might almost smell their fragrance."

"What, smell Adam and Eve?" said Ike.

"No, the flowers, stupid!" replied she; "my grand-'ther gave it to her as a memento mori of his undying infection, because the colors wouldn't fade, and they never have, though children are destroying angels, and they made the mischief among the crockery, as they always do now-a-days."

She had held the teapot in her hands as she spoke, and now she gazed in silence upon the picture of Adam and Eve, partially concealed in the bushes, and she revelled in the memory of the past, and wondered if her grandmother ever came back to look at that old teapot

5

that she had preserved so carefully, as an heir-loom; then, carefully brushing off some dust that rested upon it, she replaced it, and charged Ike impressively to keep it most sacrilegiously for her sake. He said he would, as plain as his mouth full of preserved plums would let him, and wiped his mouth on the sleeve of his best jacket.

SYMPATHY.

"HERE's fresh halibut!" cried the fish-vender, beneath Mrs. Partington's window.

"I know it is, you poor cretur!" said the estimable lady, looking after him with a commiserating expression; "I know it is; and I believe it is the seventh fresh *haul about* that he has made by here to-day; and he speaks so pitiful, too, when he is telling us of it, it makes my very heart ache for him."

She caught not the *deep* significance of the cry; but her benevolence, always on the alert, construed it into an appeal for sympathy. Heaven's blessings on thee, Mrs. Partington, and, with reverence be it wished, where hearts are regarded, may you turn up a trump.

PAUL'S GHOST.

PAUL'S GHOST.

IT was just in the nigh edge of a summer evening, and
Mrs. Partington, who had worked hard at her knitting
all day, began to feel a little dozy. She felt, as she
described it to her neighbor, Mrs. Battlegash, "a sort of
alloverness;" and those who have felt as she thus described
it, will know the precise sensation;— for ourselves, never
having felt so, we cannot explain it.

It was a sort of half twilight, when the daylight
begins to be thick and muddy, and a time when ghosts
are said to be round fully as plenty as at the classic hour
of midnight. We never could see the propriety of re-
stricting ghostly operations to this sombre hour, and, as
far as our experience goes, we have seen as many ghosts
at "noon of day" as at the "noon of night."

She never told us why, or if she were thinking of
ghosts at this time; indeed, all we know about the ghost
was from Mrs. Battlegash, and we shall have to give the
narration as we had it under Mrs. B.'s own hand : —

"Says Mrs. Part'nton, says she, 'Mrs. Battle,' she
always calls me Battle, though my name is Battlegash
—my husband's name, and his father's — says she, 'Mrs.
Battle, I 've seen an apprehension; ' and I thought she
was agoing to have an asterisk, she was so very pale and
haggard like ; and says I, 'What 's the matter?' for I felt
kind of skeered. I had heered a good deal about the
spirituous manifestations, and did n't know but they had
been a manifesting her. Says I, 'What's the matter,' agin,

and then says she, as solum as a grave-yard, ' I 've seen Paul!' I felt cold chills a crawlin all over me, but I mustard courage enough to say, ' Do tell!' 'Yes,' says she, ' I saw him with my mortal eyes, just as he looked when he was a tenement of clay, with the very soger clo'es and impertinences he had on the last day he sarved his country in the auxillary.'

"I tried to comfort the poor cretur by telling her that I guessed he did n't keer enough about her to want to come back, and as his estate had all been settled sacreligiously, it would be very unreasonable indeed in him to come back to disturb her.

"'Where did you see him?' says I. ' Out into the yard,' said she. 'When did you see him?' says I. 'Just now,' said she. ' Are you shore it was he?' said I, determined to get at the bottom of it. ' Yes,' said she, ' if ever an apprehension did come back, that 'ere was one. P'raps it is there now.' Then says I, 'Ruth,' says I, ' le's go and see.'

"She riz right up, and we walked along through the long entry into her room, and looked out of her back window, and there, shore enough, was a sight as froze my blood to calves-foot jelly. There was the soger cap and coat, as nateral as life, with the tompion atop. My heart come up into my mouth, so that I could have spit it out just as easy as not. Mrs. Part'nton, says she, ' What do you think of it? is n't it his apprehension? But I 'm determined to speak to it.'

"I tried to persuade her not to, but she insisted on it, and out she went.

"'Paul!' said she, ' what upon airth do you want,

that you should come back arter it, so apprehensively ?'
The figure was setting on the top of the pump when she
spoke, and it did n't take no notice of her. 'Paul!' said
she, a little louder. Then slowly and solemnly that 'ere
cap turned round, and instead of Paul, Mr. Editor, if
you 'll believe it, it was Ike, the little scapegrace, that
had frightened us almost out of our wits, if we ever had
any. That boy, I believe, will be the means of somebody's death. Mrs. Part'nton grew very red in the face,
and razed her hand to inflict corporal punishment onto
the young corporal, but the boy looked up kind of
pleasantly like, and she could n't find the heart to strike
him, though I told her if she spared the rod she would
spile that 'ere child. It is fortnight for him that he is n't
a child of mine, I can tell him."

Here Mrs. Battlegash's narrative ends. We can fancy
the scene in the yard: the youngster in the corporal's
coat, the red face changing to pleasant equanimity, the
raised hand, indicative of temper, subsiding, as the waves
do when the wind ceases to blow, and peace, like the
evening star above them, pervading and giving grace to
the tableau.

5*

IKE SO TENDER-HEARTED.

"THERE, don't take on so, dear," said Mrs. Partington, as she handed Ike a peach he had been crying for. He took the peach, and a minute afterwards was heard whistling "Jordan" on the ridgepole of the shed. "He is sich a tender-hearted critter," said she to Mrs. Sled, smilingly, while that excellent neighbor looked at him through the window with two deprecatory eyes —"He is so tender-hearted that I can't ask him to go out and draw an armful of wood or split a pail of water without setting him crying at once."

She paused for Mrs. Sled's mind **to** comprehend the whole force of the remark concerning Ike's lachrymosity.

"And he's the most considerable boy, too," resumed she, "that ever you see; for when we had the inclination on the lungs, he would n't take a bit of the medicine Dr. Bolus had subscribed, 'cause he knowed it would do *me* good, and said he'd full as lieves take molasses!"

She went on with her knitting, and Ike became lost in the foot of a stocking that she was toeing out. Those grapes on the trellis opposite where Ike is sitting look tempting!

MRS. PARTINGTON says there must be some sort of kin between poets and pullets, for they both are always chanting their lays.

LOOK UP.

PERHAPS it would not make a rap's difference, one way or the other, in a man's fortunes, whether he looked up or down; but we always fancied that there was a reason for the superstition that made a man's habit of looking down an augury of his success in life; as if his mind dwelling, with his eyes, continually on the earth, would better enable him to know how to make money, as a man who dwells in the dark can see better in the accustomed darkness, than one who comes directly in from the light. He keeps his eyes on the ground, and no stray fourpences or cents escape his eagle vision. Every rag is marked to see if it may not be a bill in disguise, and the hope to find a pocket-book or two, while passing along the street, seems to be continually present in his mind. His eyes grow heavy with looking down, and when at last there is no longer occasion to look down, — when he has found all the fourpences and pocket-books that he has sought for, — then the light is painful to him, and he turns to the earth again, before he is dead. Habit makes it his only happiness, and he goes to seeking for pocket-books and fourpences again.

If this be the result of looking down, the result of looking up must be, we should suppose, the opposite of this. Lifting the eyes above the world brings one to view things far better than fourpences. As much difference between them as the difference between a star of the first magnitude and a gold dollar. The eyelids turned up, the sunlight streams down upon the mind, and prepares therein a soil for the reception of good seed, that shall grow up and bear fruit.

Look up! Who ever thinks of groping about the foundations of Bunker Hill Monument, when there are so many pleasures of vision to be gained by climbing to its summit? The higher the look, or climb, the broader the view from the lofty position one gains. The most beautiful and delicate work of a structure is placed at the top. The fruit that is sweetest is always the nearest the sun. These are facts that belong to every-day life, to say nothing of that spiritual looking-up required to give light to the soul; a commodity which some few people possess, and seem desirous of benefiting.

But don't, in looking up, lose all memory of earth; for you can't drop your body as you can your coat, with your wish, and soar off on the wings of the spirit. When you look up, keep part of an eye directed to earth, and avoid the coal-holes and cellar-ways that are open for your unwary feet. A too deep absorption in things above the earth may make the star-gazer conscious of a pain in the back from a too sudden contact with the " cold, cold ground," as we saw a printer served on a cold morning (though whether he was heaven-seeking is questionable), and who looked very simple as he gathered himself up after the prostration.

Let the upward look characterize us all, — with the eye to accidents mentioned above, — and secure for us a name for aspiring above the grovelling things of the world, and five of us out of six may be deserving of it. Look up!

A SOLEMN FACT.

OUR plants are most fla-
grantly odious," said
Mrs. Partington, as she
stooped over a small oval
red table in a neighbor's
house, which table was covered with cracked pots filled
with luxuriant geraniums, and
a monthly rose, and a cactus,
and other bright creations,
that shed their sweetness upon
the almost tropical atmos-
phere of a southerly room in April, while a fragrant
vine, hung in chains, graced the window with a curtain
more gorgeous than any other not exactly like it. Mrs.
Partington stood gazing upon them in admiration.

"How beautiful they are!" she continued. "Do you
profligate your plants by slips, mem?"

She was told that such was the case; they were propa-
gated by slips.

"So was mine," said Mrs. P. "I was always more
lucky with my slips than with anything else."

Bless thy kind old heart, Mrs. Partington! it may
be so with you, but it is not so with all; for the way
of the world is hard, and many slips are made, and
for the unfortunates whose feet or tongues slip on the

treacherous path, a sentence generally awaits which admits small chance of reversal,— a soiled coat or a soiled character sticking to them until both are worn out. Dear old lady! your humble chronicler remembers that many of the young and beautiful are *profligated* by slips, — slips so gradual that propriety could hardly call them such at first, — which end, heaven and earth and perdition know how deep.

NEW REMEDY FOR A DROUGHT.

—

MRS. PARTINGTON was in the country one August, and for a whole month not one drop of rain had fallen. One day she was slowly walking along the road, with her umbrella over her head, when an old man, who was mending up a little gap of wall, accosted her, at the same time depositing a large stone on the top of the pile.

"Mrs. Partington, what do *you* think can help this 'ere drought?"

The old lady looked at him through her spectacles, at the same time smelling a fern leaf.

"I think," said she, in a tone of oracular wisdom, "I think a little rain would help it as much as anything."

It was a great thought. The old gentleman took off his straw hat, and wiped his head with his cotton handkerchief, at the same time saying that he thought so too.

"HEAR THAT VOICE."

DID the reader ever know a man grown, and big at that, with a very small voice, that almost squealed in uttering itself, and gave a most ridiculous aspect to what was perhaps of great importance, as matters of life and death, the reading of a will, an exhortation to virtue, or an anxious inquiry concerning the health of friends? Of course he has, for there are many such voices about. An agent of a large manufacturing establishment in New Hampshire possessed this peculiarity of voice to a remarkable degree, which once was the cause of a most mortifying and ludicrous mistake. A man came to the factory to get employment, — a great burly fellow, with a voice like young thunder, — and saluted the agent, who was a small man, by the way, with the question, "Do you want to hire?" in a tone that seemed to shake the room in which they stood. Starting at the sound, and with a face expressive of nervous irritability, he drawled out, in his squeaking, querulous manner, as if looking at each word before he uttered it,

"No — I — don't — know — as — I — do."

The man, not understanding his peculiarity, attributed the strange tones to another cause, and kindly extending his huge hand, as one might suppose a friendly bear would under like circumstances, patted the little agent on the head, and soothingly uttered,

"Well, well, my little fellow, don't *cry about it ;* don't take on so, if you can't hire me ! "

The contact of crude humanity with his delicate nead operated as magically upon the agent as did the touch of Captain Cuttle's hook upon the refined flesh of Dombey, and frightful was the yell with which he met the mechanic's sympathy in a command to leave the room, and awfully vehement was the manner in which he slammed the door to as the good-humored fellow passed into the street.

MRS. PARTINGTON PENNED.

A FRIEND, returned from a visit to New York, presented to Mrs. Partington a gold pen which had been entrusted to him for her. The present was duly examined and admired, and turned round, and pulled out, and held up to the light, and a receipt for pew-rent was brought out from the black bureau, on the back of which to test its quality, and she made a straight mark to the right, and then crossed it with another straight mark of equal length, and then said it was charming.

"But who are they?" said she, speculatively. "I don't know them, I'm shore."

The friend blandly explained that they knew her very well, and that this present was a tribute of regard for her many virtues, which, like the odor of ten thousand flowers, is borne across the entire land. The giver was eloquent — touching.

"Ah," said she, "it is very kind to remember a poor widowless body like me! What friends I have got!

I hope that Heaven will be rewarded for their kindness to me!"

It was a fervent aspiration, and though the letter of her prayer might seem to divert the reward from its true object, still its spirit conferred it rightly. She opened the old black bureau-desk in the corner, and placed the gold pen carefully by the side of the paste shoe-buckles, and hoop earrings, — valuable relics of bygone times, — and then securely locked the desk, as she saw Ike looking curiously into the window, with his nose flattened close against the glass.

THE SODA FOUNTAIN.

"THERE it goes again!" said Mrs. Partington, as she became conscious of the sublimity of a soda fountain one warm day. "There it goes again, I declare, fizzin away like a blessed old locomoco on the railroad. Don't say anything about Nigary now, — that is n't nothin in caparison to this, — and it a'n't *bad* beer nuther; but how in natur they can draw so many kinds out of one fassit, that 's the wonderment to me!" and she readjusted her specs, and took a new survey of the mystery, while Ike, unwatched, was weighing his knife and five jackstones in the bright brass scale on the other counter.

6

GIVING REASONS.

THE various reasons which some folks always have ready for their accidents and misfortunes, or as palliatives for their faults and follies, are very amusing. Many stories are told of such: one we remember of a boy who had played truant, and gave, as the reason for his absence, that his father kept him at home to help grind the handsaw. A toper, accounting for a bad cold he had, said he had slept on the common, and forgot to shut the gate. Another soaker, who was found in the gutter, with the water making a free passage over him, when asked how he came there, replied that he had agreed to meet a man there.

In our printing-office days, when we had to work for a living, it was our luck to work with a queer old fellow, who bore the name of Smith, or some such odd title. He was a very unhappy man, and never smiled unless he had the whole office in a snarl, and then he would chuckle right gladly. He was always fancying that his office-mates were imposing upon him, and a perfect flood of bile would he throw off at times for imagined wrongs. His position was by a window, fronting the east, and over this window he claimed absolute dominion, to shut it up or have it open, as he just pleased, maugre the fretting of those who were annoyed by his obstinacy. He assumed the office of a thermometer for the men, and graduated the heat according to his own feelings. If the wind was east he would as surely have the window open as that he would have it shut if it blew pleasantly from the west.

One day, with the wind blue east, the window was open all day, and much audible complaint was made by all hands, but without any effect. It was with a feeling nearly akin to exultation they saw him enter the office next day with indubitable signs of having a cold upon him; — his nose looked "red and raw," and his voice sounded as if he had two tight-fitting cork stoppers in his nostrils. The window that day was not opened, you may depend. One of the men undertook to remind him that his cold was in consequence of the wind blowing upon him.

"Do it aidt," said Smith, "but I hug by hat up by the widnder, ad last dight whed I put it od, it was brib full of east wid."

A SMALL TRADE.

"Cold day, Mr. Smith," said old Roger, in the Dock Square omnibus to his neighbor, who assented very politely. "And yet," continued Roger, "cold as it is, I have just seen a man in State-street, who does not wear gloves."

"Ah!" responded Smith, struck with the singularity of the statement, "why not, pray?"

"Why," chuckled the old man, "because he hasn't any hands."

Mr. Smith smiled.

ON LOCOMOTION.

"So they've got you on the stage, Mrs. Partington,"
said we to the old lady, after seeing her name, on a
theatre bill, as one of the characters in a new burletta.

"On the stage!" replied she, and a gleam of memory
passed over her face like a ray of sunshine over a faded
landscape, and she looked out of the window, and down
the street, until her eye rested on an omnibus moving
quickly along, in the pride of paint and gold, and she
took passage in it, in fancy, and went along with it.
"Yes," said she, "they did get me on the stage, because
it caused a nonsense in my stomach to ride inside; and
what a queer figure I did make on it, to be sure! But
that, dear, was five and twenty years ago, and it is so
queer they should remember it. O, them stages! I've
heerd of people riding by easy stages, but I never saw
one. The easiest way that I ever rid was on a pillory
behind Paul, there. Easy stages, indeed! why, it shook
me as if it would shake the sensuality all out of me, and
I never got over it for a week. How different it is
now!" — and she looked at the omnibus just passing her
door, — "all you've to do is to get into an ominous, all
cushioned nicely, with a whole picture-gallery round it,
to see for nothing, and afore you know it you are where
you want to go. Stages ——"

"But it is the National stage," we said.

"Well, well," replied she, hastily, "'taint no difference; only the national stage carried the mail, and

t'other the female passengers; one was jest as bad as t'other, and I don't know but worse."

"But they've got you in the theatre, the National Theatre," we persisted, and showed her the bill.

She looked at it a moment, and wiped her specs, and looked at it again in silence, as if her mind had n't got back from the hard journey it had just taken. At that moment a crash of glass called her hastily to the kitchen. The floor was covered with fragments of that brittle article, and a large ball hopped under a chair, as if ashamed of itself; while Ike was seen, through the broken window, making tracks speedily for the shed. We left her picking up the glass, so that he might not get it into his bare feet when he came in. Depend upon it, he had to take a severe "talkin to" when she caught him.

THE LARGEST LIBERTY.

"Now go to meeting, dear," said Mrs. Partington, as Isaac stood smoothing his hair preparatory to going out on Sunday. He looked down at his new shoes, and a thought of the green fields made him sigh. A fishing-line hung out of one pocket, which Mrs. Partington did n't see.

"Where shall I go to?" asked Ike.

Since the old lady had given up her seat in the Old North church, she had no stated place of worship.

"Go," replied she sublimely, as she pulled down his jacket behind, "go anywheres where the gospel is dispensed with."

6*

Such liberality is rare. Bigotry finds no place in her composition, and the truth, in her view, throws its light into every apartment of the Christian edifice, like an oysterman's chandelier into his many booths. The simile is not the very best, but the best to be had at present.

MRS. PARTINGTON IN COURT.

"I took my knitting-work and went up into the gallery," said Mrs. Partington, the day after visiting one of the city courts; "I went up into the gallery, and, after I had digested my specs, I looked down into the room, but I could n't see any courting going on. An old gentleman seemed to be asking a good many impertinent questions, — just like some old folks, — and people were setting round making minuets of the conversation. I don't see how they made out what was said, for they all told different stories. How much easier it would be to get along if they were all made to tell the same story! What a sight of trouble it would save the lawyers! The case, as they called it, was given to the jury, but I could n't see it, and a gentleman with a long pole was made to swear that he 'd keep an eye on 'em, and see that they did n't run away with it. Bimeby in they come agin, and then they said somebody was guilty of som-'-'- r, who had just said he was innocent, and did n't know nothing about it no more than the little baby that never had subsistence. I come away soon afterwards; but I could n't help thinking how trying it must be to sit there all day, shut out from the blessed air ! "

This experience is a beautiful exhibit of judicial life. True enough, Mrs. Partington; how easy might be the determining of cases, were but one side of the story told ! But, alas for perplexed jurymen ! there are unfortunately two sides, and the brain is racked to judge between them — Conscience holding the light trembling-ly, lest Honor be compromised, and Mercy pointing with raised finger to its fountain, as if endeavoring to draw attention from Justice, who stands, sword in hand, to urge her claim. " To well and truly try " is the solemn duty fastened by an oath, and the Commonwealth reposes in blessed security upon the broad responsibility of twelve honest men. God save the Commonwealth !

"RIGHT" AND "LEFT."

" THERE never was a time when the divine *right* of kings could be better shown," said old Roger, em-phasizing the word " right " significantly.

" Why?" asked the little man from the provinces, looking up.

" Because," replied he, " there will soon be none of them *left*."

An audible "*Whew!*" whistled along the table, and one distinct knock from each boarder, denoted equivocal approbation. The dessert was dispensed with.

A LITTLE TRUTH WELL PUT.

So you 've come down to attend the adversary meetings," said Mrs. Partington, as she surveyed the three trunks and two valises and a basket that the cab had just left, and the owner of them all, a gentleman in black, with a ghostly-looking neckcloth.

"Ah!" said he, humoring her conceit and smiling, for he expected to stay some days, "the adversary *we* meet we subdue with the weapons of the spirit."

"That is just what dear Deacon Sprig said when he captivated the crazy Ingen with New England rum, and then put him in bride'll. Says he, 'I 'll subdue him with the sword of the spirit'—he was sich a queer man! These meetings are excellent for converting heathens and saving the lost, and I do hope, after they have saved everybody else, that they will try and save a few more of their own that need teaching. There is a great many round here that want looking after more than the heathen do ; and we must look after our own first, or be worse than the infiddles.''

A pair of yarn stockings and a box of butter stopped her mouth for the time, and the old silver spoons marked '' P. P.'' and the antique china were brought out — articles that were only used on state occasions.

MUSICAL CRITICISM.

—

'' How did you like the concert ? '' asked Frank, of Mrs. Partington, at the Oratorio. '' Very much, indeed,'' said she; '' I liked everything about the Ontario but the consecutives ; the corrosives I thought were sublimated, but the consecutives I thought was dreadfully out of tune.'' Frank explained to her the object of the recitative, and smiled a little at the queer mistake she had made in musical terms. Bless thee, Mrs. Partington ! thy genius in its extravagance is never retarded by terms.

LIFE ON THE ROAD.

ONE summer, during the very hot weather, our Ellen, whose life could number seventeen happy summers, and nearly the same number of winters, took it into her little roguish head that she would like to go to Hampton Beach.   And when such a whim had once got *into* her head, the question might well be asked how could it be got *out*.   It would be hopeless to attempt it, provided any one were so inclined; but no one said a word, and Ellen *did* go.   She and her little friend Charlotte, who was on a visit to Ellen, started for the Beach, with lots of precautions and dough-nuts from Ellen's mother, for there is not a better soul between here and Great Hill than that same mother of Ellen's.

The horse and the wagon, bearing its charming freight of two pretty girls, moved swiftly and safely over the road to the Beach, and many a musical echo reverberated through the woods, and along the meadows, and by the hill-sides, and from the hill-tops, as they passed along.

The day was very pleasantly spent by the sea-shore, and when wearied with rambling over the fine, smooth beach, and sporting in the breakers like naiads, they started on their return home, with hearts as light and eyes as bright as when they set out in the morning.

Their horse was a spirited animal, which could ill brook a whip, and was also emulative to a great degree in competing with other horses for mastery on the road. In fact, he would allow no horse to go by him, and made

it a matter of principle — if horses are ever governed
by principle — to go by all on the road. They had
got perhaps half way home, when they overtook an
oldish sort of a man who was driving a fast horse.
"Billy," Ellen's horse, stuck up his ears, and "put
her," with an evident determination of going by. The
old 'un stirred his beast up to the strife, and away they
went over the road as swift as the swallows — neither
having the advantage. Ellen laughed at the sport, and
held the ribbons with the tact of a veteran Jehu. The
contest was soon decided, for the old chap raised his
whip and slightly touched " Billy" with the lash.

Billy impetuously kicked at the insult, but darted
like lightning along the road, distancing his competitor
in a twinkling. The old man was seen no more by the
victors ; but over the road they still flew, Billy heeding
neither rein nor word. The remembrance of the insult
put him to his speed, and he dashed along with terrific
velocity.

Men rushed out, and threw up their hands, and cried
" Whoa ! "

Women screamed, and prophesied *woe* to them.

Dogs barked as they skimmed along.

But no fear was felt by our Ellen in her peril. Her
pulse was quick with the excitement, but no fear mingled
with it. Her cheek was red as the rose, and her eyes
laughed, as her ringing voice told the people to get out
of the way. She wound the ribbons round her hands,
and to keep the middle of the road was her only care.

Bravo ! Ellen — bravo ! and the brave heart and
strong arm gave her the victory. A two-mile heat, the

quickest ever ran in our county, stands recorded to her fame.

This is n't much of a story, but it shows what a true woman can do and should do in an emergency. It will not do for Ellen's husband to treat her badly, we can tell him, when he gets her. His bones would n't be entirely safe.

FANCY DISEASES.

"DISEASES is very various," said Mrs. Partington, as she returned from a street-door conversation with Dr. Bolus. "The Doctor tells me that poor old Mrs. Haze has got two buckles on her lungs! It is dreadful to think of, I declare. The diseases is *so* various! One way we hear of people's dying of hermitage of the lungs; another way of the brown creatures; here they tell us of the elementary canal being out of order, and there about tonsors of the throat; here we hear of neurology in the head, there of an embargo; one side of us we hear of men being killed by getting a pound of tough beef in the sarcofagus, and there another kills himself by discovering his jocular vein. Things change so, that I declare I don't know how to subscribe for any disease now-a-days. New names and new nostrils takes the place of the old, and I might as well throw my old herb-bag away."

Fifteen minutes afterwards Isaac had that herb-bag for a target, and broke three squares of glass in the cellar window in trying to hit it, before the old lady knew what he was about. She did n't mean exactly what she said.

DAGUERREOTYPES.

"WHAT artfulness!" said Mrs. Partington, as she held her miniature in her hand, done in the highest style of the daguerrean art. The features were radiant with benevolence; the cap, close-fitted about her venerable face, bore upon it the faded black ribbon, the memento of ancient woe; the close-folded kerchief about her neck was pinned with mathematical exactness, while from beneath the cap border struggled a dark gray lock of hair, like a withered branch in winter waving amid accumulated snows. The specs and box were represented upon the table by her side. The picture was like her, and admiration marked every line of her countenance as she spoke.

"What artfulness here is, and how nat'rally every liniment is brought out! How nicely the dress is digested!"

She was talking to herself all the while.

"Why, this old black lutestring, that I have worn twenty year for Paul, looks as good as new, only it is a little too short-waisted by a great deal. O, Paul, Paul!" sighed she, as she sat back in her chair and gazed, with a tear in her eye, upon an old smoke-stained profile, cut in black, that had hung for many a year above the mantel-piece. "O, Paul! what a blessed thing this is, where Art helps Natur, and Natur helps Art, and they both help one another! How I wish I had your dear old phismahogany done like this! I 'd prize it more than gold or silver."

7

She sat still, and looked alternately at the daguerreo-type and the profile, as if she hoped the profile would speak to her; but it still looked rigidly forward, thrust-ing out its huge outline of nose as if proud of it, and then with a sigh she reclasped the case and deposited the picture in the upper drawer of the old black bureau in the corner. Ike was all the while burning holes through a pine shingle with one of Mrs. Partington's best knit-ting-needles.

THAT AND THAT.

"You do make that child look like a fool, wife, with all that toggery on him," said Mr. Fog angrily, as they were starting out for a walk. "Dear me," says Mrs. Partington, meeting them at the door, "what a doll of a baby, and how much he resembles his papa!" Mr. Fog coughed, and they passed along.

ON POLITICS.

—

"As regards these electrical matters," said Mrs. Partington, just before election, — she lived on a main street, and the cheering and noise of parties passing her door kept her awake o' nights, — "I don't see the uŝe of making so much fuss about it. Why don't they take some one and give him their sufferings, if he has n't got any of his own, and let him be governor till he dies, just as they do the judges, and arterwards too, as they sometimes do them, for they might as well be dead, a good many of 'em? O, this confusion of noise and hubbub! My poor head aches o' hearing of it, and Isaac has got sich a cold, looking out of the window at the possessions without nothing on the head. And then what critters they all be, to be sure! — their newspapers are brim full of good resolutions, but ne'eraone of 'em did I ever know 'em to keep. They are always resolving, like the showman's resolving views, and one resolution fades away jest as quick as another comes. If I could have my way, I would " —

"Hooray! here they come!" cried Ike, breaking in upon the old lady's remarks, and banging his slate on the floor, and throwing up the window with a vehemence that broke two squares of glass.

"Hooray!" came up in a big chorus from the street, filling Mrs. Partington's little chamber, to its utmost capacity, with "hooray," the great element of political life.

"There they go agin," cried she, "with their drums and lanterns, like crazy critters, and keeping folks awake when they ought to be in the arms of Murphy!"

Ike pulled in his head and dropped the window, and the good old lady mended the fracture of the glass by a hat and a pair of pants of Ike's, with the threat of severe punishment if he ever did so again. But do you suppose she would have kept it? Ike knew better. When the glazier came in the next day to mend the window, she had to tell him the story of how it was broke, but all the blame was on the politicians.

"Don't crowd so, good woman," said old Roger, at the Lowell Institute, as he was waiting his turn to give his name. "Don't crowd so!" and, looking over his shoulder, he met the reproachful glance of Mrs. Partington herself, who was there for the same purpose. He immediately gave way to her, and the next morning found himself not divisible by 7, nor anything like it. "So much for politeness!" growled old Roger; "she'll get all the Natural Religion now; and *much good may it do her!*" You would have smiled to see the spiteful manner in which the little man said this.

BEAUTIFUL REFLECTION INTERRUPTED.

" Dear me ! " said Mrs. Partington ; and so she *is*
dear, — not that she meant so, — because under that black
bonnet is humility, and self-praise forms no part of her
reflection.   It was a simple ejaculation, that was all ;
our word for it.   " Dear me ! here they are going to have
war again over the sea, and only for a Turkey, and it
don't say how much it weighed either, nor whether it
was tender ; and Prince Knockemstiff has gone off in a
miff, and the Rushin bears and Austriches are all to be
let loose to devour the people, and Heaven knows where
the end of it will leave off.   War is a dreadful thing —
so destroying to temper and good clo'es, and men shoot
at each other jest as if they was gutter purchase, and
cheap at that."

How sorrowfully the cover of the snuff-box shut, as
she ceased speaking ! and the spectacles looked dewy,
like a tumbler in summer-heat filled with ice-water, as
she looked at the profile of the corporal, with the sprig
of sweet fern above it, and the old sword behind the
door.

What did Ike mean as he stole in, and deposited some
red article under the cricket upon which her feet rested,
and then stole out again ?

A hissing sound followed — crack ! snap ! bang !
whiz ! went a bunch of crackers — and Mrs. Partington,
in consternation and cloth slippers, danced about the
room, forgetful of distant war in her present alarm.

Ah. Ike !

7*

APPOINTING INSPECTORS.

—

"INSPECTORS of customs!" said Mrs. Partington, energetically, as she laid down the paper chronicling some new appointment. Here was a new idea, that broke upon her mind like a ray of sunshine through a corn barn.

"Inspectors of customs!" and she looked up at the rigid profile of the old corporal, as if she would ask what he had to say about it; but that warrior had hung there too long to be now disturbed by trifles, and he took no notice of her.

"Inspectors of customs!" continued she, as she turned her attention to the old black teapot, and then turned out the tea, which celestial beverage gurgled through the spout, in harmony with her reflections, not too strong; "that's a new idea to me. But, thank Providence, I ha'n't got no customs that I had n't as lives they'd inspect as not; only I'd a little rather they would n't. I wish everybody could say so, but I'm afeard there are many customs that won't bear looking into. Well, let every tub stand on its own bottom, I say — I won't cast no speciousness on nobody. But I don't see what they wanted to appoint any more for, and be to so much suspense when every place has so many in it that will inspect customs for nothing. If they'd only make my next-door neighbor, Miss Juniper, now, an inspector of customs, they would n't need another for a long ways, that's mortally sartin."

She stirred her souchong as she ruminated, untasting, and Ike helped himself, unheeded, to the last preserved pear there was in the dish.

MRS. PARTINGTON AT TEA.

"ADULTERATED tea!" said Mrs. Partington, as she read in the Transcript an account of the adulteration of teas in England, at which she was much shocked. "I wonder if this is adulterated?" and she bowed her head over the steaming and fragrant decoction in the cup before her, whose genial odors mingled with the silvery vapor, and encircled her venerable poll like a halo. "It smells virtuous," continued she, smiling with satisfaction, "and I know this Shoo-shon tea must be good, because I bought it of Mr. Shoo-shon himself, at Redding's. Adulterated!" she meandered on, pensively as a brook in June, "and it's agin the commandment, too, which says —— don't break that, Isaac!" as she saw that interesting juvenile amusing himself with making refracted sunbeams dance upon the wall, and around the dark profile, and among the leaves of the sweet fern, like yellow butterflies or fugitive chips of new June butter. The alarm for her crockery dispelled all disquietude about the tea, and she sipped her beverage, all oblivious of dele-tea-rious infusions.

SIR, YOU OWE ME A CENT.

—

"THER things may be great,"
said old Roger with a nod,
"besides what's called so;
some very *little* thing, if 't is
done well, can be a great one;
in impudence, say, for instance. Yesterday a boy
asked me pitifully for a four-
pence; I gave him what I
thought to be one, and passed
on.   Presently I felt a twitch
at my coat-tail, and looked
round, and there stood the boy.
'Sir,' says he, 'you *owe me a cent* — this 'ere won't
pass for but five cents — it's crossed!' I gave the
little rascal a shilling at once; I could n't help it.   The
thing was sublime, — admirable; hang me if it was n't."
And the little man struck his cane violently on the
ground, and laughed happily at the supreme impudence
displayed in the affair.

GUESSING AT A NAME.

"DRIVE him out!" screamed Mrs. Partington, as Ike whistled in an immense house-dog, who perambulated the kitchen, dotting the newly-washed floor with flowers of mud, and audaciously smelling Mrs. Partington's toes, as the old lady stood up in a chair to avoid him.

"Drive him out. What is his name, Isaac?"

"Guess," replied Ike.

"I can't, I know. Perhaps it's Watch, or Ponto, or Cæsar — what is it?"

"Why, Guess."

"I tell you I can't guess. Perhaps it's Hector, or Tiger, or Rover — what is his name?"

"Guess."

"O, you provoking creatur! I'll be tempered to whip you within an inch of your skin if you provoke me so. Why don't you tell me?"

"I did tell you the first time," whined Ike, pulling the dog's ear with one hand while he wiped his dry eyes with the other, "his name is Guess."

The old lady was melted by his emotion, and, as soon as the dog was sent out, some nice quince jelly settled the difficulty.

"He is sich a queer child!" murmured she; "so bright! I suppose 't was because he was weaned on pickles."

Ike ate his preserves in silence, but his eye was on the

acorn on the post of the old lady's high-backed chair, and he thought what a nice top it would make if he could saw it off some day.

BURNING WATER.

—

" WELL, this is a discovery ! " exclaimed Mrs. Partington smilingly, as she stood with a small picture in her right hand, her left resting upon the pine table, and her eyes fixed upon the flame of a glass lamp, that sputtered for a moment and then shot out a gleam of cheerful light that irradiated every part of the little kitchen, revealing the portrait of Paul upon the wall and Ike asleep by the fire. She spoke to herself — it was a way she had — and she met with no contradiction from that quarter. " This is a discovery. This lamp was almost burnt out, and I 've filled it up with water, and it burns like the real ile." The experiment was perfectly triumphant; the problem of light from water was demonstrated; and yet, with this vast fact revealed to her, Mrs. Partington, with a modesty equal to that of the great philosopher who picked up a pocket-full of rocks on the shore of the vast ocean of Truth, smiled with delight at her discovery, nor once thought of putting out a patent or selling rights — was entirely willing all might burn water that could.

A STRIKING MANIFESTATION.

"I CAN'T believe in sperituous knockings," said Mrs.
Partington, solemnly, as some things were related to her
which had been seen, that appeared very mysterious.
"I can't believe about it; for I know, if Paul could come
back, he would revulge himself to me here, and
would n't make me run a mile only to get a few dry
knocks. Strange that the world should be so supersti-
tional as to believe sich a rapsody, or think a sperrit can
go knocking about like a boy in vexation. *I* can't
believe it, and I don't know's I could if that teapot
there was to jump off the table right afore my eyes!" She
paused, and through the gloom of approaching darkness
could be seen the determined expression of her mouth.
A slight movement was heard upon the table, and the
little black teapot moved from its position, crawled
slowly up the wall, and then hung passively by the side
of the profile of the ancient corporal! The old lady
could not speak, but held up her hands in wild amazement, while her snuff-box fell from her nerveless grasp
and rolled along upon the sanded floor. She left the
room to procure a light, and, as soon as she had gone,
the teapot was lowered by the invisible hand to its
original station, and Ike stepped out from beneath the
table, stowing a long string away in his pocket, and
grinning prodigiously.

IKE AND THE ELEPHANT.

"WELL," said Ike, looking the elephant directly in the eye, at the same time doubling up his huge fist, as big as a half-cent bun, and putting on an air of defiance, after the animal had stolen his gingerbread; "well, you got it, did n't you, you old thief, you! I s'pose you think you 've done thunderin' great things, don't you? For my part, I don't call it no better 'n stealing. O, you may stand there and swing that ridic'lous-looking trunk o' your'n just as much as you 're a mind to; you can't skeer a fellow, *I* tell *you!* This is a free country, old club-feet; and you an't agoing to take any more liberties here like that. I can tell you it won't be safe for that Ingee-rubber hide o' yourn, if you do! You take my gingerbread away agin, if you dare, that 's all! You just try it, you ongainly reptile, you! O, you may look saucy, and pretend you don't keer, but you just say two words,—just knock that chip off my head,—and if I don't give you fits my name an't Ike Partington, that 's all! Just put down that big Ingee-rubber bludgeon, and I 'll black your eyes for you, you old tough-leather! You darsn't say a word, you ill-mannered old hunch! I 'd knock your eye-teeth out, if you did. O, take it up, if you 're a mind to; you need n't think to bully it over me, because you 're a little bigger'n I am, I can tell you. We don't stand no such nonsense as that, round here. If 't warn't for that p'leceman looking here, I 'd pitch into you like a thousand o' bricks. *I* would n't get out o' your way as people do when you come along, and I should like to see you just step on my toes — why can't you just try it now, will you? I guess I'd make you hear thunder with them leather-apron ears o' your'n, you big overgrown vagabond, you! 'T a'n't no use o' talking to you, but I shall be here, and, if you don't mind your eye, I'll lick you like blazes afore I go out."

Here Isaac undoubled his hands, and, shaking his head threateningly at the huge animal, he went over to get a look at the monkeys; while the elephant lazily swung his trunk from side to side, and good-naturedly fanned himself with his big ears, as if he had n't minded a word the little fellow had said.

A SUBSTITUTE.

" I HAVE N'T got any money," said Mrs. Partington, as the box came round at the close of a charity lecture; " but here 's a couple of elegant sausages I have brought that you can give the poor creturs! " The box-holder looked confounded — the people smiled. With her view of charity, she saw nothing wrong in the act. Bless thee, Mrs. Partington! angels shall record the deed on the credit side of thy account, and where hearts are judged shall thy simple gift weigh like gold in the day of award.

8

WHOLESOME ADVICE.

"Isaac," said Mrs. Partington, as that interesting juvenile was playing a game of "knuckle up" against the kitchen wall, to the imminent danger of the old clock which ticked near by, "this is a marvellous age, as Deacon Babson says, and perhaps there 's no harm in 'em, but I 'm afeard no good 'll come out of it — no good at all — for you to keep playing marvels all the time, as you do. I am afeard you will learn how to gambol, and become a bad boy, and forget all the good device I have given you. Ah! it would break my soul, Isaac, to have you given to naughty tricks, like some wicked boys that I know, who will be rakeshames in the airth if they don't die before their time comes. So, don't gambol, dear, and always play as if you had just as lieves the minister would see you as not." She handed him a little bag she had made for him to keep his marbles in, and patted his head kindly as he went again to play. Ike was fortified, for the next five minutes, against temptation to do evil; but

> " Chase span, in the ring,
> Knuckle up, or anything,"

are potent when arrayed against out-of-sight solicitude, and we fear that the boy forgot. There is much reason in the old lady's fear.

A GHOST STORY.

In the vicinity of a town not many miles from Boston was a dark glen, by the roadside, reputed to be haunted. A traveller had been found here, many years before, frozen to death, and his troubled spirit, with a disposition to trouble everybody else, was said nightly to visit the scene of his mortal termination, to have a "melancholy satisfaction" all alone by himself, or with but such auditors as he could press in to participate in the "services of the evening." An old fellow, who resided in the town, and was fully imbued with the superstition, had been one night to a husking, where the milk-punch had circulated with more than common generosity, and though "na fou," he had enough on board to make him comfortable and happy and

> ———— "glorious,
> O'er all the ills of life victorious."

Towards the hour of breaking up, the conversation turned upon the ghost, by whose dark hunting-ground our friend had to pass, over a road raised up amid an alder swamp, whose sad gloom could hardly be dispelled by a noon-day sun, and where nothing but a ghost of the most simple sort would wish to abide.

> "Wi' tippenny we fear nae evil,
> Wi' usquebae we 'll face the devil,"

Burns said; and milk-punch we suppose to be about the same in its courage-inspiring properties. Our hero snapped his fingers at danger from ghosts and unholy angels, and cared for neither a "bodle." It was a mile-walk, good, to the spiritual precinct, and, thinking on his way that it would be the part of prudence to prepare for emergency, before he came to the dark gulf he was to pass, he gathered a small artillery from a stone wall, determined, if assaulted, to do battle manfully, for the credit of the punch.

He had crossed a little brook that murmured beneath the rude bridge above it, and had fairly got through the dangerous part, as he considered it, of his journey, and muttered to himself, in rather a tone of disappoint-ment, "I guess he must be sick; fog is n't good for him," when, lo! almost directly in the path before him was an object that made him come to a stand at once. It was all ghostly white, and he had barely time to look at it, when a hideous groan came towards him on the night air, which the milk-punch could hardly counteract in its effect on his nervous system. Rallying, however, he selected a missile and let fly at his ghostly obstructor; another groan, like the last bellow of expiring nature, answered this assault. He hurled another huge stone, and, gathering courage from the excitement, he blazed away in a manner that would astonish either human or superhuman antagonists, but without any apparent effect upon the adversary, who stood his ground manfully, or, perhaps we should say, ghostfully. As the last stone of his ammunition was expended, however, with a cry that echoed fearfully through the alders, the ghost rushed towards him, and a violent shock laid him sense-less upon the ground, a vanquished man. He was found the next morning pensively sitting by the road-side, contemplating the scene of his night's exploit, with his head in his hand.

He told his story, and pointed to the scattered missiles for proof of what he had done ; and he was believed, for " to give up the ghost" was out of the question. But, on going home, a small white two-year-old bull was seen grazing by the road-side, and suspicion for a moment crossed their minds that this might have been the ghost, after all, seen through the medium of the punch ; but this would have been voted rank heresy against the ancient institution of ghosts, and they held their peace.

A DANGEROUS POSITION.

" Don't lay in that postur, dear," said Mrs. Partington to Ike, who was stretched upon a settle, with his heels a foot or two higher than his head. " Don't lay so ; raise yourself up, and put this pillow under you. I knew a young man once who had a suggestion of the brain in consequence of laying so — his brains all run down into his head ! " and with this admonition she left him, to practise, soon after, the hazardous experiment of tying his legs in a bow knot round his neck, as he had seen Professor Baldwin do.

8*

A LESSON ON SYMPATHY.

"WHAT a to-do they are making about this Cosset!"
said Mrs. Partington, smilingly. The news had reached
her ear of the triumphs of Kossuth, and the name had
assumed a form, and that form recalled a train of peculiar and characteristic associations, and she went on
like an eight-day clock: "A cosset is a pretty thing in
a family where there's children, and they are dear
critters for girls that has n't got sweethearts to invent
their young affectations on; but what's the use of making
sich a fuss about it?"

"But this is Kos-*suth*, aunt, the great Hungarian,"
said Ike, tremendously, who was well posted up in passing matters; "who has come over here to ask our sympathy, and enlist us in behalf of his country."

"Well," said she, as the new light dawned upon
her, "they may have our sympathy in welcome, 'cause
it don't cost anything; but we must n't 'list and give
'em money, — that would be agin our constitutions!"

And the prudent dame drummed thoughtfully on her
snuff-box cover, with her eyes fixed upon the vane of
the Old South, while Ike amused himself by scratching
"KOsSuTH," with a fork, on the end of the new
japanned waiter.

HOW IKE DROPPED THE CAT.

—

ow, Isaac," said Mrs. Partington, as she came into the room with a basket snugly covered over, " take our Tabby, and drop her somewhere, and see that she don't come back again, for I am sick and tired of driving her out of the butter. She is the thievinest creatur! But don't hurt her, Isaac; only take care that she don't come back."

Ike smiled as he received his charge, and the old lady felt happy in getting rid of her trouble without resorting to violence. She would rather have endured the evil of the cat, great as that evil was, than that the poor quadruped should be inhumanly dealt with. She saw Ike depart, in the dusk of the evening, and watched him until he became lost to view in the shadow of a tree. It was a full half hour before he returned with his empty basket, and an unusual glee marked his appearance, — it sparkled in his eye, it glowed in his cheek, it sported in his hair, — and Ike looked really handsome, as he stood before the dame, and proclaimed the success of his mission.

"Did she drop easy, Isaac?" asked the old lady,

looking upon him kindly, "and won't she come back?"

"She dropt just as easy!" said Ike, letting his basket fall on the floor, and shying his cap upon the table, somewhat endangering a glass lamp with a wooden bottom that stood thereon; "she dropt just as easy! and she won't come back — you may bet high on that."

"But you did n't beat and mangle her, Isaac, did you? If you did I should be afraid she would come back and haunt us — I have heard of such things;" and she looked anxiously in his face ; but, detecting there no trace of guilt, she patted him on the head, and parted his hair, and told him to sit down and eat his supper, which the young gentleman did with considerable unction.

"Isaac! Isaac!" screamed Mrs. Partington, at the foot of the little stairway that led to the attic where the boy slept, the next morning after the above occurrence. "Isaac!"—and he came down stairs slowly, rubbing his eyes as he came. She had disturbed his morning nap.

"Isaac," said she, "what is that hanging yender to a limb of our apple-tree?" One scattering tree, as she said, constituted her whole orchard, unless she counted the poplar by the corner.

"I can't see so fur off," said Ike, still rubbing his eyes.

"Well, *I* should think it was a cat; and it looks to me like our Tabby. O, Isaac! if you have done this!" and a tone akin to horror trembled in her voice.

"I'll go and see if it's her," said Ike, as if not hearing the last part of her remark; and he dashed out of the door, but soon came back, with wonder depicted on every feature of his expressive countenance. "O, it's her! sure enough, it's her!" cried he, "but I *did* drop her!"

"Well, how could she come there then?" and the good old lady looked puzzled.

"I'll tell you how I guess it was," said Ike, looking demurely up. "I guess that she committed suicide, because we was going to drop her; they are dreadful knowing critters, you know."

"True enough," replied the old lady, while something like a tear glistened in her eye — her pity was excited; "true enough, Isaac, and I dare say she thought hard of us for doing it; but she hadn't ought to if she'd have considered a minute."

Ike said no more, but went out and cut down the supposed suicide, with a serious manner, and buried her beneath her gallows, deep down among the roots of the old tree, and she never came back.

The old lady told the story to the minister, and Ike vouched for it, but the good man shook his head incredulously at the idea of the suicide, and looked at the boy. He very evidently understood how the cat was *dropped*.

STOPPING A 'BUS.

MRS. PARTINGTON had watched three quarters of an
hour for an omnibus, and she swung her umbrella as one
drove up, and the driver stopped his horses near where
she stood.

"Now, Isaac," says she, feeling in her reticule
for a copper, away down under the handkerchief, and
snuff-box, and knitting-work, and thread-case, and
needle-book, "be a good boy, dear, while I am gone,
and don't cause a constellation among the neighbors, as
some boys do, and there's a cent for you; and be sure
you don't lay it out extravagantly, now; and be keerful
you don't break the windows; and if anybody rings at
the door, be sure and see who it is before you open it,
because there is so many dishonest rogues about; if any
porpoises come a begging give 'em what was left of the
dinner, Heaven bless 'em, and much good may it do
'em! and —— why, bless me! if the omnibus has n't
gone off, and left me standing here in the middle of the
street.   Such impudence is without a parable."

Her spectacles gleamed indignantly down the street,
after the disappearing 'bus, and, for a moment, anger had
the mastery; but equanimity, like twilight, came over her
mind, and she waited for the next 'bus, with calmness on
her face, and her green cotton umbrella under her arm.

AFTER A WEDDING.

"I LIKE to tend weddings," said Mrs. Partington, as she came back from a neighboring church, where one had been celebrated, and hung up her shawl, and replaced the black bonnet in the long-preserved bandbox. " I like to see young people come together with the promise to love, cherish, and nourish each other. But it is a solemn thing, is matrimony, — a very solemn thing, — where the pasture comes into the chancery, with his surplus on, and goes through with the cerement of making 'em man and wife. It ought to be husband and wife ; for it a'n't every husband that turns out a man. I declare I shall never forget how I felt when I had the nuptial ring put on to my finger, when Paul said, 'With my goods I thee endow.' He used to keep a dry-goods store then, and I thought he was going to give me all there was in it. I was young and simple, and did n't know till arterwards that it only meant one calico gound in a year. It is a lovely sight to see the young people plighting their trough, and coming up to consume their vows."

She bustled about and got tea ready, but abstractedly she put on the broken teapot, that had lain away unused since Paul was alive, and the teacups, mended with putty, and dark with age, as if the idea had conjured the ghost of past enjoyment to dwell for the moment in the home of present widowhood.

A young lady, who expected to be married on Thanksgiving night, wept copiously at her remarks, but kept on hemming the veil that was to adorn her brideship, and Ike sat pulling bristles out of the hearth-brush in expressive silence.

MRS. PARTINGTON IN THE MARKET.

"I WONDER what they mean by a better feeling in the market?" said Mrs. Partington, looking up from the newspaper which she was reading, and the problem deeply agitated her mind, revealed in the vibration of her cap-border. Her address was directed to nobody in particular. It was a little private wonder, got up for her own amusement. The market, and the deaths and marriages, were Mrs. P.'s favorite study in the Weekly Chronicle, but some of the mercantile phrases were at times imperfectly understood. "I wonder what they mean? I'm shore *I* don't feel any better there, and I don't believe anybody does but the butchers, and that's when they are pocketing the money, — things is so dear! But," continued she, brightening up, "I should like to see the trade embracing ten hogsheads of tobacco, that I see here printed about. That must have been a real tetching sight." She thought of Paul, and the association brought out the cotton handkerchief with the Constitution and Guerriere upon it, and she discontinued.

PARTINGTONIAN PHILOSOPHY

PARTINGTON PHILOSOPHY.

BEFORE the railroad company bought and tore down the Partington mansion, and uprooted and overturned the old family shrines without regard to their sacredness,— the Vandals! — turning the good old heart that worshipped there out upon the world to seek new ties amid new scenes, it was Mrs. Partington's delight to gather friends about her at Thanksgiving time, and the time-honored season passed very happily. Amid the festivities her benignity would beam with such a radiance, that the red seed peppers upon the wall looked ruddier in its genial glow, and the bright tin pans upon the shelf seemed brimful of sunshine, and smiled out upon all who looked at them.

There were fine times at the Partington mansion at Thanksgiving, you may depend. She did n't keep Christmas,— she was puritanical in her religious notions, and 'tended the Old North meeting-house for a third of a century, and took pride in saying that she had never been to *church;* a nice distinction which we leave the old folks to make,— Christmas was a church holiday, unsanctioned by a governor's proclamation, and she would none of it; she scented in it the garment of the disreputable Babylonish female, mentioned in the Apocalypse, and avoided it. But it is Thanksgiving that we are speaking about now —— Well, well, what has all this to do with patience ? —— Have patience, darling, and we 'll tell you an instance of patient resignation under disappointment, not surpassed since Newton's dog Diamond committed an incendiary act, and his master gravely informed the quadruped that he was not probably aware of the extent of the damage he had committed; which was doubtless the fact.

It was the custom with Mrs. P. to shut up a turkey previous to Thanksgiving, in order that he might be nice and fat for the generous season. One year the gobbler had thus been penned, like a sonnet, with reference to Thanksgiving, and anticipations were indulged of the "good time coming;" but, alas! the brightest hopes must fade. The turkey, when looked for, was not to be found. It had been stolen away! Upon discovering her great loss, Mrs. P. was for a moment overcome with surprise — disconcerted; but the sun of her benevolence soon broke the clouds away, and spread over her features like new butter upon hot biscuit, and with a smile, warm with the feeling of her heart, she said — "*I hope they will find it tender !—I guess we can be thankful on pork and cabbage !*"

"Say, ye severest, what would ye have done"

under such circumstances? You would, perhaps, have raved, and stamped, and swore, and made yourself generally ridiculous, besides perilling your soul in the excess of your anger. But Mrs. P. did n't, and there is where you and she differ. She stood calmly and tranquilly — a living lesson of philosophical patience under extreme difficulty. We cite this example that the world may profit by it.

FILIAL DUTY *vs.* WASHING-POWDER.

"Children of the present day," sighed the Rev. Adoniram Spaid, as he was visiting Mrs. Partington during the spring anniversaries — "children of the present day, ma'am, sadly ruffle the bosoms of their parents."

He crossed his legs as he spoke, and tied his handkerchief in a hard knot over his knee, at the same time looking at Ike through the back window, as that young gentleman was performing a slack-rope exercise upon the clothes-line, endangering the caps and handkerchiefs that swung like banners in the breeze. Mrs. Partington suspended washing, and looked round at her visitor, at the same time wiping her hands to take a pinch of snuff.

"Yes, sir," she said, "I think so ; but it is n't so bad, either, as it used to be before the soap-powder was found out."

Mr. Spaid quietly protested that he could not see the relevancy of the remark.

"Why," continued she, inhaling the rappee, and handing the box to the minister, "then it was a great labor to wash and do 'em up; but now the washing-powder makes it so easy, that the children can rumple bosoms or anything else with perfect impurity. We don't make nothing of it. I consider washing-powder " — holding up a pair of Ike's galligaskins that had just gone through a course of purification — "as a great blessing to mothers."

The minister smiled, and thought what a curious proposition it would be, in the "Society for the Mitigation of Everything," to recommend washing-powder as an auxiliary to other operative blessings, and thanked Mrs. Partington for the hint.

A SERIOUS QUESTION.

OLD ROGER came down stairs, one Sunday morning, with a face unusually animated, and stood, with his hands behind his back, playing nervously with the tails of his coat. The breakfast was waiting for him, the fish-balls were getting cold, the coffee was evaporating; but he did n't seem to care. He leaned over the back of the landlady's chair, and asked her, in a whisper, if she could tell him why a dyspeptic was out of immediate danger when his disease was most distressing. She looked earnestly at the top of the teapot a few moments, and then said that for the life of her she could n't tell. A curiosity was evinced by the boarders, and they asked what it was. They all gave it up, too. "Why," said he, looking very red, "it is because he can't di-gest then." Drawing his chin within his stock, the old fellow laughed lustily, and in his paroxysm threw his arms around the landlady's neck for support; but she threw them off very indignantly, for the boarders were all looking at her. He then sat down to breakfast with a good appetite.

RATHER A RASCAL.

"MRS. PARTINGTON, your neighbor, Mr. Gruff, is
rather irascible, I think," said the new minister on his
first visit to the old lady, as he heard Gruff scolding Ike
for throwing snow-balls at his new martin-house. Gruff
kept a grocery over the way, and was in a constant
quarrel with every boy in the neighborhood. Mrs. Partington looked at the minister through her spectacles
inquiringly before she answered.

"*Rather* a rascal!" said she, slightly misapprehend-
ing his question, and patting her box affectionately; "yes,
indeed, I think he is, a great rascal! He sold me burnt
peas for the best coffee, once, and it was n't weight,
nuther. When they built our new church, somebody
said there was a nave in it, and I know'd in a minute
who they meant. Why " ——

"I mean," interrupted the minister, blandly, laying
his white hand gently on his arm, "I mean that he is
quick-tempered."

"O, that's quite another thing — yes, he is very,"
and she changed the subject. But that word "irascible"
ran in her head for an hour after he was gone, and
when Ike came in she told him to take down the old
Johnson's Decency and find the defamation of it.

9*

THE SENSITIVE MAN SEES A BLOOMER.

—

THE Sensitive Man came in, one day, just after dinner, threw himself into a chair, and fainted. After a mug or two of Cochituate water had been dashed in his interesting face, he came to a little, gazed wildly upon the circle that surrounded him, and said, in a sort of unearthly whisper, " Where is she ? " Nobody knew what he meant. The fog, a moment later, rolled from his soul, and he was enabled to explain, with the aid of some slight stimulant.

A crowd in the street had obstructed his path, as he walked pensively along with his eyes cast down. Looking up, a vision of beauty burst upon his ravished sight, and he stood entranced as he gazed upon it ; and when it passed away with the crowd, he climbed upon an omnibus and watched that object, through his tunneled hand, until it became indistinct and lost in the distance. That object was a BLOOMER ! He had long ardently wished for this opportunity. In visions of the night had angels in short dresses and trousers thrust themselves among his sleeping fancies, to the bewilderment of his waking thoughts. It had become the great idea of his mind, and all his other thoughts bowed to this, as did the sheaves of the Israelitish brethren to the sheaf of Joseph of old. He had at last seen a Bloomer. The climax of his earthly desire was attained. The driver of the 'bus, callous to the emotion of his bosom, asked him " what 'n thunder he was a-looking at, up there ? " The Sensitive Man made but one step to the ground, so buoyant was he, and he bounded like cork. He could have leaped over the State-House. Little boys and sedate passengers stepped back dismayed, and a gentleman in a black coat and white neckcloth looked around anxiously after a policeman. What were policemen to the Sensitive Man ? Those terrific functionaries were nothing ! Even the cold reality of a watch-house floor would be soft as down, could he carry with him the consciousness that he had seen a Bloomer. He looked to see if her passing figure had not left its impression, in aerial portraiture, upon the impalpable atmosphere. He looked upon the pave to detect the print of her charming foot upon the insensate bricks. But she had fled, like some bright exhalation of the morning, and he turned back sorrowing. A coach came nigh running over him. The tension of his spirit relaxed, — enduring only to bring him within the precinct of his vocation, when his too sensitive nature gave out, and the result was as explained above.

And hourly, since, has he longingly gazed from the window, in ardent hope of seeing again the beauteous vision which had enthralled him, and disappointment,

———— " like a worm in the mud,
Feeds on his damaged cheek."

POWER OF ATTORNEY.

WHEN the widow Ames had been notified that her share of the Paul Jones prize-money would be paid her upon presenting herself at the Dummer Bank, she debated in her own mind, — though the debate never was reported, — whether she should go herself or give a power of attorney to some one else to receive the eleven dollars and sixty-two cents that was her share. In this strait she called on Mrs. Partington, who she knew had authorized a person to settle the Beanville estate for her when the Beanville Railroad had driven her from the homestead.

"Go yourself, dear," said the old lady, bringing the poker down emphatically upon the bail of the tea-kettle, as she was clearing out the ashes from the stove; "don't trust to nobody but yourself, for,"— raising the poker, — "if you give anybody power of eternity, depend upon it you won't never see the final conclusion of it."

The poker fell again upon the harmless tea-kettle, which seemed to sing out with reproach for the outrage, and Ike, who was looking slyly into the back window, wondered if Mrs. Ames was n't sitting on a favorite piece of spruce gum of his, and whether it would n't stick her to the chair so that she could n't get up. It showed that the boy had a reflective turn of mind.

THE NEW DRESS FOR LADIES.

"A new custom for ladies!" said Mrs. Partington, when a friend spoke to her about the proposed innovation in dress. The sound of "costume" came to her ear indistinctly, and she slightly misapprehended the word. "A new custom for ladies! I should think they had better reform many of their old customs before they try to get new ones. We're none of us better than we ought to be, and"——

"Costume, ma'am, I said," cried her informant, interrupting her; "they are thinking of changing their dress."

"Well, for my part I don't see what they want to make a public thing of it for; changing the dress used to be a private matter; but folks do so alter! They are always a changing dresses now, like the caterpillar in the morning that turns into a butterfly at night, or the butterfly at night that turns to a caterpillar in the morning, I don't know which"——

"But," again interrupted her informant, "I mean they are a going to have a new dress."

"O, they are, are they?" replied the old lady; "well, I'm sure I'm glad on it, if they can afford it; but they don't always think enough of this. A good many can't afford it — they can't! But did you hear of the new apperil for wimmin that somebody is talking about?"

" Why, my dear Mrs. P.," said he, smiling, "that is just what I was trying to get your opinion about."

" Then," returned she, " why did n't you say so in the first place ? Well, I don't know why a woman can't be as vertuous in a short dress as in a long one ; and it will save some trouble in wet weather to people who have to lift their dresses and show their ankles. It may do for young critters, as sportive as lambs in a pasture ; but only think how I should look in short coats and trousers, should n't I ? And old Mrs. Jones, who weighs three hundred pounds, would n't look well in 'em neither. But I say let 'em do just what they please as long as they don't touch my dress. I like the old way best, and that 's the long and the short of it."

She here cast a glance at the profile on the wall, as if for its approval of her resolution; and an idea for a moment ·seemed to cross her mind that he, the ancient corporal, would not know her, were he to visit sublunar scenes and find her arrayed in the new dress; and her compressed lips showed the determination of her heart to abide by the old costume, and she solemnly and slowly took an energetic pinch of snuff, as if to confirm it.

PSYCHOLOGY.

SENSITIVE people talk about feeling, in the presence or atmosphere of a man, the peculiar disposition that governs him, — whether a gentle or a stern one, whether a hypocritical or a knavish one. We have realized, in some degree, what the feeling must be, as we have, at times, elbowed our way among the gentlemen who throng about State or Wall street. The atmosphere was so hard that we shrank at once into our empty pocket, — a thing which finds no sympathy in those diggings, — and escaped as fast as possible. We could read every disposition that we rubbed against, like a book, or as well as the most subtle magician could do it. The *dollar* was the idea that every brain was working and struggling to coin itself into ; the dollar gleamed in every eager glance of the eye, and was heard in every word ; the dollar was the sun that shone and the air that blew ; and though celestial choirs had been at hand, chanting the music of the spheres, unless it had the right *chink* to it, it would not have been regarded. Let sensitive ones who have no money go down upon 'change and try the experiment. It will not make them any poorer, though most certainly they will not be any richer by it.

MATTER OF FACT.

—

" SHAKSPEARE's well enough," said Mr. Slow, "but he don't come up to my idee of po'try. There is too much of your hifalutin humbug about him. What he says don't seem to 'mount to nothing. As for Falstaff, he's a miser'ble and disreputable old fellow, and Hamlick's as mad as a bed-bug. Why did n't he knock his old father-in-law over, and done with it, and not make sich a hillibolu about it? Shakspeare is n't what he is cracked up to be, and if he does n't improve, I would n't give two per cent. for his chance of immortality. Who b'leves this 'ere, for instance?

> ' Orpheus' lute was strung with poets' sinews,
> Whose golden touch could soften steel and stones,
> Make tigers tame, and huge levithians
> Forsake unsounded deeps to dance on sand! '

That's all gammon. Poets' sinews, indeed! Dare say 't was n't nothin' but catgut; and as for its softening steel and stones, and taming tigers, and making levithians dance on the sand, that 'ere 's all bosh, and too ridic'lous for any man to b'leve."

Mr. Slow looked fearfully oracular as he said this, and the subject was suspended.

THE CAT AND KITTENS.

BEFORE Ike dropped the cat, it was a matter of much annoyance to Mrs. Partington, upon coming down stairs one morning, to find a litter of kittens in her Indian work-basket, beside her black Sunday bonnet, and upon the black gloves and handkerchief, long consecrate to grief. Ike had left the basket uncovered, during a search for some thread to make a snare to catch a pigeon with. Her temper was stirred by the circumstance, as what good, tidy housekeeper's would not have been by such an occurrence?

"I'll drownd 'em," said she, "every one of 'em! O, you wicked creatur!" continued she, raising her finger, and shaking it at the cat; "O, you wicked creatur, to serve me such a trick!"

But the cat, happy in the joys of maternity, purred gladly among her offspring, and looked upon the old lady, through her half-closed eyes, as if she did n't really see any cause for such a fuss.

"Isaac," said the dame, "take the big tub, and drownd them kittens."

There was determination in her eye, and authority in her tone, and Ike clapped his hands as he hastened to obey her.

"Stop, Isaac, a minute," she cried, "and I'll take the chill off the water; it would be cruel to put 'em into it stone-cold."

10

She took the steaming kettle from the stove, and
emptied it into the tub, and then left the rest to Ike.
But she reproached herself for her inhumanity long
afterwards, and could not bear to look the childless cat
in the face, and many a dainty bit did that injured
animal receive from her mistress.   Mrs. Partington
perhaps did wrong, as who has n't at some period of life?
Perfection belongeth not to man or woman, and we would
throw this good pen of ours into the street, and never
take another in our fingers, could we pretend that Mrs.
Partington was an exception to this universal rule.

A POINT SETTLED.

DR. DIGG — for whose researches the world can
never be grateful enough — has been studying out the
genealogy of the great family of Co., which occupies
such a distinguished mercantile position.   This family is
scattered the world over, and almost every sign in every
city bears the name of one of them as partner.   He
traces their genealogy back to Jericho, of Palestine
(modern Jeremiah Co., or, for shortness, Jerry Co.),
whom we find frequently mentioned in ancient books.
The doctor expresses the belief that the exclusive business habits of the family may be attributed to their
Jewish extraction.

MORAL TRAINING.

—

"Moral training," said Mrs. Partington, "is the best, arter all." She had heard some one in the omnibus speaking of moral training, and her benevolence gave it into the charge of memory until she got home, and memory revolved it, and pondered it, and reviewed it, and fancy construed it to mean something about the military training that was to come off the next day.

"I hope it will be a moral training, I'm shore," said she; "for I see the Gov'nor is to be there in his new suit, and I hope they'll make their revolutions well before him. I do admire the millintery, where the sogers in their fancy unicorns look jest like a patchwork quilt. They wasn't moral trainings in old times, when men put 'enemies into their heads to steal away their hats,' as Mr. Smooth, the schoolmaster, used to say Your Uncle Paul had a good deal of millintery sperrit sometimes, Isaac."

Ike had remained very quiet while she was speaking "What upon airth are you doing there, Isaac?' cried she.

The young gentleman readily told her he was painting a horse, at the same time displaying an animal, nominally of that description, done beautifully in blue, which he appeared to look on with much satisfaction.

"But what are you painting it with? As true as I'm alive you've got your Uncle Paul's tompion that he used to wear in his cap so long ago, and you're using up all my bluing!"

That pompon, saved for so many years, to be used for such a purpose! Ah, Ike, Ike! we fear the old lady will have sad times with thee yet. Why didst thou, yester even, secrete the large ball of yarn for thine own purposes, which to-morrow she will seek for in vain? Say, why?

A LITTLE TRUTH.

"THERE'S something for us all to do," is the heading of a poem in the papers — a subject which seems to have more of truth than poetry in it. There are exceptions, however, to the rule; for a very seedy gentleman with a very red nose told us, one day, that he could n't get a thing to do. The man appeared strong, and so did his breath. But there are many worthy people who cannot find their proportion of the "something for all to do," and suppose some philanthropist is doing it for them.

HAIR-DRESSING.

"WHAT a queer place this Boston is!" said Mrs. Partington, when she first came here from the country. "I was walking along the street just now, and saw on a sign 'Hair-Dressing.' 'Something like guano, I guess, for the hair,' said I to myself. 'I declare, I'm a good mind to look at some.' So I went in and asked a dear, pretty young man, smelling as sweet as catnip, to let me look at some of his *hair manure*, — I wanted to be as polite as possible. Gracious! how he stared at me, just as if I'd a been a Hottenpot, or a wild Arad. 'I mean your hair-*dressing*,' said I.

"'O, ah, yes!' said he; 'set down here in the big chair, mem, — scratch, perhaps, mem!'

"'Scratch,' said I, completely dumbfounded; 'you saucy fellow! I can do all my own scratching, and some of yourn, too, if you say that agin, — scratch, indeed!' — and I went right down the stairs."

She never before had hinted that she stood in need of any hair tonic, though everybody knew that she had worn a wig for twenty years.

MRS. PARTINGTON says that it makes no difference to her if flour is dear or cheap, she always has to pay the same price for half a dollar's worth.

10*

OMNIBUS-RIDING.

'T IS a rainy morning, and, health considered, we think we 'll ride. The 'bus heaves in sight, and we look anxiously through the dusty windows, to see a dense packing of humanity, in one long lane that has no turning, occupying the inside. The driver pulls up as we wave our cane, — he has been watching us for some distance, calculating on the chances of a summons, — and, peering down from his perch, through the ticket-hole, ascertains that there is room for *one more.* There always is. We take heart at the announcement, and mount the steps, while the door swings open to admit us. " Calculated to hold twelve persons " beams upon us from the front of the vehicle, whether nature in framing the " persons " bore the 'bus-maker's limit in mind or not. It *must* hold twelve, irrespective of size. There are but *eleven* inside, and we make the twelfth, but where to sit? Six lean " persons " occupy one side, and five fat ones the other. Of course our place is with the five, and they seem conscious of it, — they have read the arbitrary inscription, — and crowd one another, and squat their sides to the smallest squeezable limit to admit us, and, just as the 'bus starts, we fall plump between a very fiery-looking old gentleman, and a lady of unromantic years, and biliously wicked-looking withal. Something cracks in the old gentleman's pocket, and a growl greets us from him, while, with half of our " per-

son " resting upon the lady's carpet-bag, we are made
sensible of a sharp elbow, and the ejaculation " O,
Lord ! " uttered in a tone between a prayer and a reproach. Of course we 've a right there, for, is n't the
coach bound to hold twelve, and won't we give " one pull
for the right " before we 'll give it up ? That 's a beautiful face opposite, — a glimpse convinces us of this, —
but we cannot stare at her; good manners forbid it !
There is a glass beneath the driver's seat, and here the
pretty face in duplicate appears, and we gaze upon it
unnoted.

We are now reminded of the presence of the collector
of the tickets, who touches our shoulder, and looks
significantly without saying anything. He was never
known to say anything but twice in his life, it is said, —
once to inform a man in the 'bus that it was cold, and
again, in a confidential whisper, to hint that it was
unpleasant. We struggle to reach the pocket which
contains our ticket; but the mass that hems us in won't
move, and, in a spasmodic effort to entrap the card,
three buttons are sacrificed, and a bonnet disturbed in its
position. We laugh at some pleasant allusion of our
own about clumsiness; but the laugh appears only upon one
side, and we relapse into silence, and look in the glass
beneath the driver's seat. Thank Heaven ! the big man
here pulls the string, and sturdily tramples over quiescent toes in his egress. Then the lady with the carpet-
bag pulls vehemently, in a vain effort to jerk the driver
through, and she gets out. Then another, and another,
until all are gone but us, — the pretty girl last, — and
we are captain of the ship, all the difficulties of our

outset merged in the triumphant consciousness that we
have *room*.   What do we care now about how many the
'bus will hold?   We snap our fingers at the insulting
rule that would curtail humanity, and gaze upon the
other inscription, that enjoins the pull for the right;
then pull the string magnificently, the coach stops, and
we descend among the pedestrians, not a whit inflated by
our momentary exaltation.

AURIFEROUS MEDITATIONS.

"Golden airs of Californy," said Mrs. Partington,
as she read in the Post an advertisement of some new
music; "such airs, I should think, would be very re-
plenishing, and I wish a draft of 'em would blow this
way.   What a country that Colifarny is!" murmured
she, in a half reverie, in which golden visions, like the
sunshine reflections on the kitchen wall, from her teacup,
were dancing through her brain.   "What a queer thing!
where gold is so plenty they pick it up in quarts on
American Forks, — Connetticut ones, I dare say; but
spoons, I should think, would be a good deal better."
Of course it would.   Strange that the miners didn't
think of this in the first place.   Many a valuable suggestion of hers has benefited the world; though the
world was not aware of its indebtedness until she said,
"I always thought so;" and this coming late, she never
got the credit for it.

IKE AND THE ORANGES.

"I can't conceive," said Mrs. Partington, standing up on tiptoe, and pushing aside the antique wash-bowl that stood on the front shelf in the old cupboard in the corner, and rattling the papers of seeds, and the teacups, and the plates, and looking into the dark corners, and feeling in, also, to be certain. When she said she "could n't conceive," it was but part of the sentence that she wished to speak; the earnestness of her search had suspended the remainder of it.

"I can't conceive where those oranges are," said she, "that the young ladies sent me — Heaven bless 'em ! — they were so good to lucubrate the throat with when it 's dry and hot with the information that comes with a cough. It is strange where they have gone. If I believed in superhumorous things I should say the spirits had got 'em ; but they would n't take mine when they could go so easy where they grow and get as many as they want."

She stopped her search amid the dust, and regaled her nose with dust of a more fragrant character.

"What are you doing, Isaac ? " said she, as she saw him forming a star out of an orange upon the closet door, and using up her pump tacks. The boy pointed to his handiwork, and the delight she felt for his genius blinded her eyes to the possibility of how he might have come by the oranges.

PATRIOTISM.

A YANKEE gentleman, convoying a British friend around to view the different objects of attraction in the vicinity of Boston, brought him to Bunker Hill. They stood looking at the splendid shaft, when the Yankee said,

"That is the place where Warren fell."

"Ah!" replied the Englishman, evidently not posted up in local historical matters; "did it hurt him much?"

The native looked at him, with the expression of fourteen Fourth of Julys in his countenance. "Hurt him!" said he, "he was *killed*, sir."

"Ah! he was, eh?" said the stranger, still eying the monument, and computing its height, in his own mind, layer by layer; "well, I should think he would have been, to fall so far."

The native tore his hair, but it gave him a good opportunity to enlarge upon the glorious events connected with the hill, and the benefits therefrom flowing to our somewhat extensive country, and he soon talked himself into good-humor.

KEEP your eyes wide open for the truth; let it come down into your mind like the sunlight, to illumine all of its dark corners. "Buy the truth, and sell it not."

DULL BUSINESS.

A LONG time ago, in an old town we wot of, there lived a man of humble means, — there are some poor people there now, — and, in pity for his need, he was made sexton of the church of which he was a member. The times were dull, his salary was low, and he found it hard work to make both ends meet. He called upon the members of the church, but they could not or would not do anything for his relief. As a last resort he called upon the minister and told him his troubles, and how hard he found it to get along. The minister heard his story, but, instead of relieving his wants, or telling *him* how to do it, went to arguing with him about the unreasonableness of his complaint.

"Why," says he, "don't you have, besides your salary, a number of perquisites? Are you not paid for ringing the bell on the Fourth of July and other public celebrations? And are you not paid, too, for your services at funerals, when any occur in our society?"

"True," said the dolorous sexton, looking up solemnly; "but I have little hope from this source, for, confound it, none of our society ever die!"

The poor fellow went away sorrowing, thinking, probably, that Providence was rather hard on him in not killing off half the parish that he might have the profit of burying them.

ANTIQUITY IN A SHOWER.

Mrs. Partington attended the dedication of Mount Hope Cemetery, in Dorchester, and got wet with the rain. No sheltering umbrella was there to hold its broad surface above her venerable head; and the rain, all regardless of her august presence, poured down relentlessly. But we will let her tell the story in her own way.

" The seminary would have been dictated, but, by an imposition of divine Providence, the bottles of heaven were uncorked and the rains fell as if another delusion was agoing to destroy the world. The lightning blazed horridly, and everybody was filled with constipation. Not a shelter to be had! I tried to lean over and get my bonnet under a gentleman's umbrel, in front of me, and the water all run down into my back like a spout, till I was satiated through and through like an old boot. Cold chills run over me as if I had an ager, and, O dear! look at that bonnet."

Certainly the faded remnant had wilted, the pasteboard that formed the crown had relaxed and shook flabbily as we held it, and irreparable decay seemed written upon it.

" It never will be fit to be seen again ! " said she, and we fancied a tone of deeper sorrow in her words, as she looked straight up at the stiff old corporal on the wall, whom this antique crape commemorated. Heaven bless thee, Mrs. Partington ! we thought, and felt round our capacious pocket for a dollar to leave with her, but, as it usually happens when our benevolence comes on, we found none, and came away with a paper pinned to our coat-tail by that " everlasting Ike."

THE NATIONAL EPIC.

" 1 CAN'T see through it," said Mrs. Partington, with a reflective nod of her head, and her eyes earnestly bent upon the keyhole of the closet door, as if that were the object she could not see through. She had just learned the report of the committee upon the prize poem proposition of Mr. Latham, and the loss of $500 to the musical genius of the country. "I can't see why somebody could n't have written an epic poem, when there is so many beautiful epicac poets in the country. Dear me, the older I grow, — and I never shall see fifty-seven again, — I 'm convinced that genius is n't thought half enough of, and that versatanity of talent and great power of versuffocation is n't rewarded as it ought to be." This was said in compliment to Wideswarth, who, it was half suspected, had put in for the prize, and he bowed modestly, as he placed his hand in the vicinity of his heart, and felt in his vest pocket for a tooth-pick.

11

MRS. PARTINGTON AND THE MAINE LIQUOR BILL.

MRS. PARTINGTON was in the gallery of the House of Representatives when the Maine liquor law was under discussion. The member from Cranberry Centre was very attentive to the old dame, and replied to her questions concerning the Maine liquor law, and spoke of the various provisions of the bill. " Provisions ? " said the kind old dame, tapping her box gently, " I never heerd there was any provisions mentioned in the bill; though I dare say there is, for Paul used to say that give old Mr. Tipple a pint of rum, it would be vittals and drink and house-rent for a week; and I b'lieve it was so, for, only give him rum enough, he 'd never ask for bread. I remember, too," continued the old lady, raising her voice, as she saw Mr. Batkins about to interrupt her, — " they used always to put rum and tobacco into their provision bills, in old times, when they went a fishing, and I s'pose this putting provisions into the liquor bill is 'bout the same thing." She looked at Mr. Batkins, and smiled, as she saw him looking smilingly at her, and they both smiled at each other.

" The provisions meant, mem," said the member, impressively, " are provisions of law."

" Ah ! " replied the old lady, musingly, as she took the third pinch, and handed the box to Mr. Batkins, " yes, yes, I 've heerd of folks bein' bread to the law

afore, though a good many of 'em is more like vegetables. But " —— Here the speaker's mallet attracted
her attention, and she listened to the reading of part of
the liquor bill, watching carefully for the items. " Is
that the liquor bill? " asked she, in an incredulous tone,
of her friend, the member ; " is that it ? " He assured
her that it was. " Well," continued she, as she rose to
go, " I must say that I never see a bill made out in that
way afore."

Mr. Batkins handed her out, and she remarked to
Mr. Verigreen, whom she met on the stairs, that she had
come to hear the liquor bill, and they were reading a
new chapter, that she 'd never read, in the book of
Acts.

TAKE THINGS EASY.

" I NEVER knowed anything gained by being in too
much of a hurry," said Mrs. Partington. " When me
and my dear Paul was married, he was in such a tripi-
dation that he came nigh marrying one of the brides-
maids instead of me, by mistake. He was such a queer
man ! " she continued. " Why, he joined the fire apartment, and one night in his hurry he put his boots on
hind part afore ; and, as he ran along, everybody behind
him got tripped up. The papers were full of crowner's
quests on broken legs and limbs, for a week afterwards,"
— and she relapsed into an abstraction on the ups and
downs of life.

CARRIED AWAY WITH MUSIC.

—

EVERYBODY will remember the organ-grinder's little child, who was carried around, seated upon the instrument his father was tuning, his young heart well satisfied with things as they were, so he enjoyed his musical throne.   We regret to say that this babe of tender years was once made the subject of as cruel a joke as was ever seen in print.   Our friend, Old Roger, was concerned in it, too, and with his kind feelings 't is a wonder he could have done it.   PHILANTHROPOS observed Old Roger standing upon the sidewalk, good-humoredly beating time to a lively air performed by the man of the organ, and observing the dexterity with which he would pick up a cent and not lose a note.

"Sir," said Philanthropos, "observe the hard fortune of that babe, thus chained to such a destiny; a child with a soul to save thus risking its safety by breathing continually such abominable *airs*."

"I know it," said Old Roger, in his way; "I know it, and yet the little fellow seems to be entirely *carried away* with the music."

Philanthropos immediately left him.

MRS. PARTINGTON IN TROUBLE.

"TRYING the French sea-steamer!" said Mrs. Partington, as she read in the foreign news an account of trialtrips made by the French steamships. She has always had a deep interest in the French, since Mr. Lay Martin, as she calls Lamartine, has been driven out of the provisional government, and the people have got to go back to frog soup again. "What can they be going to try them for?" continued she. "I never knowed that steamboats could be arranged for murder and such things before, though I don't see no reason why they should n't, seeing so many murders come from their arrangements. And I wish they'd try 'em all before they do the mischief, and condemnation 'll be a warning to 'em, just as it would if we could try all of the murderers, and hang 'em off aforehand, and save the lives of their innocent victims. Isaac!" she screamed, as a snow-ball struck the window, "don't throw your snow this way!" and she rushed out to save her glass. Alas! she was a moment too soon, for a snow-ball struck her cap as she issued from the door, tore it from her head, and bore it, with its strings hanging down, far from her. Her hair, all unconfined, danced madly in the wind, and Mrs. Partington for a moment looked every witch way. Virtue is of little account unless it be tried, nor is patience. Mrs. Partington calmly "digested" her cap on her head and went in.

11*

INFLUENZA.

"I DECLARE, I b'lieve I'm going to have the influ-wednesday," said Mrs. Partington, tenderly enveloping her nose in her cotton bandanna, previous to a blast that would have done credit to Sam Robinson's stage-horn in the old time. "'T is a dreadful feeling to have your head as big as a bucket of water, and your nose dropping like the eaves, and your flesh all creepy with cold pimples, like a child with the mizzles. Paul's sister's child, she that married with a Smith, had the distemper-ature so bad that they had to put cork stoppers in his nostrils to keep his brains from running out!"

She was here "brought up" suddenly with a fit of coughing; the knitting-work was laid by for the night, and she went up stairs with a hot brick for her feet, and a little preparation of something hotter for her stomach.

AN ANSWER.

"WHAT do they call them dancers the *corpse de ballet* for?" asked Mr. Verigreen of old Roger, at the theatre. The old fellow was watching them intently from the parquette, with a double magnifying opera glass, and did n't wish to be disturbed, but answered: — "Because no *live* dancers can jump half so high as they can."

MUTTON CUSTARD.

"As regards this mutton custard," said Mrs. Partington, as she held up the spoon with which she was stirring the preserves, and let the treacle trickle back into the kettle in syrupticious ropiness, and stirred it again till the little yellow eyes that bubbled on the top seemed to snap and wink at Ike who sat whittling a stick and looking intently at the operation, till his mouth watered again. "Mutton custard!" and she smiled as the idea stole across her mind, like the shadow of a cloud in summer over a green meadow full of dandelion blossoms and butter-cups. "Some new regiment for sick people, I dare say; but I hope it 'll be better than the custards that widow Grudge used to make for the poor, God bless 'em! with one egg to a quart of milk, and sweetened with molasses, and thought that Heaven itself was too small an emuneration for what she had done. But mutton custard"—

"It is Martin Koszta," said Ike, who had read the name to her in the Post of that individual when he arrived in Boston; "Koszta, the Hungarian."

"Well," continued she, "it might have been worse, as the girl said when she kissed the young minister by mistake, in the dark entry, for her cousin Betsey, — a mistake is no haystack, Isaac."

Isaac silently admitted the truth of the remark as he

thrust the stick he had been whittling into the kettle, and then made a drawing of the equatorial line across both cheeks in warm molasses.

MRS. PARTINGTON ON THE "RELIGIOUS TEST."

"The religious taste among politicians!" exclaimed Mrs. Partington, as her opinion was asked on the great question that was then agitating the people of New Hampshire; and she smiled incredulously as she answered, "I never heerd that they had any religious taste at all, nor religious feeling, nuther, for that matter. We see that all the politicians this 'ere way that ever had any religion has give it all up. There is Parson Trot, who used to compound the gospel up in the old church, has come out a politicioner, and where is his religious taste, now, I should like to know? and there's lots just like him " ——

"But, dear madam," quoth the interrogator, blandly, "I did n't mean *taste*, — it was test that I spoke about."

She inhaled a large thumb and finger full of her favorite before she spoke. "Their testiness," said she, "is quite another thing, and none of 'em a'n't no better 'n they ought to be."

The inquirer left, decidedly impressed with the originality and truth of her remark.

MRS. PARTINGTON'S IDEA OF HUMOR.

—

"WHAT is your opinion of the humor of Hawthorne, Mrs. Partington?" asked a young neighbor that had been reading "Twice-Told Tales."

"I don't know," said she, looking at him earnestly; "but if you have got it, you 'd better take something to keep it from striking in. Syrup of buckthorne is good for all sorts of diseases of that kind. I don't know about the humor of Hawthorne, but I guess the buckthorne will be beneficious. We eat too much butter, and butter is very humorous."

There was a slight tremor in his voice, as he said he would try her remedy, and a smile might have been perceived about his mouth, next day, when she asked him, with a solicitous air and tone, how his humor was.

—

A GREAT CURIOSITY.

—

DR. DIGG, in a lecture before the Spunkville Lyceum, stated it as an interesting fact, and as indicative of the progress of the age, that he had, in a recent journey among the Green Mountains, discovered a SAGE CHEESE. We hope the doctor will be induced to give a paper upon the subject to the world. Cheeses have often been noted for their activity, but none of them, we believe, have ever been distinguished for their profundity.

MRS. PARTINGTON ON EXTRADITION.

"EXTRADITION of Sims!" said Mrs. Partington, as she paused a moment before the bulletin board of the Commonwealth, during the great excitement; "I don't see what they want an extra edition of Sims for, when they had so much trouble in getting off the first one!"

"'Ere's the Commonwealth, fourth edition!" bawled a newsboy in her ear.

She raised her umbrella with a menacing air, for the noise was strange to her, when her good genius stayed her hand; the umbrella, — the old green cotton one, — descended gently as a snow-flake, and the kind old lady invested two coppers, American currency, in a last week's paper which the urchin chanced to have on hand.

IRREVERENT.

ONE of our preachers, in his sermon, spoke of those who do business, as travelling along the level plain of life. Old Roger happened to be there, and the old fellow reached over to his neighbor, and whispered, "It may be a plain for some, but for myself I have always found it up-hill work." The neighbor laughed at Roger with the back of his head, but kept the part grave that was towards the minister.

INDIGNATION MEETING.

—

HE enforcement of the law re-
quiring our canine friends and
fellow-citizens to wear collars
about their necks — a servile
mark, which no dog of spirit could for a moment consent
to wear — caused, as might be supposed, much growling
among them; and many teeth were shown, and much
dogged determination was evinced to resist the law.
Acting upon this feeling, the more energetic of the Canin-
ites went round among their brethren counselling them
to withstand the law, and telling them, besides, that the
rights of universal puppydom were in their keeping, and
asking them, in tones of earnest entreaty, if they would
see those rights sacrificed without a struggle.

This appeal was effectual, and a meeting was forthwith
assembled at the old slaughter-house, on South Boston
flats, to discuss the great question of resistance. It was
composed chiefly of dogs whose necks had never chafed

with the ignominious badge of ownership; of hard-faring dogs, bone-gnawing dogs; of dogs not nursed in the lap of luxury or pampered by the indulgence of favoring masters; none of the silk-eared and soft-footed aristocracy; but there were the Huge Paws from Roxbury Neck, the Shagbarks from the North End, and the Tough and Roughers from West Boston, and many of minor note. Not a smile marked their meeting, not a tail wagged, not a bark disturbed the stillness, and anybody with half an eye could see that each heart was nerved with mighty resolution.

The meeting was organized by the choice of CÆSAR, the biggest dog present, for president; and PLATO, a lean dog in specs, who had been very active in getting up the meeting, and who was known to be an excellent reporter, was appointed scribe. Some said, in an under tone, aside, that the scribe had nominated himself, but his well-known modesty precluded the possibility of this, and it may be set down as a slander.

The chairman, on taking his seat, stood up, and, after wagging his tail in silence for some moments, expressive of his deep emotion, he then proceeded to make a speech describing the object of the meeting, characterized by all the profundity, eloquence, brilliancy, and power, that has rendered the name of Cæsar immortal, and that has more or less marked the efforts of every chairman of every meeting since when the memory of man or dog knoweth not the contrary. We regret very much that we have not this great speech to print. In recommending union in their action, he related an original anecdote about an old man and his sons and a bundle of sticks, which was received with tremendous applause.

There was a struggle for the floor as the chairman ceased, and, amidst much yelping, it was assigned to CATO, an old setter, who called upon his hearers to keep cool and not be in too much of a hurry; they would accomplish more by masterly inactivity than by thrusting their necks in the way of the danger; they must remember the conduct of an ancient member of their race, — he must refer to it, although it was humiliating to think that a dog should be such a fool, — who dropped a piece of beef he had in his mouth for its shadow in the water. Prudence, with both eyes wide open tight, would remove them out of the way of trouble; as a last word he would advise them to lay low and look out for bricks — a species of dog-bane inimical to canine constitutions.

A heavy old, dark-browed dog here arose, who commenced to bay violently against the law and those who were enforcing it. He was astonished, he was paralyzed, he was dumfounded to hear dogs counsel coolness in this crisis! The policemen are upon us! We have already felt our tails within their degrading fingers! I hold them and their leader in detestation! *He!* I would bark at the woman who does his washing, I hate him so! I would point at him in State-street, though not naturally a pointer! I would show my teeth at him wherever I met him! His excitement overpowered him, and he sat down.

PONTO, a large, gnarly, hard-looking dog, here arose, and it was doubtful for a time if he could be heard, for the noise and confusion which prevailed among the oppo-

12

sers of the law. He was for law and order. Law was too sacred a thing to be handled without gloves; it was the palladium of our liberty. If the law was oppressive, as it doubtless was, he would suggest, in his reverence for law, that they grin and bear it; if their necks were a little chafed, the evil would be mitigated by the reflection that the law was inviolate. Individual grievance was nothing in comparison with this grand idea. Everything that is legal is right; what is wrong in the individual may become right in law. Did the law require him to fasten the collar upon his own neck or upon the necks of those with whom he was allied, he would not hesitate to do it, in his regard for the law; he would " ——

He was here pulled down by his tail, when, amid the shaggy hair which thickly covered his neck, a collar was discovered, fitting closely to the skin! Amid the confusion attending this discovery, he sneaked away.

A sandy-haired dog, named CARLO, next took the floor, and snarled ominously as he commenced. He had but few words to say. He would ask them if they were going to allow this law to be enforced? For his part he would fill his pockets with pistols, and with a twenty-four-pounder under each arm would he go alone to oppose it!

His remarks produced an immense sensation among the younger portion of the audience. A cry was here made for "BONES." A venerable dog arose, whose appearance excited respect. He gained his feet with much difficulty, and it was perceived that he had a wooden leg, and bore about his person sundry other marks of dilapidation.

"My brethren," said he, when the cheering which had greeted him had subsided, "you have before you but a sorry dog; but such as I am is all that was left over from that fatal nineteenth of April, when so many of our race were served up cold. I was then young and ardent. At the first howl of danger, I left the bone I was gnawing, and threw myself into the front rank of the defenders of my race. Alas! my friends; I soon found that I was barking up the wrong tree, and discovered, too, that canine sagacity, however good it might be in saving children from drowning, or worrying cats, could never cope with humanity armed with clubs and actuated by the love of money. In a bloody fray my leg was broken with an ignominious brick; in another my termination was curtailed; in another my right eye closed in darkness on the world forever. With this view of the power of man, and of our own weakness, I would counsel caution — submission, even — for the present, resting in the assurance of the fulfilment of the ancient prophecy of the good time coming, when 'every dog shall have his day!' when, basking in the broad sunshine of beneficent law, we may catch flies in peaceful security, fearing not the butcher's art, fearing not the urchins' mischief, who, so reckless of our feelings, persist in ornamenting our extremities with cast-off culinary utensils."

This speech produced a great sensation, awakening the president, who had fallen asleep during the pathetic part of it; and a few sensitive pups near the door were so deeply affected that they had to go out and take a little whine to restore their strength. The scribe, who had prepared a series of resolutions before he came, concluded not to submit them, and let them drop back in his pocket, to read some other time to private admirers; and the meeting dissolved.

HOW TO GET OUT OF AN OMNIBUS.

GIVE the string a sudden jerk at the same instant you start from your seat to make for the door. The motion of the coach will afford you an excellent opportunity of testing your powers of navigation, and will not in the least annoy you, although it may be annoying to those whose corns you tread on. If you are timid of falling into the laps of your fellow-passengers, incline your body forward, as if about commencing to swim, and place your hands upon projecting knees on each side, until you are at a right distance from the door, and then make a sudden and energetic plunge at it, as if attempting to carry it by storm. We have seen a lady attempt this mode of egress, and by skilful management contrive to sit on seven masculine laps before she reached the door It saves time to start a trifle before pulling the string; you might lose a full sixteenth of a minute by waiting for the coach to stop, and that is something where "time is money" and money is two per cent. a month!

A LITERAL CONSTRUCTION.

"Preachers," said a reverend gentleman, "should be careful, in doing their Master's service, never to exceed their commission, or take anything but the Bible into their mouths."

"Bless me!" thought Mrs. Partington, as he said this; "I don't see how he could find room for anything more very well; though some mouths are a great deal larger than others. I remember my poor Paul and his brother were digging a cellar once, when Paul threw some dirt in his brother's mouth. 'Paul,' says he, 'you 've filled my mouth half full of dirt.' His brother had a very big mouth. 'Have I?' said Paul; 'well, just spit it outside, and we shan't have any more to dig.' Ah, Paul was such a queer man! He was the beatermost creatur."

What a joyous gleam shot from her specs as this reminiscence crossed her mind, giving the very iron of the bows the semblance of gold in its light! But the reflection cost her the whole of the fourthly.

12*

A LEGITIMATE CONCLUSION.

OLD Mr. Brown and his son George were engaged in the haymow, when the conversation turned upon California, and the young man expressed a strong desire to go. The old man said he should n't go. They talked about it, reasoned about it, grew mad about it, and the end of it all was, that George shoved his venerable progenitor down over the mow, through a hole in the barn floor, into an apple binn, to the imminent risk of the venerable gentleman's neck, and then ran away, leaving his father in the binn among the apples. The old man, some months afterwards, told the minister the story, and the reverend very profoundly said that he thought children who showed such disrespect to their parents never came to a good end. "No, *sir!*" said old Mr. Brown, firmly, striking his hoe with energy into the turf, — "no, *sir!* depend upon it, that boys who throw their fathers down into apple binns don't go to Heaven by a great sight."

AN EPIGRAM. — Upon the election of General Pierce the usual changes were made in the various subordinate offices, with the usual anxiety among the outs and ins, expressed by the following : —

> "The office-holders are all in a sweat,"
>   Said an office-hoper, with exultation ;
> "True," said old Roger, "I never yet
>   Saw such a General Piercepiration."

QUESTION ANSWERED.

"Where is the fire?" asked Mrs. Partington of a fireman, from an upper window, as the bells were waking the night with their clangor.

"In ——," was the ungallant response, naming the hottest title of perpetual warmth. "Dear me!" said the old lady, not comprehending him; "is it so far off? I wish it was nearer for your sake! But he'll get there soon," she muttered to herself, "if he goes on as he does now;" and she went to sleep again, invoking blessings on the guardians of public safety.

THE TEST REFUSED.

Mr. Jabez Brattle, the elocutionist, was introduced one day to Prof. ——, and expressed himself much pleased at making that gentleman's acquaintance. Mr. Brattle stated to the professor that he was an ardent admirer of his works, and that he could repeat "Evangeline" and the "Golden Legend" from beginning to end. He commenced the former, and had not got more than half through before the professor was seen dashing wildly up School street; and, in fifteen minutes by the Old South, he stood upon Cambridge Bridge, thankful at his escape from a bore.

A WHOLESOME LESSON.

"A DOG is a very singular animal," said the owner of Fido to old Roger, after they had marked the affectionate gambols of the faithful creature, who now, in weariness, had come to lie at his master's feet; "a very singular animal. Now you see I will flog him severely (suiting the action to the word); and now you see him licking my hand in return."

Old Roger was moved.

"Yes," said the old man severely, "and were I the dog I would give you a different sort of licking from that. He is the noblest animal of the two, and ought to change places with you. Let me tell you, sir, that a man who by a mere accident occupies the superior position, and out of pure wantonness abuses the power he may possess, or presumes upon that power to hurt the helpless, is a scoundrel, sir! That dog, there, is a king to him."

And the old man turned away, leaving Fido and his master to experience perhaps the benefit of the lesson. There is a moral in it.

A BOOTLESS CASE.

"I wish I could find something to help my corns," said Mr. Verd, despondingly; "they ache so!"

"I 'll tell you what 'll cure 'em," said one of the boarders. "Wear large boots, — 'bout two sizes larger 'n you now wear, — and your corns 'll be better."

Mr. Verd wore No. 12s, already, and, as he cast his eyes towards his feet, upon hearing this advice, he sighed piteously, for the remedy seemed bootless.

"Young man," said old Roger, wiping his mouth on his napkin, "I pity your case, if you depend upon that; for, to carry out the plan recommended, the streets would surely have to be widened, and land is very dear in Boston."

It was touching the young man upon a sore spot, and he left off complaining from then.

PERHAPS TRUE.

A paper begins a paragraph eulogistic — "Price, the immortal friend of mothers," &c. We are assured, by a friend at our elbow that knows, that price is no object with some mothers; and that however much it may be pretended that Price is the mother's friend, it is a notorious fact that price is obnoxious to fathers.

OLD ROGER'S NEW HAT.

"FOR heaven's sake, old woman, get off my hat!" said Roger at the concert, as he saw a two hundred and fifty pounder settle on his new ventilated castor. *Old woman!* It was an ungallant expression, but the circumstance would seem to justify it. A new hat was a new era in his existence, and this was one of the latest. Recovering himself, and pressing over his knee as best he might his crushed tile, the wrinkles but too apparent, he calmly continued, "I wouldn't object to your trying it on, ma'am, were there the least chance of its fitting; but it is evident that it isn't large enough. *I* never saw a hat worn in that way before, and *I* don't want to furnish one to experiment upon, either."

The hat was put on, but how like an apothecary's 'prentice long indented it looked, contrasted with its previous fair proportions! The opera is very destructive to hats, especially where they throw them at the singers.

CHRISTMAS REFLECTION.

—

"I wish you a merry Christmas
And a happy New Year,
With your stomach full of money,
And your pocket full of beer,"

yelled Ike, as he skipped into Mrs. Partington's kitchen, where the old dame was busily engaged in cooking breakfast on Christmas morning.

"Don't make such a noise, dear," said the kind old lady, holding up her hand; "you give me a scrutinizing pain in my head, and your young voice goes through my brains like a scalpel knife. But what did the good Santa Cruz put in your stocking, Isaac?"

And she looked at him with an arch and pleased expression, as he took out of his pocket a jacknife, and a humtop painted with gaudy colors. Ike held them up joyously, and it was a sight to see the two standing there, she smiling serenely upon the boy's happiness, and he grateful in the possession of his treasures.

"Ah!" said she, with a sigh, "there's many a home to-day, Isaac, that Santa Cruz won't visit, and many a poor child will find nothing in his stocking but his own little foot!"

It might have been a grain of the snuff she took, it might have been a floating mote of the atmosphere, but Mrs. Partington's eyes looked humid, though she smiled upon the boy before her, who stood trying to pull the cord out of her reticule to spin his new top with.

REFLECTION ABOUT MOSQUITOS.

—

"THERE! now I hope you 've got it, you everlastin' torment!" said Mrs. Partington, angrily giving Margaret, her young neighbor, who was in spending the evening with her, a smart slap on her forehead, and nearly throwing her from her chair; at the same time knocking the Britannia lamp from the table by her violent motion.

"What 's the matter?" inquired Margaret, alarmed; for such conduct was very unusual, and the oil from the lamp had marred her new calico.

"It 's only a pesky musketeer, dear," said the old lady, relighting the lamp; "it 's only a musketeer, and I can't see the use of 'em, the tormenting creaturs! They say the Lord makes everything for some good purpose; and so I think that these sort of annoysome reptiles must be made by somebody else, I do."

The remark may be thought irreverent by some, but the old lady was excited, and the heat of these warm, mosquito-teeming evenings ought to excuse more, even, under such annoyance as she was suffering.

A PASSABLE JOKE.

OLD ROGER was at the concert one evening, and as he sat awaiting the commencement of the performances in a slip where there was room for one more, a gentleman came along, and tapping him on the shoulder told him in a whisper that he should like to pass inside of him. Old Roger looked at the stranger a moment; he was a large man, very large.

"Upon my word, sir," said the old fellow, "I don't think you can, for I have just eaten a hearty supper, and from appearances I should judge that you wouldn't sit well on my stomach."

This was said loud enough for people in the adjacent seats to hear, and in an instant eleven double spy-glasses were levelled at him. The gentleman looked very red at first.

"I mean," said he, pointing to the vacant seat, "will you allow me to pass by you to that seat?"

"Certainly, sir," said Old Roger gravely, "and I am rejoiced to find that your request is so much more passable than I first regarded it."

The stranger immediately tendered Old Roger his hat, which he magnanimously declined receiving.

13

A PORCINE EXPOSURE.

—

"Could n't you get *young* pork, ma'am, to bake with your beans?" said old Roger, somewhat cynically, as he sat at table one Sunday.

"They told me it was young!" said the landlady.

"Well, it may be so, but gray hair is not a juvenile feature, by any means, in our latitude, ma'am," continued he, fishing up a gray hair, about a foot and a half long, with his fork. "He *may* have been young, but he must have lived a very wicked life to be gray so soon."

As he spoke he looked along the table, and a slight emotion was visible among the boarders; and the man who sat opposite, with his mouth full of the edibles with which he had been endeavoring to smother a laugh, grew dark with the effort, and then collapsed, scattering dismay and crumbs amid the nicely-plaited folds of old Roger's shirt-frills.

———

Spunk.—"*I* would n't be so bothered about *my* meals," said a jour printer to a brother typo, who had to wait pretty often for dinner that did n't pay for waiting; "if I boarded out I 'd have my dinner ——— just as soon as I could get it."

A NAVE IN THE CHURCH.

"A NAVE in our church!" screamed Mrs. Partington, as her eye rested on a description of the new edifice, and the offensive word struck terror to her soul; "a nave in our church! who can it be? Dear me, and they have been so careful, too, who they took in, — exercising 'em aforehand, and putting 'em through the catechis and the lethargy, and pounding 'em into a state of grace! Who can it be?" And the spectacles expressed anxiety. "I believe it must be slander, arter all. O, what a terrible thing it is to pizen the peace of a neighborhood deterotating and backbiting, and lying about people, when the blessed truth is full bad enough about the best of us!"

What a lesson is here for the mischief-maker to ponder upon! Truth lent dignity to her words, and gave a beam to her countenance, reminding one somewhat of a sunset in the fall on a used-up landscape.

MRS. PARTINGTON, one Fourth of July, was much incommoded by the crowd that rushed to see the procession. She said she "did n't see the least need of scrowging so, for she dared say the procession was full long enough to go round.'

A QUEER ASSOCIATION.

—

IT was with a strong emotion of wonder that Mrs. Partington read in the papers that a new wing was to be added to the Cambridge Observatory.

"What upon airth can that be for, I wonder? I dare say they are putting the new wing on to take more flights arter comics ahd such things, or to look at the new ring of the planet Satan,—another link added to his chain, perhaps; and, gracious knows, he seems to go further than he ever did before."

She stopped to listen, as the sounds of revelry and drunkenness arose upon the night air, and she glanced from her chamber over the way, where a red illuminated lantern denoted "Clam Chowder." Why should she look there just at that moment of her allusion to Satan? What connection could there be in her mind between Satan and clam chowder? Nobody was near but Ike, and Isaac slumbered.

THE PUNDIT PUNNED.

Dr. Digg and old Roger were holding an animated conversation upon the subject of California, the Doctor contending that the chances were against the emigrants thither getting recompensed for their trouble; "for," said the Doctor, "the ground is all occupied, and those coming last have small chance of procuring a lucrative field for their operations."

"My dear sir," said old Roger, with animation, "I can assure you it is not so; for I am informed by an intelligent returned Californian that every man who goes to the mines has his *pick*."

The Doctor, however, still contended for his point, and could not see how it could be possible, and thought old Roger's friend must be mistaken.

13*

PUNCH IN THE HEAD.

OLD Sherry came home one night when it was so near morning that the line dividing the night from the morning was legitimately debatable, and having taken an extra glass or two previous to leaving the company he had been with, he was somewhat dull of apprehension, and the houses seemed walking around him unaccountably, and the streets, by some sort of undulatory motion that he had never before noticed, seemed determined to throw him down; but he got home safely.

So far, well; but he had lost his night-key, or it was in the pocket of his other pants, in the wardrobe, within ten feet of the spot where Mrs. Sherry was probably at that time reposing; whose snore he even fancied he heard jarring the latch of the outside door. It must be one or the other, for he felt in his pockets for it in vain. He did n't like to alarm the house, nor the people in it, for a quarter of a century's experience of the quality of Mrs. Sherry's temper led him to know that her welcome to him, in his present plight, would be more warm than agreeable, even if she consented to let him in at all.

It at last occurred to him that a window in the rear of the house could be opened from the outside, and he at once resolved to gain an entrance in this manner, then creep up stairs to bed, and say nothing to anybody. Accordingly, with this burglarious idea in his mind, he went round to the back of the house. The window was a lit'le above his reach, but he found a barrel somewhere,

PUNCH IN THE HEAD.

and by skilful manœuvring got it beneath the window and elevated himself upon it. He tried to lift the sash, and it slid up easily to the desired height, where he secured it with a stick. Mr. Sherry congratulated himself upon this triumphant achievement under difficulty. The outposts were won — another step, and he would be master of the citadel. Already was his foot raised to take this last step ; his head and shoulders were within the window, when the treacherous barrel, losing its equipoise in the exertion Mr. Sherry was making, fell over ; his luckless elbow touching the stick that sustained the window, it fell with a crash upon Mr. Sherry's broad shoulders, and he found himself in a trap from which he could not escape.

Mr. Sherry's maiden sister, a romantic damsel of thirty-five, had heard the noise, and as she awaked from her slumber the idea of thieves flashed across her mind. She had been dreaming of brigands and robbers, and the noise occurred just where a heroine was forcibly carried from her paternal home by ruffians in masks ! Upon the spur of the moment she darted into her nephew's chamber, contiguous to hers, and told him, in a big whisper, that robbers were breaking into the house, and added the gratuitous and sanguinary information that they would all be murdered in their beds !

While she went to impart this gratifying news to the rest of the household, the young man arose, and, without stopping to dress himself, seized a big stick and went stealthily down stairs. He opened the door softly of the room from which the noise proceeded, and, beholding the supposed burglar in the window, the young Sherry gave his parent's head a couple of whacks with the stick, when a cry from that suffering specimen of suspended animation revealed to the young man who the victim was, and, with the assistance of the rest of the family, who had now assembled, the two hundred pounds of old Sherry were soon housed.

Such a lecture as he received ! ′Either the lecture, or the debauch, or the cane, perhaps the whole combined, gave him a severe headache the next morning, and he was constrained to keep his bed. He summoned his son to his bedside, and with an expression of grave authority he asked the young man if he did n't think he was a graceless rogue to be punchin' his parent's head in the way he did — if he was n't really ashamed of himself ! The young Sherry made up a mouth, in which much fun blended with considerable that was serious, and replied that his respected sire would never have got any punch in his head from him, had it not been for the punch he had got in his head before he came home. The old Sherry admitted the corn, turned over and slept on it.

MATTER OF FACT AND SENTIMENT.

—

SAID Augustus, as he gazed from Mrs. Partington's little window, his finger pensively resting upon a cracked china teapot upon the sill, — "Here is a spot in which to cultivate the flowers of poesy; here the imagination may soar on unrestricted wing; here balmy zephyrs rising from embowering roses waft ambrosial sweets "—

"Them is beans planted in the window," said the old lady, interrupting him. "What you say is very true; there's nothing better for a sore than balmy-gilead buds in rum; and it's so handy to have 'em in a temperance neighborhood, too, where people are too good to keep rum in the house themselves, but leave it all to be borryed of the neighbors. How glad I am always to have it for 'em! They are so kind, too, always advising me to give up keeping it in the house; but, dear me, what would the poor creturs do if I should? I may be committing sin in keeping it; but a bad use of a thing makes all the trouble after all."

Augustus was moved; but there was so much of the " earth earthy " in her remark that he was silent.

"I should like to know what he meant about embowelling roses," murmured she to herself; "peppermint would be better if he has the colic."

She looked at him earnestly, but there seemed no token of pain, and she forbore to speak.

COMMISERATION FOR CLERKS.

—

"SHOPKEEPERS is not enough thought of," said Mrs. Partington, after having been out making some purchases. "How they do toil and how they suffer! One dear pretty young man, with a nice black coat on and a gold chain and a starched collar, with a carrivan on his neck, told me with tears in his eyes that he was selling to me at less than he gave for it; and I bought it out of pity, though I knowed I could get it five cents a yard cheaper next door. Talk about Moses being executed on one string, indeed! These poor creturs are Rogerses, every one of 'em, by the yard-stick, and are all the time a dying."

There's a constant flow of the milk of compassion in her breast-inexhaustible; like the purse of the gentleman in the story, the more that is taken from it the more remains. The allusion to Moses was drawn from an advertisement of a prodigy violinist, who was to play a violin solo, from the oratorio of "Moses," upon one string.

THE BOUQUET.

"Look here!" exclaimed Mrs. Partington, in a tone of triumph, as she returned from answering the door-bell, bearing in her withered hand a bouquet of generous proportions and exquisite beauty, with her name written in fair characters upon an accompanying card. "Look here, at the bucket of flowers somebody has sent me. How charmingly it smells, as well as looks! And the colors is all blinded together, too, so prettily!"

At this stage of her admiration, a small billet dropped upon the floor.

"And here," she continued, "is a letter besides, written in a beautiful hand, from somebody with ornamental corners." "From your valentine, TIMOTHY TOBY," closed the missive.

She said not another word, took one more inspiration from the "bucket," and busied herself in preparing the large-mouthed honey-bottle for its accommodation. It might have been from the projecting lily spear, it might have been from a grain of subtle maccaboy coming in contact with her eye, and it might have been from some deeper cause, but a tear escaped the area of the right eye of her specs, and stood for an instant in pellucid lustre on her cheek-bone, before passing away through the channels time had worn in her face.

MRS. PARTINGTON ON VENTILATION

"WE have got a new venerator on our meeting-house," said Mrs. Partington; "but how on airth they can contrive to climb up there to let the execrations go out is more than I can see into. But it is sich a nice intervention for keeping a house warm!"

"What sort of a ventilator is it?" asked we, anxious to get an inkling of the old lady's philosophy.

"It is one of the Emissary's," replied she, sagely, "and it is ever so much better than Professor Epsom's, because a room is kept so warm and comfortable by it, — not the least danger of taking cold from draughts of too fresh air. It will be a great accusation in cold weather."

"But how will it do in summer?" we again asked. The dame, for a moment, was puzzled. She had not thought of this contingency.

"O!" cried she, after a few moments' reflection, aided by the merest trifle of maccaboy, at the same time proffering us the box; "I suppose, then, they will stop it up altogether, and open the windows."

It was an idea worthy of the profound black bonnet and far-seeing specs before us. She left us then. We watched her from the window, and felt anxious about her rheumatism, as we saw her right foot sink in a puddle, in an attempt to reach a Canton street omnibus.

Any one who breathes the suffocating air of our concert rooms, will be reminded of Mrs. Partington's "venerator" for keeping a room warm.

OUR RELATIONS WITH MEXICO.

"OUR relations with Mexico!" said Mrs. Partington, contemplatively, and her glance turned upward to the wall, where the portrait of the deceased corporal, in rigid pasteboard, looked straight forward, as if indicating a bee-line of duty that she should follow, — a sort of pictorial cynosure, to which she always looked for guidance. "Our relations with Mexico!" said she; "some of the poor creaturs, maybe, left there in the late hospitalities, too poor to get back. If I was President Pierce, now, I'd send right away and bring 'em all home by express. The Mexicans had better not trouble any of our relations, I can tell 'em!"

Of course she could tell 'em. There was no doubt of it. Mrs. Sled believed she could, and Ike, who was busy in transforming the old lady's new clothes-stick into a bat, did n't say a word. If there is a weakness in Mrs. P.'s character, — and as a chronicler we should be false to our trust to say that there was not, — that weakness is love for her relations; continually manifesting itself in blue yarn stockings and souchong tea.

14

THE FIRST OF APRIL.

"I NEVER see the like!" said Mrs. Partington, as she slammed to the front door, with a noise and jar that set everything to dancing in the house, and the timid crockery stood with chattering teeth upon the little "buffet" in the corner. It was wrong in her to say she had never seen the like, for this was the fifth time that she had been called to the door by a violent ringing, within half an hour, and had found no one there. Hence anger — so rarely an occupant of her mind, but so justifiable now — prompted the slamming of the door and the remark, "I never see the like!"

It was the first of April, and the occurrence was the more annoying for this reason. She stood still by the door and watched stealthily for the intruder; tapped her box easily and regaled her olfactories with a dusty oblation, and held still. The peal of the bell again startled her by its vehemence. She opened the door and looked out, but no one was to be seen. As she turned away, a string attached to the bell-wire, extending from the banister, met her gaze, and, sitting quietly upon the stairs, with a grin on his face that had a world of meaning in it and a world of fun in it, sat *Ike!* How the spectacles sparkled in the rays of her indignation! She went for the rod, which had long rested on the shelf, but it had been manufactured three days before into an arrow by Ike, and, as the chance of finding it diminished, her anger cooled like hot iron in the air, and the rogue escaped.

AN INQUIRY ANSWERED.

"DOES Isaac manifest any taste for poetry, Mrs. Partington?" asked the schoolmaster's wife, while conversing on the merits of the youthful Partington. The old lady was basting a chicken that her friends had sent her from the country.

"O, yes!" said the old lady, smiling; "he is very partially fond of poultry, and it always seems as if he can't get enough of it." The old spit turned by the fire-place in response to her answer while the basting was going on.

"I mean," said the lady, "does he show any of the divine afflatus?"

The old lady thought a moment. "As for the divine flatness — I don't know about it. He's had all the complaints of children, and when he was a baby he fell and broke the cartridge of his nose; but I hardly think he's had this that you speak of."

The roasting chicken hissed and sputtered, and Mrs. Partington basted it again.

BAILED OUT.

    " So, our neighbor, Mr. Guzzle, has been arranged at the bar for drunkardice," said Mrs. Partington; and she sighed as she thought of his wife and children at home, with the cold weather close at hand, and the searching winds intruding through the chinks in the windows and waving the tattered curtain like a banner, where the little ones stood shivering by the faint embers. " God forgive him and pity them ! " said she, in a tone of voice tremulous with emotion.

    " But he was bailed out," said Ike, who had devoured the residue of the paragraph, and laid the paper in a pan of liquid custard that the dame was preparing for Thanksgiving, and sat swinging the oven door to and fro as if to fan the fire that crackled and blazed within.

    " Bailed out, was he ? " said she; " well, I should think it would have been cheaper to have pumped him out, for, when our cellar was filled, arter the city fathers had degraded the street, we had to have it pumped out, though there was n't half so much in it as he has swilled down."

    She paused and reached up on the high shelves of the closet for her pie plates, while Ike busied himself in tasting the various preparations. The ·dame thought that was the smallest quart of sweet cider she had ever seen.

HAVE YOU GOT A BABY?

A BACHELOR friend of ours was riding, upon a time, through the state, when he overtook a little girl and boy, apparently on their way to school. The little girl appeared to be five or six years old, and was as beautiful as a fairy. Her eyes were lit up with a gleam of intense happiness, and her cheeks glowed with the hues of health. Our bachelor looked at her for a moment admiringly. She met his glance with a smile, and with an eager voice saluted him with,

"Have you got a baby?"

He was struck aback by the question, and something like a regret stole over his mind as he looked upon the animated and beautiful little face before him.

"No," he answered.

"Well," she replied, drawing her tiny form proudly up, "*we have*," and passed on, still smiling, to tell the joyous news to the next one she might meet.

What a world of happiness to her was concentrated in that one idea — the baby! And in her joy she felt as if all must have the same delight as herself; and it was a matter of affectionate pride to her, that lifted her little heart above the reach of ordinary care; for in the baby was her world, and what else had she to crave? Such was the reflection of our friend, and he remembered it long enough to tell it to us.

14*

A HOME TRUTH.

"WHAT a to-do they make about treating the slaves bad at the south!" said Mrs. Partington; and everybody strained their ears to catch an opinion that perhaps was fraught with the destiny of millions. There was a slight tremor in her voice, a sort of rumbling before the "bustin'" of the volcano, and her eye looked troubled as a lake by a fitful gust. "What a to-do they do make about it, to be sure! But some of our folks don't do much better. I know a poor old colored man here in Boston that they treat jest like a nigger. People a'n't no better than scribes, pharisees, and hippogriffs, that say one thing and do another."

There is truth in thy remarks, O, most estimable Mrs. P.! Our philanthropy, we fear, if weighed in the just balance, would be found often sadly wanting.

A SEASONABLE PUN.

"FINE gloves, them!" said old Roger, as he held out his hand, encased in a new pair he had just bought. An assent was expressed. "But," continued he, "can you tell me why a man is more likely to get taken in, while buying gloves in winter than in summer?" They could n't. "I 'll tell you, then; it 's because they are more apt to get worsted."

VARICOSE VEINS.

—

"WHAT is the matter with Mrs. Jewks, doctor?' asked Mrs. Partington, as Dr. Bolus passed her house. She had been watching for him for half an hour through a chink in the door, and people who detected the end of a nose thrust out of the chink aforesaid, stopped an instant to look at it, strongly inclined to touch it and see what it was.

"She is troubled with varicose veins, mem," replied the doctor, blandly.

"Do tell!" cried the old lady; "well, that accounts for her very coarse behavior, then, and it is n't any fault o' her'n, arter all, poor woman, 'cause what is to be will be, and if one has very coarse veins what can one expect? Ah, we are none of us better than we ought to be!"

"Good morning, mem," said Dr. Bolus, as he turned away, and the old lady shut the door.

"No better than we ought to be!" What an original remark, and how candid the admission! The little front entry heard it, and the broad stair that led to the chamber heard it, and Ike heard it, as he sat in the kitchen, daubing up the old lady's Pembroke table with flour paste, in an attempt to make a kite out of a choicely-saved copy of the Puritan Recorder. "We are no better than we ought to be" — generally.

MRS. PARTINGTON ON VACATION.

" FIVE weeks' vexation in August!" said Mrs. Partington, when she heard that the school had a vacation
for five weeks; "five weeks' vexation! It is a trying
season for mothers, and wearing and tearing to their
patience and the jackets and trousers of the children.
Talk about the relaxing from study! I don't believe
it's half as bad as the green apples they get in the
country. But I do love to see the little dears enjoying
themselves, frisking about like pigs in clover, as happy
as the days is long. What an idea of freedom there is
in a little boy with his face and hair full of molasses and
fun and good-nature! Be still, you good-for-nothing!"
cried she, as Ike attempted to take her snuff-box; " Be
still, I say!"

But it was not in anger; for she felt in her capacious
pocket, and, from away down under her snuff-box, and
thimbles, and bone-buttons, and needles, and pin-cush-
ions, and beeswax, she brought up a ball of variegated
hues, and smiled as she gave it into his eager hand, and
bade him be a good boy.

TORCHLIGHT PATRIOTISM.

"Hooray! hooray!" yelled Ike, as he dashed in at the front-door with a lighted torch, swinging it over his head, and spattering the oily fluid around upon the tables and chairs, a drop even falling upon the snow-white table-cover that lay folded up on a shelf. The smoke of the torch filled the kitchen, and rolled along the snow-white ceiling in murky volume, to the great annoyance of Mrs. Partington, who always said if there was anything on "airth" that she held in utter "excrescence," it was "ile."

"What's to pay now?" said the dame rising, and she heard, through the floor, the noise made by the "unterrified democracy" in torchlight procession assembled. Paul was a democrat, and her sympathy kept time with the martial music.

"Quite a furor," said we to her as we recognized her. A tremendous cheer interrupted us.

"A *few* roar," said she, smiling, "I think it is a good many roar. Ah!" continued she, "I do love to see the unclarified democracy in possession, with their torches a blazing and their patrickism a busting."

She felt patriotic. Her face was momentarily lit up with the emotions of her soul and the light of a Roman candle, and then the venerable countenance melted away in the darkness, as the candle, after making a great effort to sustain itself, became exhausted and snuffed itself out.

MRS. PARTINGTON ON SUFFRAGE.

"How these men do talk about exercising their right of sufferings!" said Mrs. Partington; "as if nobody in the world suffered but themselves. They don't think of our sufferings. We, poor creturs, must suffer and say nothing about it, and drink cheap tea, and be troubled with the children, and scour and scrub our souls out; and we never say a thing about it. But a man comes on regularly, once a year, like a Farmer's Almanac, and grumbles about his sufferings; and it's only then jest to choose a governor, arter all. These men are hard creturs to find out, and a'n't worth much after you have found 'em out."

This was intended as a lesson to Margaret, who was working Charlotte and Werter on a blue ground, at her side; but Margaret had her own idea of the matter, and remained silent.

DOWN WITH THE TYRANT.

"Ha! ha! Down with the tyrant! Death to the Spaniard!" shouted Ike, as he rushed into the kitchen, brandishing Paul's old artillery sword that had hung so long on the wall. He struck an attitude, and then struck the upright portion of the stove funnel till it rung with the blow, and Mrs. Partington, with amazement on her countenance and the glass lamp in her hand, stood looking at him. Ike had been reading the thrilling tale of the "Black Avenger, or the Pirate of the Spanish Main," and his "intellects," as Sir Hugh Evans might say, were absorbed by the horrible.

"Don't, Isaac, dear," said Mrs. Partington, and she spoke in a gentle, but firm tone. "You are very scarifying, and it don't look well to see a young boy acting so. It comes, I know, of reading them yellow cupboard books. You should read good ones; and if you won't touch that again I will let you have my big Bible, king James's aversion, with the beautiful pictures. I declare, I don't know what I shall do with you if you carry on so. I am afraid I shall have to send you to a geological cemetery to get the old sancho out of you."

The point of the sword was lowered as it was making a passage for a dark spot in the centre panel of the door; the eye of the boy, so fiercely lit by the spirit of the "Black Avenger," became mild and laughing, as he said he was only "making b'lieve," and Mrs. Partington gave him a penny as she disarmed him. What a visible emotion of peanuts became manifest as he grasped the copper and made tracks for the door, and climbed over the snow drifts to reach the grocer's opposite !

MRS. PARTINGTON AND THE CLERK.

"Is the steamer signified, sir ?" asked Mrs. Partington at the telegraph station.

" Yes 'm," replied the clerk, who was busily engaged turning over the leaves of his day-book.

"Can you tell me," continued she, "if the queen's encroachment has taken place yet ?"

"Some say she is encroaching all the time," said the clerk, looking pleasantly at the old lady, and evidently pleased with his own smartness.

"That is n't possible," responded the venerable dame; "but," said she to herself, "how could *he* be expected to know about such things? and yet there is no reason why he should n't, for all the bars to science, 'notamy and them things, is let down now-a-days, and Natur is shown all undressed, like a puppet-show, sixpence a sight !"

" Good morning, sir," said she, as he bowed her out; and as she passed down the stairs her mind, grasping the manifold subjects of the telegraph, queen, and facilities in science, became oblivious in a fog.

THOUGHT FOR THANKSGIVING DAY.

THIS day, long celebrated in New England, again returns, amid whose festivities the heart expands itself and awakes anew to cheerful life. Though the whole year has bound it with selfish fetters, and it has pursued unremittingly its aim of worldly gain or worldly advancement, on this day all the avenues to its genialities are thrown open, and troops of kindly feelings, long strangers, come thronging back to their early home, as their possessors return, on this glad season, and revisit the source from whence they sprung.

It is a time of glee and a time of thankfulness, — the twin feelings of the season. The joy of meeting after long separation; the gathering of friendly faces about the generous board; the hilarious song and the graceful dance; the sports of childhood, and the heart-mingling of youth old enough and willing to love, — all *are* worship, and offerings of thankfulness, where sweet innocence lends its charm.

It was known, months ago, that Tom was to come home from the city to Thanksgiving. He had been gone a whole year, and when his great red face had disappeared it seemed for a while as if the sun had ceased to shine. His first letter was an event in the lives of " the old folks at home," and Tom's sisters; and Tom's sisters had to carry the letter all round the neighborhood, that people might see how well he could write, and what

15

proper words he used, and how he crossed his t's and minded his i's. But Tom has written many letters since, and the novelty has worn off; but the affection around the old homestead is as bright as ever. And Tom is actually coming home to Thanksgiving, and the girls will pinch his red cheeks and tease him with their kindnesses as they used to do. His last letter tells his father that he must have the mare at the depot by six o'clock. The girls insist that they will drive down to meet him; they're not afraid of a horse, not they, and go they will. The house is swept, and the wood is piled up in the best-room fire-place, and the floor is newly sanded, and the chair with the new tidy that 'Bella has knit is in its place for Master Tom when he comes; for Tom has got to be a character, and it is a question if more preparation could be made for a king's reception. The old folks talk of his coming, and a softer expression than usual mingles in their voices, and the clock is watched for the hour of his appearing. Here they are at last! And the red-faced boy gets out. Father! Mother! God bless you both! — and he is a child again, — the child of the old homestead, — and he loves every stick in the old house better than ever before.

It is not time to talk yet about the big city, — that is served for the evening, when they are seated round the cheerful fire. Now he must answer the questions about his health, and if his last stockings fitted, and what he thought when he heard his aunt Deborah had got married, and if his cousin John had given him the little Bible his old schoolmistress sent him, — they knew he had, because Tom had said so in a letter home, — and if he heard that his cousin Sally had got a baby! Heavens! how the questions pour in upon him, and will, until he gets his turn to ask, and theirs comes to answer.

This is a picture-sample of a thousand such. Freights of happiness are borne on every railroad car; the steam whistle of the locomotive conveys a thrill of pleasure to many a listening heart; the hum of business palls the ear that listens for happiness, and the shutters are put up for one day, — the heart's jubilee.

Though sin and excess may mark and mar its hilarity, an aggregate of joy remains to it commensurate with the virtue that remains to us. The noise of the turkey is heard in the land; ovations are made to the genius of plenty; groaning tables pave the way to groaning stomachs, and thankfulness works its way out between the scant apertures left in compact stomach stowage.

Heaven give the rich heart to help the poor, and to make them thankful on this day, in spite of the three hundred and sixty-four other days of hardship and privation!

PEACE INCULCATED.

"BETTER is a crust of bread and quietness therewith than a stollid ox and strife," said Mrs. Partington, as she heard the noise of wrangling in a neighbor's house. It was a Sunday morning, and Ike was cleaning his shoes by the door with the clothes-brush. "Why can't folks live in peace, without distention? How much people have to answer for that causes animosity in a neighborhood! Thank Heaven, I've never done anything of the kind that my conscience acquits me of."

With what a feeling this was uttered! And the sunlight came into the window, and looked through her specs down into her soul, and it was as calm there as the bottom of a well, not disturbed by Ike's whistling "Old Dan Tucker" as an accompaniment to his brush.

HUMAN NATURE.

SEAT eleven millionaires in an omnibus, and seat between them one old woman who has but five coppers in the world, which she intends to invest in that one ride. When the collector comes in, and the old lady takes out her antique wallet to pay him, it is curious to observe the avidity and eagerness with which the millionaires watch her operations, and peep over to catch a glimpse at the interior of the wallet. That is human nature.

MR. STEADFAST'S SOLILOQUY.

WELL, my mind 's at last made up. I 'm going against rum, this 'lection. I 've made up my mind on that pint, and there 's no shaking me. When I say my mind 's made up, folks may know what to depend upon. Yes, I go against rum. It 's time we looked about us. It 's time the people got their eyes open to the evil, — and I 'm one of 'em. But (stopping suddenly) the party ! — what would the party say ? I did n't think of that before. The party, of course, must be looked to. What could we do without party ? Where would the Union be, and our institutions and what-do-ye-call-its, if it was n't for the party, I should like to know ? Party is our egeus, our pal-pal-what 's his name. But I can't go against rum without going against party. If I vote against rum, and the temperance inspectors and constables and things are chosen, where would our institutions be, and our destiny as a nation, and the respect of people abroad, who we don't care a copper about ? And then, if I vote for party, and rum triumphs, it would go on, undermining our moral institutions and our physical constitutions. So, hang me, betwixt 'em both, if I know what to do ! I have it. I 'll make a compromise between cold water and rum, and make it half rum and the other half rum-and-water. That 's the ticket, and my mind 's made up to vote it When my mind 's made up, there 's no moving *me !*

15*

MRS. PARTINGTON RURALIZING.

Mrs. Partington and Ike were huckleberrying in the country, and a large swamp was wearily canvassed to find the quart which she bore in her five-quart pail. She despaired of filling it.

"Look here, aunt," said Ike, in a sort of confidential whisper, "look in there and see what a lot of 'em."

There was a smile upon the face of the boy, that betokened mischief, or it might have been a gleam of satisfaction at the prospect of filling the pail; but certainly a smile was round the little mouth, and the eye caught it, and a roguish twinkle like a sunbeam lay sparkling there.

"I see!" said the old lady, and a moment later the log-cabin bonnet, borrowed for the occasion, was seen above the tops of the bushes, its restlessness indicating its wearer's activity. Ike remained outside.

Fizz-z-z — Buzz-z-z! — what was that? — a humble-bee, as we are a sinner. Another and another. The log cabin was besieged, and Mrs. Partington rushed frantically from the bushes, swinging the tin pail and crying "Shoo! shoo!" with all her might. It was a trying time for the widow of Corporal Paul. And Ike did not escape, for a big humblebee attacked him, and he roared heartily with a sting upon his cheek. The laugh disappeared.

At the recital of their troubles at home, people regarded the matter as a trick of Ike's; but how could he have known about the humblebee's nest being in there? Mrs. Partington avowed that she "never was so frustrated by anything in her born days," and the people believed her. She thinks, notwithstanding the bees, that she would like to have a "villain" in the country, and become an "amatory" farmer.

VENTILATION.

In the course of his rambles in the country, Mr. Spotgam called at a poor-looking house by the road-side to inquire the whereabouts of a trout brook which he supposed to be in the vicinity. Some pretty children attracted his attention, and he stepped inside the door to play with them, and invest a few cents in their affection. Their father came in a moment afterwards, and appeared somewhat confused to find a stranger in his humble domicile.

"Warm, sir," said he, wiping his forehead; "wife, throw up the window, and let us have a mouthful of fresh air."

Mr. Spotgam looked at the window about to be thrown up, and saw with pain that every square of glass had been broken out. His mind turned to a nice mathematical calculation, in which he endeavored to make out the difference between the quantity of air received through an open window and one with no glass in it, and gave it up in despair.

LETTER FROM IKE, IN THE COUNTRY.

—

HILLTOP, Sept. 10, 1852.

DEAR BOB — I wish you was up here, and the way we would train you wouldn't be slow. There is boys enough up here, but they don't know nothing. When I first come they didn't know how to play jack-stones! But you'd better believe I soon made 'em fly round. I've found enough to do since I've been here. We've got a boat, and we go out swimming every day. The boat tips over ever so easy, and don't you think, the other day, when we were out with the girls, we tipped over right where the water was overhead, and we all had to get onto her bottom. I wasn't at all skeered, though everybody said they knowed I did it on purpose. But you know I wouldn't.

We've had some prime fun out a gunning. We didn't kill anything only some tame pigeons; but we put some green beans into the gun and shot the dog, and he ki-hi'd just as if he didn't like it. I can fire at a mark first-rate. I wish you could see the goose I made with wheel-grease on the newly-painted barn-door, — it's peppered brim full of holes. There's lots of apples and peaches, and if you was here we'd be in among 'em. There's some over there in the pasture just like some in our garden, but them in the pasture is best, and they belong to the old captain, and he's a cross old fellow, and I should like to fix him, cause he set his dog on me t' other day, because I fired an apple at one of his hens, and broke a square of glass. He's a real cross old chap, and has n't got no friends.

There's some fine ponds here, and lots of mud turtles, but all that is humbug about their leaving their shell when you put a coal of fire onto their backs, because I've tried it. It makes 'em go it, though, I tell you. Our dog is first-rate for catching of 'em, and I got a dozen of 'em t' other day to bring home, and put 'em in a barrel, and forgot all about 'em, and there they stayed for ten days. I put 'em in the water again, and away they went. Don't you think, Bob, I caught a big bull paddock and harnessed him the other day, and you should have seen him kick when I let him go.

I don't like the oxen they have here, because they don't laugh, and when they are hauling anything they seem to do it unwilling like, and look surly and cross. Reasoning with 'em don't do no good. I ride the horse to water and drive the geese out of the corn. Up in the corn yesterday I found what I thought was a great big water-melon, and when I got over the wall and cut it it turned out to be a green punkin.

They have begun to make sweet cider, and I don't see

what people ever want to make sour cider for when this is so nice.

I s'pose school begins soon, and the old woman will want me to come home; but I don't want to a mite.

Tell Jim Jones I've swapped my jackknife, and got a bran-new hawkey that I cut myself in the bushes.

Good-by, Bob.   Write to me if you've had any fun this summer, and I am yours in clover.

IKE PARTINGTON.

OUT OF PLACE.

"DOES your arm pain you much, sir?" asked a young lady of a gentleman who had seated himself near her, in a mixed assembly, and thrown his arm across the back of her chair, and slightly touched her neck.

"No, miss, it does not; but why do you ask?"

"I noticed it was considerably out of place, sir," replied she; "that's all."

The arm was removed.

TENDER NAMES.

THERE are people, in the romantic period of their lives, who delight in bestowing tender terms upon objects of their affection, borrowed from the pretty things of nature or fancy, such as " My Rose Bud," " My Pink," " My Diamond," " My Lily," or some such nice and delicate name. Of all that we have ever heard, however, the Irish term, " My Bloomer," sounds to us the best.

These terms are all well enough when used in private endearment, but when uttered in the presence of others they operate with a most nauseating effect. Fancy a man, brimfull of the charms of his Dulcinea, to whom he has given some romantic appellative, coming into a tailor's shop, among the forty girls there employed, of whom his heart's hope is one, and asking if his " Rose Bud " is present, or addressing her as his " Rose Bud," if she be there. If the girl has any sense she will prove a " Rose Bud " with a thorn when she gets him out somewhere.

We had a friend who was smitten with this mania for pretty names, and had adopted the romantic one of " My Light " for his idol ; and for several years she had lighted his path and his pocket in the way that lovers understand. It grew near the period when the word was to be spoken that should make them " one flesh," when, calling at her dwelling one evening, he asked the housegirl, who met him in the entry, if his " Light " was in.

" No," said she, " your light has just *gone out* —
with Mr. ——," naming an old rival.

Jealous pains seized him; he rushed to his boarding-
house, dashed madly up stairs, three at a time, opened
his drawer, and, seizing a —*pen,* wrote a letter that
extinguished his "Light" forever.   It was a severe blow
to his spirit, and in six months from the time of his
disappointment the poor fellow committed matrimony
with another and a more steady "Light," the flame of
which burns undimmed even now.

LEARNING TO RELISH IT.

WE were surprised to see Mr. Slow at an opera one
evening.   Leaning over the back of his seat, we remarked that we had an impression that he did n't like
opera music.

" I never did," said he, " till lately ; but I 've been
eddicating for it.   It can be done.   Talk about natur's
having all to do with it! that 's all humbug.   Natur
don't have any more to do with it than she does with
learnin us to eat tomatoes, nor sardines, nor olives, —
but by eddication we come to like 'em.   That 's jest the
way with opery music.   The first time you don't like it;
then you get another taste, and it 's better ; then you go
a little further, and it 's first-rate.   There 's nothing like
eddication.   Natur is well enough in her place, but
eddication does the job."

Mr. Slow looked grave as he uttered this oracular
wisdom, and his auditors admired.

PHLEBOTOMY A DISEASE.

"Do you think people are troubled as much with fleabottomry, now, doctor, as they used to be before they diskivered the anti-bug bedstead?" asked Mrs. Partington of the doctor of the old school who attended upon the family where she was staying.

"Phlebotomy, madam," said the doctor gravely, "is a remedy, not a disease."

"Well, well," replied she, "no wonder one gets 'em mixed up, there is so many of 'em. We never heard in old times of tonsors in the throat, or embargoes in the head, or neurology all over us, or consternation in the bowels, as we do now-a-days. But it's an ill wind that don't blow nobody no good, and the doctors flourish on it like a green baize tree. But of course *they* don't have anything to do with it, — they can't make them come or go."

The doctor stepped out with a genteel bow, and the old lady watched him till his cabriolet had turned the corner, her mind revolving the intricate subject of cause and effect.

16

HIRSUTE ORNAMENTS.

—

"Well!" said Mrs. Partington, as she leaned forward, with her hands resting on the window ledge, and peered out into the street through a chink in the blinds. It was n't a *deep* well, expressive of content or satisfaction, but it was an ejaculatory well, that found expression at some object which she had witnessed in the street. "Well," said she, "I hope that man is married, I declare I do; because, if he is n't, I 'm sure he never will be, for a dreadfuler looking creature I never did see, with them mustychokes on his mouth — nobody would n't have him. I 've heerd 'em say that Heaven's best gift to man was woman; I should say that the next best gift was a razor to such a man as that. Folks did n't take pride in looking bad in old times!"

She turned thoughtfully to the wall, where hung in military rigidity that profile, the cherished gem of bygone art, the counterfeit presentment of manly grace.

"Ah, Paul!" sighed the dame, "you was an ornament of your specie, and the cheapest among ten thousand, or *more!*" She emphasised the "more," as if the contrast was very great indeed between Paul and him who had passed. But the profile took no notice of what she said; its gaze, chained to perpetual straightforwardness, looked never to the right or left; though, at times, she said it bore a kinder expression about the mouth. But this must have been her fancy, which gave to every object she looked upon the hues of her own benignity.

MRS. PARTINGTON AND PROBATE.

—

"O, WHAT trials a poor widow has to go through!" sighed Mrs. Partington, rocking herself in a melancholy way, and holding the morsel of maccaboy untasted between her thumb and finger; "terrible trials; and O, what a hardship it is to be executioner to an intestine estate — where enviable people are trying every way to overcome the widow's might; where it's probe it, probe it, probe it, all the time, and the more you probe it the worse it seems! The poor widow never gets justice, for if she gets all, she don't get half enough. I have had one trial of it, and if ever I should marry again, if it should so please Providence to order it, I'll make my husband fabricate his will before he orders his wedding-cake; — I'll take Time by the foretop, as Solomon says, you may depend upon it."

She here revived a little, and the subtle powder passed to its destination, and reported itself home by an emphatic sneeze.

———

EXTRACT from a great unwritten poem of 1051 verses, entitled "Ye Constabel" : —

> "Ye constabel from one man took
>   A large and ample fee,
> I'll now take one from ye t'other side,
>   Said ye constabel, said he."

DOMESTIC PURITY IMPUGNED.

—

"Have you got any rooms to let here, marm?" said a little man to Mrs. Partington, who occupied half of a house, the other half of which was to let, and to whom was entrusted the care of answering the door-bell.

The rooms were shown.

"They are not large," said the little man, depreciatingly.

"No, sir," replied she, "they are not very ruminous; but here are two little bed-rooms contagious that perhaps you did n't see."

He looked in, and, in a supercilious tone, muttered, "*Bugs!*" implying want of cleanliness, — a reflection on the purity of the premises in her charge!

There is a point, as she says, where patience ceases to be virtuous, and she had found it. Indignation choked her utterance; and the little man fortunately departed before it found vent. It was great, the way in which she slammed the door to after him, and ejaculated "*Bugs!*" till the empty rooms in echoing it seemed full of *bugs*. It was a sublime moral spectacle.

DID IT HURT YOU MUCH?

WHILOM there did dwell a barber in one of the most populous streets of this city, the hues of whose insignia by the street door, red and white, were typical often of his customer's chins as they came under his professional hand. Suds was a little fellow, but many a huge six-footer did he have, unresisting, by the nose, and many a fierce eye quailed beneath the gleam of that blade whose edge so many had keenly felt. It was a sublime spectacle to behold him while enjoying his momentary triumph, — his face absolutely shiny between the combined influence of sweat and exultation, — his razor, urged by the fervor of his excitation, whirling through seas of snowy lather with the rapidity of thought, — his customer, meanwhile, with eyes shut, and breath suspended, awaiting tremblingly the blow that should send him forth noseless, a scoff and a reproach among men; though, thanks to mighty science, such calamity seldom happened.

A farmer, who resided in the vicinity of the city, and supplied the people thereof with fruit, was excessively annoyed by the boys, who would climb upon his wagon and bite his apples, while inquiring the price, and pretending a desire to purchase. He took a big and fearful oath, one day, — he was a very crabbed man, — that the first boy who that day took a bite should likewise take a cut with it; he swore it on his whip!

16*

He jogged on undisturbed; the urchins read "whip lash" in his demeanor, and judiciously gave him a wide berth. But Fate, that generally has to bear the odium of causing all evil, — that by many is deemed a sort of subordinate Providence, who, in conjunction with Luck, another genius of the same kidney, takes the destiny of men to work out by the job, — pulled the reins directly opposite the barber's door.

Now, Mrs. Suds had that very day charged Mr. S. to procure some fruit, — she did "long so to eat an apple," — and he, as he was looking out of his window, his last customer having departed, was minded of her request, as the wagon, with its rich and tempting load, stopped within the range of his vision. He was fond of apples himself, and, running hastily out, he stepped upon the wagon wheel, took up an apple, and bit it, and at the same time inquired the price.

Fatal bite! — to Suds fatal as the first bite in Paradise was to Adam. A whistling sound he heard in the air, and then the whip, stinging with the malignity of concentrated spite, fell quick upon his unguarded shoulders, to his deep shame, and astonishment, and pain. Jumping down as quick as he could, he stood on the pavement, an injured and indignant man, and fiercely demanded the cause of the outrage.

The farmer had mistaken him for a boy, and, profuse of apology, endéavored to appease the little lion of the brush by stating his annoyance by the boys, to say nothing of his loss by biters, and his determination to put a stop to it by the summary means he had given Suds a taste of. Suds was a reasonable man, and admitted that the farmer was nearly right, even while he shrugged his shoulders with the remembered pain, and they parted on as good terms as the circumstances would admit of.

Unfortunately for the peace of the little man, a neighbor, who loved to stir up Suds, had seen the castigation, and each day as he came to be shaved would he ask with the tenderest solicitude, " *Did it hurt you much ?* " — always after shaving, however; for his nose would certainly have been in the way during the agitation the question produced, had he asked it before. That question, so sneeringly asked ! Human nature could n't stand it, patience could n't stand it, Suds could n't stand it ; and that question was a declaration of war with all who put it to him. Continual dropping will wear a stone.

One day Suds was splitting wood in the back yard, — like a dentist working away among the old stumps, — fretting at the unrivable tenacity with which they held together, when, sticking his axe into one apparently on the point of yielding, he swung it above his head to bring it down upon a block, and thus force the axe effectively through the tough fibres. The axe, with the wood adhering, was raised aloft, — the blow was about to be struck, but, slipping from the iron, the block took another direction, and fell heavily upon the hatless poll of the unfortunate barber.

His wife had seen the whole proceeding from the window, and, rushing out to ascertain the extent of the damage, she anxiously inquired, " *Mr. Suds, did it hurt you much ?* " To say that fire flashed from his eyes would be inadequate, — chain-lightning alone could typify the glance he gave the solicitous Mrs. S. — and a small thunderbolt like a billet of wood darted upon the wings of a fierce anathema at her devoted head. She dodged the missile, and a smashed window remained a monument of his passion.

Poor Suds! he soon removed from that locality, and the little shop where he shaved, and sheared, and suffered is obliterated by the huge granite piles that indicate the progressiveness of commerce.

"FARE, MA'AM."

ow do you do, dear?" said Mrs. Partington, smilingly, shaking hands with Burbank, in the Dock-square omnibus, as he held out his five dexter digits towards her.

"Fare, ma'am!" said he, in reply to her inquiry.

"Well, I'm shore, I'm glad of it, and how are the folks at home?"

"Fare, ma'am!" continued he, still extending his hand. The passengers were interested.

"How do you like Boston?" screamed she, as the omnibus rattled over the stones.

"Fare, ma'am!" shouted he without drawing back his hand; "I want you to pay me for your ride!"

"O!" murmured she, "I thought it was some one that knowed me," and rummaged down in the bottom of her reticule for a ticket, finding at last five copper cents tied up in the corner of her handkerchief — the "last war" handkerchief, with the stars and stripes involved in it, and the action of the Constitution and Guerriere

stamped upon it.   But the smile she had given him at
first was not withdrawn — there was no allowance made
for mistakes at that counter — and he went out, with a
lighter heart and a heavier pocket, to catch t' other coach.

PAYING PROMPTLY.

"IF there is any place in this world where I like to
ransack business more than another," said Mrs. Partington, with animation, untying from the corner of her handkerchief a sum of money she had just received, "if there's
any place better than another it's a bank.   There's no
dillydalliance, and beating down, and bothering you with
a thousand questions, till you don't know whether your
heels are up or your head is down; all you have to do is
to put your bill on the counter, and they pay it without
saying a word."

The old lady had presented a check for a quarter's
pension-money, received on account of Paul, who, in the
"last war," served a fortnight in fortifying Boston
harbor, and got mortar in his eyes, which hurt his
"visionary organs" so that he took to glasses.

"MEMENTO MORY."

BEFORE Old Roger left boarding at No. 47, he for-
feited all regard of the quiet inmates of the house by the
perpetration of the following atrocity, which was the
true reason of his leaving, and not the quality of the
bread-pudding, as many believed. Mory, the Kilby
street clerk, got married, and moved off. It had always
been a custom with Mory to pile his dishes up in a
curious manner, after he had used them, — cups, saucers,
plates, in a heterogeneous heap. A day or two after
his departure from the house, Old Roger was observed
piling his cup and saucer and plates in the same manner,
and he took those of his neighbor to add to the pile.
The boarders watched him silently, in much surprise,
and one of them, a little bolder than the rest, ventured
to ask him what he was doing that for.

" O," said Roger, very placidly, crowning the pile he
had made with the cover of the sugar-bowl, " I am only
erecting a memento *Mory*."

Mr. Blifkins, the serious man, exhorted the more
volatile boarders on the impropriety of laughing at such
an outrageously sacrilegious use of a respectable dead
language. From that day Roger had cold shoulder for
dinner, and the coldness of the landlady became suddenly manifest in cold potatoes, and in the rheumatic
condition of his room attic; so he left.

MESMERISM.

—

" Do you believe in mesmerism ? " we asked of **Mrs.**
Partington, as she dropped alongside of us yesterday
morning, like a jolly old seventy-four.

" Believe what ? " said she, sitting down in the other
chair.

The question involved an answer from us of some
fifteen minutes' length, running through the whole of
mesmerism, clairvoyance, and psychological phenomena,
like a knitting-needle running through a ball of yarn.

" O, yes," said she, " I believe all of that, and I know
a case in pint, to prove it. When Miss Jeems had her
silver-plated spoons extracted, — that was her mother's
afore her, and she sot a sight by 'em, — she come away
to Boston to see a miserymiser, I b'leve you call it.
Well, he told her jest where her spoons was, and who
stole 'em, and all about it, and the color of his hair, and
all that. Well, she gin him a dollar, and when she got
home she went right where the spoons was, and could n't
find a thing about 'em. No, no, that isn't the story,
nuther; 't is about Sally Sprague and her beau. You
see "——

At this instant the door opened, and company came
in, and Mrs. Partington, pleading an excuse that she
wanted to tend one of the " adversary meetings," subsided, like a wave upon the shore.

A SLIGHT MISTAKE.

MR. VERIGREEN, passing by the entrance to a hall where some sable minstrels were exhibiting, saw a black fellow coming out through the arch. Mr. V. stopped and looked at him earnestly, at which the colored gentleman was rather indignant, and demanded what he was looking at.

"Nothin' pertickler," said Mr. V. "I was jest lookin ter see what a plaguy difference there is betwixt you now, and last night, when you wor a singin in there. I wouldn't a b'leeved it was the same individooal."

Mr. V. put his hands in his pockets and walked along.

CONSIDERABLY TRUE.

WE find it stated in a paper that a well-bred woman, if surprised in a somewhat careless costume, does not try to dodge behind a door to conceal deficiencies, nor does she turn red and stammer confused excuses. She remains calm and self-possessed, and makes up in dignity what she may want in decoration. This is true. The most sensible woman we ever saw was one who, when her husband took us home on a washing day to look at his new house, never made one word of apology for the confusion that existed, nor once begged us not to "look round."

17

OLD BULL'S CONCERT.

—

" OLD Bull's concert ! " said Mrs. Partington, glancing up from her knitting as she read the announcement
of the grand concert on Saturday evening, and she smiled
as the ridiculous fancy ran through her mind, like a grass-
hopper in a stubble field, of an old bull giving a concert.
" And yet it is n't so very wonderful," continued she,
" for I remember a cat and canary that lived together,
and one or t' other of 'em used to sing beautifully.   But
I wonder what he plays on."

Ike suggested that he played on one of his own horns,
which seemed to be reasonable.

" I am glad he is going to *give* his concert, because,
when I went down to hear a great artisan play on a
violence, as they called it, though I found out afterwards
it was nothing but a fiddle, they were going to charge a
dollar till I told 'em I was one of the connections of the
Post, and they let me in.   I can't think what music an
old bull can make, I 'm sure.   It must be very uproari-
ous, I should think, and better fitted for overturns than
for pastureal music."

She closed her critique with a pinch of snuff, and got
on to her wires again like a telegraphic despatch, and
went ahead, while Ike amused himself by scratching his
name with a board nail in magnificent Roman capitals
upon the newly-painted panel of the kitchen door.

ANGULAR SAXONS.

"I don't know," said Mrs. Partington, and the expression, considered as a mere abstraction, was true, for there are some that have more of the world's wisdom and a better knowledge of grammar than the dame; for the school for her teaching was not one of letters. But let us hear her. "I don't know," said she, "about these Angular Saxons being any better than our old-fashioned ones."

Ike had been reading to her an article upon the destiny of the Anglo-Saxon race.

"And as for the race, Isaac," and her voice fell to a pitch of deep solemnity as she spoke, "it isn't proper at all; for when a funeral goes too quick — to say nothing about racing — it always is a forerunner, sometimes, that somebody'll die before the year's out. The old saxons were full fast enough, naturally; and arter the parish gin our saxon the surfeit of plate for his officious services, it spruced him right up, and it seemed as if it would have pleased him to bury all of 'em, he was so grateful. No, no, we don't want any Angular Saxons, Isaac, when our own are full good enough."

Ike, as she was talking, had amused himself with tying the old lady's snuff-box in the corner of his handkerchief and was experimentally swinging it around his head; and she ceased just as the box, released from the knot, dashed against the opposite side, scattering the

pungent powder in plenteous profusion upon the sanded
floor.   Of course he did n't mean to do it, and that was
all that saved him.

WATER GAS.

" WELL, that is a discovery ! " exclaimed Mrs. Partington, smilingly ; and she stood with a small pitcher in
her right hand, her left resting upon the table, and her
eyes fixed upon the flame of a glass lamp, that sputtered
a moment and then shot out a light that irradiated every
part of the little kitchen, and revealed the portrait of
Paul upon the wall, and Ike asleep by the fire.   She
spoke to herself ; it was a way she had ; she met with
no contradiction from that quarter.   " This is a discovery !   Where is Tom Paine and his gas now, I should like
to know ?   Here I 've been and filled this lamp up with
water, and it burns just as well as the real ile."

The experiment was perfectly triumphant ; the problem of light from water was demonstrated ; and yet,
with this vast fact revealed to her, Mrs. Partington, with
a modesty equal to that of the great philosopher who
picked up a pocket-ful of rocks on the shore of the
great ocean of truth, smiled with delight at her discovery,
nor once thought of getting out a patent or selling
rights.

MRS. PARTINGTON AT THE OPERA.

WE were surprised, at the opera, last evening, by having a hand placed upon our shoulder. It was a gentle touch; altogether unlike certain other touches on the shoulder that delinquent men so much dread. It came at a time when we were all absorbed by the melody of the charming Sontag, and were provoked at the intrusion.

"Will you be kind enough to lend me your observatory?" asked a voice that we thought we remembered.

Looking round, "Great heavens!" we cried, "Mrs. Partington!"

It was, indeed, that estimable dame, but yet it was not; for the black bonnet had disappeared, and a new rigolette adorned her venerable poll, beneath which every sprig of wavy gray was securely tucked. But the smile was there, as warm as a June morning at nine o'clock. She repeated the request to use the pearl and diamond-studded opera-glass, that we had hired at Fetridge's for twenty-five cents, — denominating it an "observatory."

"Is this the right pocus?" said she; "I s'pose I shall have to digest it to my sight, for my poor visionary orgies are giving out."

She levelled both barrels at the singers at once, and brought them down to her, and Pozzolini directed three successive appeals to her tenderness.

"It a'n't no use," said she, as she handed the glass;
17*

"I can't understand better with that, — I should have bought one of the lab'ratories at the door."

She beat time gracefully to the music for a while upon the cover of her snuff-box, and then went out, like an exhausted candle, to try and light on Ike, who was trading for a jacknife with another boy on the gallery stairs.

A SLIGHT MISAPPREHENSION.

Mrs. Partington was at Thackeray's last lecture, — Mr. T. had kindly sent her a card, admitting one, — and, forgetting the theme of the lecture, she leaned over the seat and asked the gentleman before her what the subject was.

"Goldsmith and Sterne, mem," was the reply ; "but he is on Sterne, first."

Mrs. Partington blushed. There was evidently a question agitating her mind as to whether she should tarry and hear a lecture from a person so ridiculously postured as Mr. T. must appear. She looked around, meditating a retreat; but the avenue to escape was blocked up, and she thought she might as well stay it out. She watched tremblingly for Mr. Thackeray, and was much relieved by seeing him standing perpendicularly before her. She thought she must have mistaken the meaning of her informant.

APOLLYON BONYPART.

"When will the world get rid of this Apollyon Bonypart?" said Mrs. Partington, as Ike threw down the paper in which he had read a comparison between the "18th Brumaire" and the "coup d'etat." In the uncertain glimmerings of her memory, she confounded the nephew and uncle, and her thought took the course the dim reminiscence pointed.

"Apollyon Bonypart! I remember all about him, and his eighteenth blue mare too. I always wondered where he got so many of 'em, — something like the woolly horse, I guess, — and when he was transplanted to Saint Domingo, Isaac, folks went up to the King's Chapel to sing tedium about it, because they were glad of it. And now he's come back agin, with all his blue mares with him."

The dropping of a stitch brought her down from the new hobby she was riding so furiously, and Ike drew a picture of a blue mare, in chalk, upon the newly-washed kitchen floor.

Mrs. Partington says she don't see why people want to be always struggling for wealth; for her part, she affirms that all she wants is food and raiment and clothes to wear to meeting.

PAUL AND POLITICS.

WAS Paul inclined to politics?" we asked of Mrs. Partington, as we saw the old dame reading a "grand rally" hand-bill at the corner of the grocery store. She asked us to wait a moment till she "digested" her specs. "Inclined to politics!" said she, and her eyes rested upon the period at the end of the last line, till she seemed to be meditating a full stop. "He was; but he wasn't a propergander, nor an oilygarchist, or an avaritionist, nor a demigod, as some of 'em are; all he wanted was an exercise of his sufferings and the use of his elective French eyes, as he used to say. Ah, Heaven rest him!" exclaimed she, as her eyes rose from the period at the bottom of the bill and rested on the top of the fence. "But did he never get an office, Mrs. P.?" we asked. "Yes, replied she, and we fancied the tone of her voice had an expression of triumph in it — enough to be perceptible, like three drops of paregoric in a teaspoonful of water — "yes, he was put one year for a hogreefer, and got neglected." As we were about asking her opinion of the new constitution, Ike came along whistling "Jordan" and swinging a pint of milk, in a tin pail, around his head, and the old lady forgot her politics in her solicitude about Ike's soiling his new cap.

A PREDICTION.

IKE came running in one day during the sleighing season, with, " O, aunt, I just now saw a little boy fall right down under a sleigh in Washington-street! "

" Dear me ! " she screamed, horror-struck; " bless my soul ! did it hurt him much ? did it kill him instantly ? "

" O, no, aunt ! " replied he; " it did n't hurt him at all, for the sleigh had n't any horse in it."

His face beamed with fun.

" Ah, you disgraceless boy ! " cried the old lady, with her finger raised, at the same time with her apron wiping away the mists that the momentary sympathy had gathered in her eyes ; "ah, you disgraceless boy ! you won't die in your bed if you tell such stories ! "

There never was a kinder creature than she; and, as she looked on his good-natured face and sparkling eyes, she patted his head and gave him an apple.

THE DESSERT.

—

"Desert, did you say?" growled old Roger, at a festival supper some time ago, to a person who sat opposite him at the table, who had called for the dessert; "come over this side, my friend, and you'll have no occasion to call for it. It's quite a *desert*, and almost a perfect *famine* here already, and has been so all the evening. Don't look at that turkey — that is nothing — that is only a promise made to the hope and broken to the stomach; for human strength cannot divide its members — they are unanimously tough." And the little man recommenced ogling a ham that was rapidly disappearing in the dim distance, and mumbled cheese crumbs to allay the cravings of unsatisfied appetite.

BOSTON MUSIC HALL.

—

When Mrs. Partington first visited the new Music Hall, she looked at the structure with great admiration. It was in the day-time, and the gas burners over the edge of the cornice met her eye. Turning to Mrs. Battlegash, who sat next to her, she remarked that everything seemed excellent "except the out-of-the-way place where they driv the nails for the ostriches to hang their coats on," and pointed to the ceiling, saying she didn't believe they could ever reach them.

TROUSSEAU OF PRINCESS WASA.

IKE read, "At Paris, the dressmakers, jewellers, and milliners have all been occupied in furnishing the trousseau of the Princess Wasa."

"Stop, Isaac," said Mrs. Partington, raising her finger, and glancing at him over the top of her spectacles; "is that so?"

He assured her that it was.

"Well," continued she, and a blush of offended modesty crossed her features, like the sun-flush on the newly reddened barn-door; "that may be the way they do things in Paris, but it isn't modest to begin with. A woman has no right to wear 'em. 'T is agin natur and decency. And what does she want so many of 'em for? She can't wear but one pair to a time, and here she has got all of the dressmakers making trousers for her, as if she was going to live long enough to wear 'em out. Ah, women a'n't what they were once!"

She rose suddenly as she spoke, and Ike, who was upon the back of her chair, endeavoring to tie a string to a nail in the big beam that traversed the ceiling, was thrown violently against the table, breaking three plates and a teacup in his descent.

STOCK OF THE REVOLUTION.

—

" WE have little left of the revolutionary stock, now,"
said the schoolmaster, as he seated himself in Mrs. Partington's back-room, and wiped his brow.   There was a
meaning in her spectacles, as they glanced upon him,
responsive to his remark, but she said not a word.   Drawing a chair towards her, she smilingly stepped upon it,
and, standing on tiptoe, reached away back into a closet
in which were kept the remnants of past service, — bottles
and paper bags, and a heterogeneous mass of odds and
ends that would have made the fortune of a showman, —
the blue stockings revealing themselves as she prosecuted
her search; but the schoolmaster did n't see them —
not he.

" Revolutionary stock!" said Mrs. Partington, and
her voice seemed choked by the dust raised in the old
cupboard, " here 's one of 'em!" and she reached out,
with a present-arms motion, an old musket-stock.   " Here
is a relict of the revolution that has survived the time
that tired men's souls; and, poor souls! I should think
they would have been tired to death with the smell of
the powder and balls.   I keep this up here away from
Isaac, for fear he should do some mischief with it, for I
don't want him to have nothing to do with fire-arms.
Is n't it a relict?"

Bless thee, Mrs. Partington! and thou art a relict,
thyself, more to be prized than stacks of arms; and, did

STOCK OF THE REVOLUTION

thy warm spirit pervade the land, war would be no longer the scourge of the nations, and men would not know fighting any more.

PHILOSOPHY OF COUNTRY HEALTH.

"PEOPLE may say what they will about country air being so good for 'em," said Mrs. Partington, "and how they fat up on it; for my part, I shall always think it is owin' to the vittles. Air may do for camamiles and other reptiles that live on it, but I know that men must have something substanialler."

The old lady was resolute in this opinion, conflict as it might with general notions. She is set in her opinions, very, and in their expression nowise backward.

"It may be as Solomon says," said she; "but I lived at the pasturage in a country town all one summer, and I never heerd a turtle singing in the branches. I say I never *heerd* it; but it may be so, too, for I have seen 'em in brooks under the tree, where they perhaps dropped off. I wish some of our great naturals would look into it."

With this wish for light, the old lady lighted her candle and went to bed.

18

THE PROMENADE.

WE sat directly in front of Mrs. Partington at Jullien's concert, one night, and were pleased to witness the marked attention that she paid to the performance. The first part had been concluded, and the " fifteen minutes' intermission for promenade," announced on the bill, had been well spent, when we felt a finger laid upon the arm that rested upon the back of the next seat, and a whispered voice was breathed into our sinister ear :

" When is he going to carry it round ? "

We looked at her inquiringly, and she looked inquiringly back again.

" Carry it round ? "

" Yes," replied she, " the promenade here. 'T is the refreshment part of the entertainment, is n't it ? "

We explained to her the meaning of the word " promenade," and, with a long drawn " O ! " like an extended cipher, she sank back into her seat. Ike was blowing peas at a gentleman's boot projecting through the lattice work of the gallery.

MRS. PARTINGTON IN THE CROWD.

"Don't go anigh it, Isaac," said Mrs. Partington, with nervous anxiety, on the day of the great railroad jubilee procession, as the carriage, bearing the big gun, came by where she and Ike were standing. She had been very nervous all the morning, and had made some curious mistakes. When the procession first came along, she waved her handkerchief at an alderman, taking him to be the president; and Marshal Tukey she thought was Lord Elgin.

"Don't go anigh it, — it's one of the pesky Paxon guns we read of; they call 'em peace-makers because they tear people all to pieces; and, depend upon it, Isaac, if a man got hit once or twice with such a gun as that, my idea is, that there would n't be much left of him. O, the wickedness of men, that they should learn war, and kill people, and spoil good clothes, and act more like Kottenpots or salvages than they do like men! They say this Mr. Paxton has got up a Christian Parish in London, and everybody is going to see it. Well, I hope he will tend it himself, and get good, and repent of the evil he has done. But, I'm sure, I hope he won't have any such machines as that, ever, to help his preaching."

The noise of the passing crowd drowned half her remarks, and, at that moment, a marshal backed his horse near where she and Ike stood, with a command to her to " stand back." It was astonishing how the flies, or something, troubled that marshal's horse all the while he stood there.

A CEREOUS MATTER.

" THERE was a cererous accident happened down here, just now, aunt," said Ike, running in hastily.

" Dear me ! " cried Mrs. Partington, dropping her knitting-work, and starting from her seat in great alarm; "what upon airth was it, Isaac ? Was anybody killed, or had their legs and limbs broke, or what ? "

" O," replied he, giving his top a tremendous twirl, that sent it round among the chairs at a great rate; " O, no ! 't was only a man capsized a box of candles, that 's all."

The old lady looked at Isaac reproachfully. He will break her heart one of these days. Her mind, at the first alarm, had flown among her balsams, and bandages, and lints, that had lain in obscurity since the poor boy next door had cut his toe off; and to be thus lowered down from her hope of usefulness was too bad. But Ike went out with his top, laughing all the while, and the old lady subsided into the old arm-chair, and went on with her knitting.

ANCIENT AND MODERN REMEDIES CONTRASTED.

"THEY don't doctor folks now as my physician learnt me," said Mrs. Partington, sagely tapping her snuff-box by the couch of a friend lying indisposed. Her gesture was very expressive, and the profundity of a whole Med. Fac. beamed from her spectacles. She took a pinch of Farwell's subtle Maccaboy in her fingers, and shut the box, and laid it away in her capacious pocket, then, with her closed forefinger and thumb raised, went on with her remarks, — "They don't subscribe for folks now as they used to. My doctor used to tell me, — and he never lost any of his patience but once, and that was an old man of ninety-seven, whose days were shortened because he had n't strength to swallow, — he used to tell me, — and I 've been with him thousands of times with sick folks, — he used to tell me, first, said he, give 'em apecac, to clear the stomach; then give 'em purgatory to clear the bowels; then put a blister on the neck if the head aches; and have 'em blooded if there is a tenderness of the blood to the head; and put hot poultices on to the feet, arter soaking 'em in hot water. There wan't none of your Homerpathics, nor Hydrapathics, nor no other pathics then, and what was done might be sure it would either kill or cure!"

She inhaled the dust with great unction, and the patient, who lay making squares and diamonds out of the

18*

roses on the room-paper, " thanked God and took courage," as heartily as St. Paul did when he saw the three
taverns, that he had fallen upon times of more physical
mildness.

MR. SLOW IN THE MOON.

MR. SLOW and Abimelech were out looking upon the
moon, as it gleamed above them in the sky. The moon,
as they gazed, passed behind a dark cloud, the edge of
which gleamed like silver.

" How beautiful ! " said Abimelech.

" Yes, my son," said Mr. Slow, solemnly, " that
'ere 's well got up. Some people say they have brighter
moons in other places than our'n, but I say that 's all
moonshine. Look at it, 'Bimelech, as it hangs up there
now, as bright as a dollar, and don't you believe any of
the gammoning stories about its being a green cheese."

" But, father," asked Abimelech, his son, " is n't the
story true about the man in the moon ? "

" Certingly, my son, certingly," said Mr. Slow, looking down at him ; " that 's all true, that is, 'cause it 's in
the primer."

Abimelech was satisfied — so was Mr. Slow.

MY LITTLE BOY.

ERHAPS he is in no wise different from everybody's little boy
— I dare say he is no taller,
or thicker, or heavier, than ten
thousand other boys who have
had existence, and been the
idol of doting papas, and mammas, and maiden aunts. He
is not an original boy in a
single particular — I don't
claim him as such; he eats
very much the same way, and
very much the same food, as
other young gentlemen of his age — sleeps the same, cries
the same, and makes up the same outrageous faces at
castor-oil. I don't care if he is n't different. But every
parent has a right, in fact he is bound, to think his boy
better than everybody's boy, by a law of nature that knows
no contravening — will admit of none. If everybody
sees in the picture I draw of my boy a sketch of his own,
let him remember it is *my* boy still, and not flatter himself that he has a prodigy that knows no equal.

My boy has the glory of more than a year of months
to brag of, three of which he has devoted to taking his
steps in the initiatory of locomotion. and excels in little

manœuvres in engineering, of his own adoption, steering warily among chairs and tables; and, though frequently broaching to and foundering under a press of eagerness in circumnavigating the kitchen, he invariably comes up all right, and forgets minor adversities in the grand triumph.

My boy is a living proof of the great truth of gravitation, as, when unlucky circumstance kicks him out of bed or throws him from a chair, he invariably strikes the floor; and my boy has had knocks enough on his head to realize a faith with regard to his profundity equal to that of Captain Cuttle in the renowned Bunsby, for the same reason.

My boy understands the moral of a whip. Thus young, will he wield the rod in terror over the back of shrinking sisterhood, nor even spare maternity in his "experimental philosophy."

My boy knows very well how to manage it when the slop-pail is within reach, and nothing pleases him more than a plentiful ablution in soap-suds or greasy dish-water.

My boy delights in experimenting in hydraulics, — now essaying to administer hydropathy by the dipper-full to a healthy floor, now sousing stockings into the water-bucket, and now putting the hair-brush into the sink.

My boy fills his father's boots with incongruities that do not belong there, and looks on gravely as the load is shaken out, wondering, apparently, why his father don't let it stay.

My boy watches his chance to pull a dish, or a cup, or a saucer, — no matter which, — from the table; he seems to have an antipathy against crockery, and vivid visions of sundered pairs remind his father daily of the havoc he has made in the once respectable " service," — here a white and there a blue, some cracked, noseless, handleless, stare him in the face.

My boy despises all conventional rules, and unheeds the suasion that would limit will; republicanism speaks through every act, independence in every look, freedom in every motion.

My boy is very decidedly partial to an ash-hole; it is a spot by him of all others to be craved; he glories in an ash-hole; thereward his inclination ever points. David of old, in his utmost woe, could n't have gone deeper into the ashes. A stove-pan is a good substitute for the ash-hole; there is a luxury in strewing the gritty dust about a clean carpet, that is not to be overlooked, and never is; there is fun in hearing it crunch beneath the feet of his mother, and fun, too, in filling his mouth with the fragments. I have thought, from my boy's predisposition to pick up gravel, that he required it to aid digestion.

My boy rejoices in a dirty face. No Mohawk chief, in the pride of war-paint, could feel more magnificent than my boy under an application of molasses, — or anything, — he is not particular; and no Mohawk would fight harder to prevent its being wiped off.

My boy takes to sugar very readily; he was very quick in taking to this; it seemed instinctive with him. I have heard of people's having a sweet tooth, but I verily believe the whole of my boy's — he has but four — are *all* sweet.

My boy is all-exacting in his demands, — *demands* sure enough, as imperious as those of a prince; and his brow frowns, and his little voice rings again, if his demands are not complied with, — principally confined, however, to the matter of victuals.

My boy is everything that is affectionate; a laugh and kiss his morning and even sacrifice, and his bright black eyes and rosy cheeks glowing in the sunlight of a happy heart. His voice greets me as I come from labor, and his arms encircle my neck in a sweet embrace, and his cheek reposes against mine in the fulness of childish love, and then I feel that my little boy is better than everybody's, and I can't be made to begin to believe at such times but that everybody must think so. In short, as Mr. Micawber might say, **my boy is a trump card** in my domestic pack.

MY LITTLE BOY.

HAT " Little Boy," of whom it was our delight and pride to speak, is no more. His sweet spirit has fled from the earth, and left an aching void in our heart, and an anguish which will be hard to allay. The music of his voice is stilled; the mild beaming of his eyes is quenched in the darkness of death; his arms are no more outstretched upon loving impulses, nor his step speedy in affection's errands; the happiness of his smile will no more impart its blest contagion to our own spirit, nor the home places be made again pleasant by his bright presence.

We were loth that he should depart. There were a thousand ties that bound him to us. We could not conceive that a flower, so fair and full of promise, should wither and die while within our grasp. We fancied that we could hedge him round with our love, and that the grim archer could not find access to our fold through the diligence of our watchfulness. We had forgotten that the brightest and fairest are oftenest the victims of inexorable Death, and that the roseate robes of to-day's joy may be usurped to-morrow by the sable drapery of affliction.

There was much to endear him to us. Perhaps no more, however, than every child possesses to a parent. He was precocious to an extraordinary degree, and his little life was full of childish manliness that made everybody love him who looked upon him. His kiss is still warm upon our cheek, and his smile still bright in our memory, replete with love and trust. We were sanguine of a fruitful future for him, and we had associated him with many schemes of happy usefulness in coming life, and with foolish pride boasted of indications that promised all we hoped. Alas! how dark it seems now, as we recall the dear little fellow in his dreamless rest. He was smiling as we laid him beneath the coffin-lid, as if the spirit in parting had stamped its triumph, on the cold lips, over the dominion of Death.

That "Little Boy" was our idol, and there were those — well-meaning people too — who would expostulate, and shake their heads gravely, and say that we *loved him too much ;* as if such a thing were possible, where a being of such qualities was making constant drafts upon our affection. It is our greatest consolation that we loved him so well, — that there was no stint or limit to the love we felt for him, — that his happiness and our own were so promoted by that affection, that it was almost like the pangs of death to relinquish him to the grave.

It seems almost a sin to weep over the young and beautiful dead; but it must be a colder philosophy than ours to repress tears when bending over the lifeless form of a dear child. We may know that the pains of earth are exchanged for the joys of heaven; we may admit the selfishness of our woe, that would interpose itself between the dead and their happiness; we may listen to and allow the truth of gospel solaces, and cling to the hope of a happy and endless meeting in regions beyond the grave; but what can fill the void which their dreary absence makes in the circle which they blessed, where every association tends to recall them?

Thus it seems when the heart is first bereft, when the sorrow is new, and we sit down in our lone chamber to think of it and brood over it. But we know that affliction must become softened by time, or it would be unbearable. And there are many reflections that the mind draws from its own stores to yield after-comfort. Memory forgets nothing of the departed but the woe of separation, and every association connected with them becomes pleasant and joyous. We see them, "with their angel plumage on;" we feel them around us upon viewless wings, filling our minds with good influences and blessed recollections; freed from the sorrows and temptations and sins of earth, and, with a holier love, they are still ministering to us.

It is one of the immunities of grief that it pour itself out unchecked; and everybody who has a little boy like this we have lost will readily excuse this fond and mournful prolixity — this justifiable lamentation. But

" We shall all go home to our Father's house —
To our Father's house in the skies,
Where the hope of our souls shall have no blight,
Our love no broken ties :

19

We shall roam on the banks of the River of Peace,
    And bathe in its blissful tide ;
And one of the joys of our heaven shall be —
    The little boy that died.''

———————

'To talk of a man worth his millions giving a few thousands of dollars in charity, is well enough,'' said old Roger; '' he should be praised for it; but what is his act compared with that of the poor woman who buys a pint of oil from her own hard earnings, and carries it in a broken-necked bottle to a sick neighbor, poorer than herself, to cheer the gloomy hours of the night? What is his act compared with hers, I should like to know? Not *that!*''

And he snapped his fingers, and felt sustained in his high estimate of the poor woman's small donation.

MRS. PARTINGTON ON REMEDIES.

"This is an age of enervation in medicine, sure enough!" said Mrs. Partington, as she glanced at the column of new and remarkable specifics; "why will people run after metaphysics and them nostrums, when, by taking some simple purgatory, they can get well so soon? It's all nonsense, it is, and if people, instead of dosing themselves with calumny and bitters, would only take exercise and air a little more, and wash themselves with care and a crash towel, they would be all the better for it."

She said this on her own experience. As for "diet drink," and summer beverages, Mrs. P. is very noted.

A NEW INSTRUMENT.

"When is he going to bring on the *wioleen?*" whispered Mrs. Partington to a neighbor, at the Melodeon, after listening through the first part of Ole Bull's concert.

"That's it, ma'am, which he is now playing on."

"Why, that's a fiddle, a'n't it? Good gracious! why can't they call things by their right names?"

And she left the hall, saying to the door-keeper, as she passed, that it was only a *fiddle* after all.

CRITICISM.

A SMALL crowd gathered before a window, recently, to admire the figure of a cat which was there as if for public inspection. Nearly every one was delighted with its likeness to life.

" But still," said Augustus, " there are faults in it; it is far from perfect; observe the defect in the fore-shortening of that paw, now; and the expression of the eye, too, is bad; besides, the mouth is too far down under the chin, while the whiskers look as if they were coming out of her ears. It is too short, too " — but, as if to obviate this defect, the figure stretched itself, and rolled over in the sun.

" It *is* a cat, I vow ! " said a bystander.

" It is *alive !* " shouted Ike, delightedly clapping his hands.

" Why, it's *only* a cat, arter all," said Mrs. Partington, as she surveyed it through her specs; but Augustus moved on, disappointed that nature had fallen so far short of his ideas of perfection in the manufacture of cats.

BLEAK HOUSE.

"DICKENS is fast getting along to the denouncement of the Bleak House," said Mrs. Partington, as she saw a paragraph mentioning the approaching denouement of the story. "Well, I should think he would have denounced it long ago, and had it prepared, for I don't believe they could have made him pay one mill of rent unless he did it at his own auction. Bleak House, indeed; and Mr. Dickson a poor man, too, with aliments enough on him to patternise a whole hospital himself!"

The picture of the Good Samaritan handing the wounded Jew a quart bottle of Sarsaparilla Bitters attracted her attention, and she delivered Ike a private lecture on the humanities, while he sat pulling the cat's tail in the dark side of the chimney-corner.

ADMIRATION FOR ELOQUENCE.

"DEAR me, how fluidly he does talk!" said Mrs. Partington recently at a temperance lecture. "I am always rejoiced when he mounts the nostril, for his eloquence warms me in every nerve and cartridge of my body. Verdigrease itself could n't be more smooth than his blessed tongue is;" and she wiped her spectacles with her cotton bandanna, and never took her eyes from the speaker during the whole hour he was on the stand.

19*

NAVES OF THE CRYSTAL PALACE.

—

" WELL," said Mrs. Partington, as Ike read the paragraph from the Post that the decorators were at work on the two naves of the Crystal Palace.   She paused at the " well " before she went further into it, and Ike stopped reading to hear what she had to say, and chewed up a part of the paper into spit-balls, which he amused himself with by throwing at the old white-pine dresser in the corner.   " Well," said she, — this is the same *well* we left some time since, — " I am glad they are taking time by the fire-lock and looking arter the knaves aforehand. Knaves in the Christian parish, indeed ! But they will get in, the best that can be done.   There's many a one, I dessay, in all parishes that has a sanctuary in his face, but with the cloak of hypocrisy in his heart.   Read on, Isaac."

And the old lady looked up at the black-framed ancient picture of Susannah and the elders, and patted her box reflectively.

MR. BISBEE'S CONFESSION.

It was a rash promise that I, Jeremiah Bisbee, had made to the youngest Miss Teel to gallant her to church. I knew that she would be offended if I did not comply, and yet how I felt! The previous evening's amusement had extended well towards daylight, and a more miserably-feeling fellow than myself never did rouse himself at the sound of breakfast-bell on a Sunday morning. But the promise was made, and the glory of a new pair of plaid pants and a red velvet vest was to blaze beside the modest beauty of Miss Seraphima in the Rev. Mr. Blunt's church.

I had no seat there, but my cousins, the Misses Titmarsh, who owned a pew in the broad aisle, had many times invited me to sit with them, informing me that there was plenty of room, and I determined to avail myself of their invitation. The pew was a very respectable one, I knew, as I had heard them many times describe it as having heavy drapery, and all the other essentials of genteel worship, just as they had inherited it from the deacon, their uncle. I had heard them describe, too, the occupants of adjacent pews, and had been given to understand that the Ogglers and Spighs, the aforesaid occupants, were the most respectable people in town, and that they felt rather envious at the superior position of " our " pew, for so the *young* ladies (forty-seven if they were a day) called it.

The day was bright, the pants fitted to a charm, the red vest gleamed in the sun, my coat was neatly brushed, and, with an unexceptionable hat, and a pair of brilliant boots, I felt myself to be " some." The sleepy feeling with which the morning commenced, was overcome by the momentary excitement of walking and talking with a charming girl; a triumph over Somnus that I thought truly wonderful.

We reached the church,— a large, venerable, sleepy pile, having a good many pews in it, the latter a characteristic, I believe, of churches generally. There was a languor upon the still air of the old church that struck me sleepily as I took my seat in the spacious, high-backed pew; the monotonous toll of the bell sounded like a lullaby, and the swelling notes of the big organ, which rose like incense to the roof, and pervaded the house, gave me a qualm that my boasted triumph outside would not be of permanent duration, opposed to the somnolent influences within.

As ill luck would have it, we had a very dull preacher, — a duller I never knew, — trite and common-place, without originality or fervor, and insufferably long. I felt sleepy at the propounding of the text, which was, as near as I remember, " Sleep on, and take your rest;" and every wakeful feeling within me began to grow heavy about the eyes at the injunction. I struggled against slumber, as a man overboard would struggle with the tide. My eyelids drooped in spite of me, and when I would open them they felt as if they were interlaced with sticks, and my sleepy soul seemed looking through a grating of wicker work. The eyes of my cousins, the

Misses Titmarsh, were wide open upon me, the bright eyes of Seraphima were upon me, the eyes of the Ogglers and Spighs were upon me, for the Misses Titmarsh had informed me in a whisper that they were here in full force, and that the new plaid pants, and the red vest, and Seraphima's new bonnet, a charming thing, by the way, would produce a tremendous envy among their opponents in the adjacent pew.

In my sleepy reflections I saw the utter disgrace that would attend upon my cousins, the Titmarshes, if I misbehaved. I thought upon them, positively, more than upon my own shame. I thought of the horror they would feel were I to speak aloud, or laugh, or tumble down, or commit any extravagance in a dream. All of the tricks I had ever practised in my sleep came up before me, frightfully magnified. What if I should practise some of them over again, or get up on the backs of the pews and go round, as Amina foots it over the tiles, in the opera?

I struggled manfully with sleep, but I found I couldn't hold out long. Hum-m-m, hummed on that long sermon! — Upon my honor, I don't believe I heard a word of it besides the text, unless it were the word "sleep," which seemed profusely scattered, like poppies, along the tedious way. I found myself rapidly sinking. The faces by which I was surrounded were melting away, the Ogglers and the Spighs were becoming oblivious, and the preacher, just taking the form of a huge black beetle impaled on a pin, was humming a dull drone on one continuous key, when, mustering resolution, I roused myself, thrust my hand hastily into my pocket to pull out my handkerchief, when, — the Ogglers and Spighs were all looking, and so were the Misses Titmarsh and Seraphima, — when, — I blush to say it, though it was the means of my becoming a reformed man, and a tolerable member of society, and the father of a large family, — when I pulled my handkerchief out, *a pack of cards*, a deposit of the previous night, came leaping out with it, and, as if actuated by the devil who invented them, they darted about in almost as many directions as there were cards, brazenly showing themselves in the holy house, to my utter confusion of face.

Had my worst enemy seen me then, he must have pitied me. I was wide awake now. The concentrated redness of every red card was painted upon my face, and the blackness of every black one was transferred to my heart. The spots on the cards, to my heated fancy, seemed bigger than a cart-wheel. I heard a suppressed titter among the Ogglers and the Spighs. Just then the eldest Miss Titmarsh fainted. " Heaven be thanked for this ! " says I ; " here 's an opening ; " and, seizing the unconscious spinster, I made for the door as speedily as possible. Placing her in charge of the sexton, I ran with all haste for the doctor. Strange that those medical gentlemen should be away at such a time ! I left an urgent order on the slates of six of them, and was told that five of the six, an hour afterwards, met in consultation on the steps of Rev. Mr. Blunt's church.

As I said before, I have now reformed, and sit just in the shadow of life's afternoon, looking back over the events of its morning, rejoicing with hopeful trust that the errors of youth may not be carried forward to the account of mature age, if repentance make atonement for the past. The Misses Titmarsh forgave me, and Seraphima, in a long life of devoted attention on my part, has quite forgot that Sunday's mortification.

GERMANIA BAND.

"How do you like the music, Mrs. P.?" asked her neighbor of the old lady, as she stood listening to the Germania band, one evening on the common, and beating time on the cover of her snuff-box.

"Beautiful!" replied she, enraptured, "oncommon beautiful! It seems almost like the music of the syrups. I think the Geranium band the sweetest of any of 'em. Can you tell me," said she, in a big whisper, "which is Mr. Bergamot?"

The name of Bergamot was associated with her rappee and hence her solicitude.

She was told that Mr. Bergman belonged to the Germania Society, and that the leader of the Germania Serenaders was Mr. Schnapp.

A smile lit up her face, revealed in the declining twilight, as she asked if he was akin to Mr. Aromatic Schnapps, the gentleman that imported so much gin. Her ear was arrested by the strains of the music, and the black bonnet waved in unison with a waltzing measure, as Isaac sat upon the grass in contemplation of a dog's tail before him, wondering what the effect would be if he should stick a pin in it.

A GOOD SUGGESTION.

ESSRS. CHANG and ENG — those interesting exotics, from whose land all the golden fountains and talking lauras, and singing trees that graced our juvenile literature were derived — were much gratified by an introduction to Mrs. Partington, one of whom assured her that he had heard of her in Siam many years ago, but the other did n't recollect about it. On informing her of their intention to go to Saratoga or Newport the coming summer, the old dame wondered at the determination.

"How crowded you will be!" said she, "accommodations are so scarce; though, I dare say, you could, upon a 'mergency, both sleep in one bed."

The suggestion was a happy one — all the difficulty was removed in an instant — and the dual gentleman smiled a thankee with his four lips, and Mrs. Partington waved a parting benediction to him with her green cotton umbrella, as he disappeared in the crowd.

CATCHING AN OMNIBUS.

"If you want to take a 'bus," said Mr. Sphynx, in his oracular manner, "you must be 'mazing sly; you must n't go boldly up to 'em, 'cause they 'll certingly be full, — room for twelve, and seventeen inside, — or the driver won't see you, if you shake your umbrel or cane at him never so much. 'Buses are queer critters — very queer; it takes sunthing of a man to understand their natur. When you want one, there a'n't one coming. Put your head out in the rain, and look every which way, you can't see hide nor hair of one. Wait till the next one comes — that 's full; so 's the next. Then you get a little miff'd, and says you, 'I 'll walk!' Start in the rain — get wet; when you get almost where you want to go, 'long comes one of 'em, like blazes — lots of room — looking at you as much as to say, 'See here, old boy! don't you wish you 'd ha' waited?' and whisks by like a racer. If you see a 'bus a little ways ahead, and run yourself into a fever to catch it, two to one it 'll be the wrong 'bus, and you 'll have to walk, arter all. Now the way to do is this: — Act jest as if you don't care a snap whether you ride or not. Be indifferent, and one 'll come right along; don't be uneasy 'bout getting a seat, and there 'll be plenty of room; conclude that you 'll walk, and you may have a whole 'bus to yourself. That 's the way to come it over 'em!" Saying which, and shaking his head profoundly, Mr. Sphynx retired.

20

IKE IN A NEW POSITION.

IKE got a situation to blow an organ in town, and one Sunday a stranger organist took it into his head that he would try the instrument a little after the congregation was dismissed. He expressed his desire to the boy, who consented to blow; for there are few more obliging boys than Ike when he is well used. He pumped away vigorously for some time, until his arm ached, when, peeping round the corner of the organ, he asked if he might now go.

"No!" said the organist, curtly, and kept on, drumming away among the dainty airs that he was taking upon himself, — now thundering among the bass notes, and now glancing playfully amid the tender trills of the pianissimos, — when, confusion to a fugue commenced, the breath of the organ gave out, and the music flattened to a dying and dismal squeal.

"Holloa!" cried the performer, "don't get asleep there — blow away!"

But no response attended his command. He grew red.

"Blow away, I say!" he cried, louder.

Still no response.

Angrily and inharmoniously the man of music arose and looked for Ike. He was not there, and the mad man of melody, as he glanced from the window, caught a distant view of a pair of juvenile coat-tails as they disappeared round a corner.

UNPOPULAR DOCTRINE.

"I was surprised, Mr. Roger, to see you speaking with that *creature*," said Miss Prim, significantly emphasizing the word.

" Why, madam ? " asked the old man.

"Because she is a low, vile creature of the town," said she, waspily.

He took her hand within his own, and looked her calmly in the eye, as he replied : — " Call her not vile ; call her miserable, rather; and as such she is more worthy of your regard and pity; for, though she may have sadly erred, she still is not all depraved ; that old spark of sympathy in her heart is there yet unquenched. I have seen her not long since watch by the sick, work for the needy, and give her money for their relief; take her own bread and give it to a poor felon in prison, and comfort a little child in its sinless sorrow; — I have seen this, and, bad as you think she is, *I* can honor her for her *virtues*. My dear madam, gain her *good* qualities, and add them to your own perfections, before presuming to sit in judgment on her *bad* ones. Besides, do you know what temptation is, ma'am ; were you ever tempted ? "

The frosty look which met his own seemed to render such a question unnecessary, and he released her hand, gently advising her to exercise more of charity in her estimate of character.

BENEVOLENCE.

PHILANTHROPOS, the day after the great Railroad Jubilee, appeared in public with two excessively black eyes. It seems that he was going by one of our principal hotels, when a large delegation arrived from out of town, and hearing the remark, "All full," his heart was touched, and, mounting upon a post, he asked the crowd if they would n't like to have a nice house to stop at, where every man could have a room to himself, and every accommodation he could desire. The response was "Yes."

"Well," said the good man, with emotion, "well, if I hear of any such I will let you know."

The people were strangers, and did not understand the benevolence of his intentions, and one or two of them expressed their disapprobation in a striking manner, which marred the good man's pleasant exterior, as above described.

On the day of the above celebration, a large locomotive was brought to a standstill in Washington street, in consequence of one of the wheels giving out belonging to the car it was on. PHILANTHROPOS, with an eye always to the interests of the mechanic, seeing the danger to which the engine was exposed, walked sentry round it all night to prevent the boys from running away with it. It was an act for which he should have been honored; but the workmen called him an ass for his pains, when they came the next morning to take it away. His indignation for a moment was awakened; despair succeeded of ever being able to benefit his race; when a small voice whispered to his conscience: "Will you abandon an eternal principle because crude humanity fails to appreciate your efforts?" and he responded promptly to the question, and turned away in search of new objects for the exercise of his benevolence.

MYSTERIOUS ACTION OF RATS.

"As for the rats," said Mrs. Partington, as she missed several slices of cake, the disappearance of which she imputed to them, "it a'n't no use to try to get rid of 'em. They rather like the vermin anecdote, and even chlorosive supplement they don't make up a face at. It must be the rats," continued she, thoughtfully, and took a large thumb and forefinger full of rappee to help her deliberation, — "it can't be Isaac that took the cake, because he is a perfect prodigal of virtue, and would n't deceive me so, for, I might leave a house full of bread with him and he would n't touch it."

Ike sat there demurely, with his right foot upon his left knee, thinking what a capital sunglass one eye of the old lady's specs would make, while a trace of crumbs was visible about his mouth. It is feared that not even chlorosive supplement, nor anything weaker than a padlock, will save Mrs. Partington's cake.

20*

MRS. P. ON THE MISSISSIPPI.

—

"WHEN will the Father of Waters come along?" asked Mrs. Partington, as she sat looking at a panorama of the Mississippi, in the last hours of its exhibition.

"The Father of Waters!" replied the individual addressed, "why, this is it that you are seeing before you."

"Goodness me! is it?" said she, "why, I've digested my specs to look arter a big man with the dropsy, and it's nothing but a river, arter all. How I wish they'd call things by their proper names!"

There was something of disappointment in her tone; but when afterwards she remarked to herself "I wonder if that water will wash?" it was a beautiful tribute from Benevolence to Genius.

———

"ENTERED at the Custom House?" said Mrs. Partington, pondering on the expression; "I don't see how the vessels ever got in; but I am glad that the collector cleared 'em right out again. It will learn them better manners next time, I think."

PROVISIONS OF THE CONSTITUTION.

"Provisions of the Constitution!" said Mrs. Partington, with an earnest air and tone; "for my part I should be glad to see 'em. Heaven and all of us knows provisions is scarce enough and dear enough, and if they can turn the Constitution to so good a use I'm glad of it. Anything that will have a tenderness to cheapen the necessities of life,"—and here she laid her finger on the cover of her box, and looked earnestly at a cracked sugar-bowl in the "buffet" in the corner, containing the onion-seeds, and the bone-buttons, and the scarlet beans, and the pieces of twine, long-gathered from accumulative paper tea-bags,—"I am agreeable to it, and if they can turn the Constitution and all the ships of war to carrying provisions, I am shore they will do more ood than they do now a good many of 'em."

She here ran down like an eight day clock, and she smiled as Ike rushed in with his arms full of votes, and his face full of fun and molasses candy, and asked her if he should n't give her a "tig whicket."

SEVERE, BUT JUST.

—

'DOLLY PRIM a spinster, indeed!" said Mrs. Part-
inton, as she heard her unmarried neighbor in the back
parlor termed thus. "I should like to know what upon
airth she spins but street-yarn; for she's gadding from
morning to night. The wheel she spins on would be
harder to find, a great deal, than the fifth wheel of a
coach!"

O! she could be severe, could Mrs. Partington; but
there was generally a commingling of the bitter and
sweet, the wormwood and molasses, in her rebukes, that
tempered acidity, and made reproof wholesome.

MRS. PARTINGTON AND PIETY.

—

DEACON SNARL, in exhortation, would often allude to
the "place where prayer is 'wonted' to be made."

"Ah!" said Mrs. Partington to herself, "there's
nothing like humility in a Christian. I'm glad you
confess it. I don't know a place under the canister of
heaven where prayer is wanted more to be made than
here, and I hope you'll be forgiven for the rancorous
butter you sold me yesterday."

She was a simple-minded woman, was Mrs. P., and
was apt to get the world mixed up with her devotion;
believing, somehow, that Christian duty prescribed
worldly justice. She had n't been long a member.

BRICKS AND STRAW.

Dr. Digg has discovered a striking analogy between the brickmaking operations of the Israelites in Egypt and those of the present day. In the first instance straw was required in the manufacture of a perfect brick; in the latter straw is an essential thing, as is shown in the imbibation of juleps, an element in the manufacture of modern bricks, where straw is invariably used. The Doctor asks when Egypt was like a dry lemon. Presuming the answer will not be forthcoming, he says, "After the *Jews* were all out of it." It is supposed he means *juice*.

MEDALLIC PROSPECTS.

"I don't see," said Mrs. Partington, as Ike came home from the examination, and threw his books into one chair, and his jacket in another, and his cap on the floor, saying that he didn't get the medal, — "I don't see why you didn't get the medal, for, certainly, a more meddlesome boy I never knew. But never mind, dear; when the time comes round again you'll get it."

What hope there was in her remark for him! and he took courage and one of the old lady's doughnuts, and sat wiping his feet on a clean stocking, that the dame was preparing to darn, that lay by her side.

MRS. PARTINGTON BEATING UP.

"THERE's poor Hardy Lee called again," said Mrs. Partington on a trip from Cape Cod to Boston. The wind was ahead, and the vessel had to beat up, and the order to put the helm "hard a lee" had been heard through the night. "Hardy Lee, again! I declare I should think the poor creetur would be completely exasperated with fatigue; and I'm certain he has n't eat a blessed mouthful of anything all the while. Captain, do call the poor cretur down, or Natur can't stand it."

There was a tremor in her voice as indignant humanity found utterance. "It a'n't Christian — it is more like the treatment of Hottenpots or heathen!"

The captain went on deck, and a sudden lurch of the vessel sent the old lady on her beam-ends among some boxes, recovering from which forgetfulness of "Hardy Lee" ensued, and this tack brought her to the wharf.

A DEAD SHOT.

"How do you feel with such a shocking-looking coat on?" said a young clerk, of more pretension than brains, one morning.

"I feel," said old Roger, looking at him steadily, with one eye half closed, as if taking aim at his victim, "I feel, young man, as if I had a coat on which has been paid for, — a luxury of feeling which I think *you* will never experience;" and then he quietly resumed the reading of the Post, and the young clerk made no further remark on the subject.

SHOCKING JOKE.

"I SEE," said old Roger to a farmer topping corn, "that to one branch of your industry you are its worst enemy."

"Why?" asked the farmer.

"Because," replied he, "you are always raising shocks for the corn-market."

"Yes," quietly replied the farmer, "but the market is always saying, 'lend us your ears.'"

Old Roger and the farmer smiled at each other as they parted.

RIDING.

WHAT a vast improvement has been made upon the old methods and means of travelling, even within the memory of the youngest of us! Recall the old staging system a moment to mind, when a day's ride was agony in its anticipation, not to be dispelled by the stern reality, over roads scarce redeemed from primeval roughness, which the jolly tongue of the red-faced driver — provided you were lucky enough to get on the box with him — was hardly capable of enlivening. What apprehension did timid insiders feel of threatening wreck at the bottom of the steep hills they rattled down! How fearful they would be of never reaching the top of the next hill, from the miserable horses giving out that were attached to the vehicle! How they trembled at the danger of having their brains knocked out against the roof of the low coach, in the rebound that anon jerked them from their seats as the stage-wheel sunk into a cart-rut!

For this latter alarm there was considerable cause, to judge by a story told us once by one of the professors of the whip. He was riding, he said, one day over the way we were then travelling, in a terrible bad season of the year, when the cart-wheels had cut the roads up into hideous gullies, into which the wheels would plunge, to the danger of all who chose to ride ; and often the passengers had to get out and lay their shoulders to the work to assist the horses in their exertions to extricate the vehicle from the mud. The day he spoke of, however, he had but one passenger,— an elderly gentleman, wearing a wig,—and, feeling his responsibility lessened by his diminished fare, he took less heed as to where he went, and dashed along over the road, whistling from absence of care, entirely regardless of horses or passenger, determined to achieve the distance to the next stopping-place in a time mentally allotted for its performance. It was one of the old-fashioned low-roofed coaches, one of the oldest of its class. A sudden cry from a child who was passing caused him to look round, and there to his horror he saw the old gentleman's bald head glistening in the sun's rays like a mammoth mushroom, his eyes glaring on him wildly, and his mouth vainly endeavoring to articulate. It was but an instant before he was extricated from his perilous situation. In one of the sudden lurches of the road he had been forced up through the canvass roof, and this closing around his neck held him there, incapable of helping himself, and he had ridden many miles in this manner before he was discovered.

"That story's just as true, now, as I tell it to you," said the driver.

21

" Don't doubt it," we replied ; " but what became of the hat and wig ? "

" I can't say anything about the hat, but I 'm very much mistaken if I did n't see that old wig, for three seasons, used as a genteel residence for a family of crows down the road here."

A very singular story, we thought, and think so still.

MRS. PARTINGTON LOOKING OUT.

" I CAN'T make it out," said Mrs. Partington one morning, when she first moved to the city, after the railroad ploughshare had upturned her hearth-stone. " I can't make it out;" and she reached further out of the window, to the imminent danger of the " embargo " returning again to her head, or of a somerset into the street below.   She had caught the sound " Here 's haddick ! " from stentorian lungs under her window, and she could not make out what the sounds meant.

" I wish I knowed what the poor critter was crying about, but I thought he said he had a sick headache; and I declare I pity the poor soul that has got such a distressing melody as that."

She drew in her head, like a clam, and shut down the window, to keep out the sounds of a misery she could not relieve.

FORESEEING THINGS BEFOREHAND.

"I WONDER who is coming here to-day?" said Mrs. Partington, at the breakfast table, turning her cups and working the tea-grounds to their oracular position. It was the 4th of July, and a procession was advertised to pass her door. "I wonder who *is* coming here to-day? Here's a horse, and a wheelbarrow, and a tub; and there's a big G and a cipher; and here's a flock of geese and a cow. The cow and the geese must mean the procession, that's clear; but what *can* the big G stand for, and the rest of 'em? It must mean our seventh cousin, Mrs. Tubbs; and it is so kind of her to remember her poor relations at such times, as she always does. Yes, it must be her, 'cause there's a *tub*, and the wheelbarrow must run for an omnibus; but what can the cipher be? I guess, though, that don't mean anything. Scour up the German silver spoons, Margaret; we must be hospitable. I dare say she would be to us if she should ever ask us, and we should go."

The prediction was fulfilled, and the fat lady occupied the front seat in Mrs. Partington's private box.

A SINUOSITY.

OLD ROGER was seated at the dinner-table by the side of Seraphima, the youngest of the five marriageable daughters. The conversation turned upon conundrums and queer comparisons. The old fellow leaned back in his chair, and, wiping the traces of soup from his mouth, said, as he took the young lady's hand in his own, "See this fair hand, now, white as a snow-flake, and rich with dimpled beauties!" — Seraphima smiled. — "Who is there among you that can tell me why this sweet hand is like the remains of that 'hock-shin' soup before us all?"

The hand was drawn back suddenly, — that fair hand, compared with a vile pile of beef sinews! The boarders were astonished at his audaciousness, — Seraphima frowned.

"You can't guess, can you?" said the jolly old fellow. "Well," continued he, "it is because there is such tendonness in it."

He pronounced it "tenderness," and Seraphima smiled again; but the boarders, who had found the meat rather hard, did n't see the relevancy of it, — they did n't know what *tendon* meant, no more 'n a cow knows about its grandmother.

THE SCIENCE OF FISH.

—

" I WONDER what this ' *itch theology* ' is," said Mrs. Partington, giving a somewhat novel pronunciation of the old science, as she read the announcement of the lecture by Professor Agassiz; " what in the name of Old Scratch *can* it be ? I suppose it must mean the itch for meddling with politics and things that does n't concern 'em, and running down their own country and relations, and praising up everybody else, and at war with everything, all the time they are preaching peace."

Some one explained that it was the science of fishes.

" Well, well," said the lady, " it 's just as well; for a minister preaching politics is like a fish out of water — he is out of his ailment."

She passed over to the deaths and marriages, and Ike ganged his hook, with an afternoon's smelting in his eye, and a ball of Mrs. Partington's piping-cord in his pocket for contingencies.

21*

ETERNAL INDEBTEDNESS.
—

" When I lent her the eggs," said Mrs. Partington, " she said she would be eternally indebted to me, and I guess she will. How can people do so ? I would go round the world on all-fours a begging before I would be guilty of such a thing. Ah, well, it takes everybody to make a world ! "

And she put in saleratus enough to make up for the non-returned eggs; her neighbor had decidedly taken a rise out of her.

BORROWING NEWSPAPERS.
—

" Shall I have the goodness to look at your newspaper one moment ? " asked Mrs. Partington at the grocery store.

" Certainly, my dear madam, with the greatest reluctance possible," replied the grocer.

They exchanged glances, and there was so much of thankfulness in her eye that he almost made up his mind to subscribe for another paper for her express accommodation.

PROMISING CHILDREN.

———

"WHAT a to-do people make because children happen to know something when they are young!" said Mrs. Partington, as she read an account of many men who had been distinguished in early years. "Now, all these together don't know so much, by one half, as Dolly Sprigg's baby. That *is* a perfect prodigal, to be sure; sich an intellect! Why, it got through its goo-googles, and into its bar-bars, afore it was seven months old, and when it wäs only a year and a half old it emptied a snuff-box down its precious old grandmother's throat as she was asleep, and came nigh suffocating the old lady afore she could wake up to conscientiousness and spit it out. There never was sich another, its mother says, — and who knows so well as a mother what a child is, that has watched over it, and seen it expand itself like a tansy blossom, and sweet as a young cauliflower?"

The old lady was always eloquent on this topic; she was a believer in prodigies, and thought Solomon must have consulted some young mother when he wrote that "every generation grows wiser and wiser."

FORGIVENESS OF WRONG.

"He called me a termagrunt, and said I was n't any better than I should be," said Mrs. Partington, as she threw her shawl into the water-bucket, and her bonnet on the floor, on her return from her landlord's, where she had vainly sought an extension of time for payment of the rent; "there never was such an aspiration cast upon one of our family before; there is no such thing in our whole craniology; and, if there is any statuary or law for slander, I 'll see if he can prove it. The terma-grunt I don't mind so much; but to be called no better than I should be—the mean, penny-catching curmudgin! But no, it 's wrong to call him names; it makes me most as bad as he is; I 'll borrow the money and pay him, I will, and show him that I don't bear mallets;" and she brightened up in the thought of this mode of revenge, bustling about and putting the house to rights in the best humor in the world. Her conduct was a sermon and seven tracts on the sublime principle of forgiveness of wrong.

What kin is that which all Yankees love to recognize, and which always has sweet associations connected with it? Why, pump-kin, to be sure.

A NEGATIVE AFFIRMATIVE.

Mr. Timms, a farmer up in the country, had a habit of putting in "Yes yes, yes yes," at every pause in his speaking, which sometimes had a ludicrous effect. The old fellow owned a fine horse, which he was very careful of, and would never lend or hire him to the most particular of his friends. A youngster of the village, who wished the horse for a Sunday ride, went over to the old man's house, to hire the animal, if possible.

"So, you want my horse, young man? yes yes, yes yes," said Timms; "and you say you'll ride him gently? yes yes, yes yes; and you'll give him plenty of oats? yes yes, yes yes; and rub him down well when you get where you are going? yes yes, yes yes; and will give me a dollar for the use of him? yes yes, yes yes. Well, upon the whole, you can't have him, — yes yes, yes yes."

The young man left sorrowing.

We see it stated in the prints, frequently, that vessels going to California *double* Cape Horn. If this is the case, by-and-by there will not be a *single* Cape Horn left.

TAKING PICTURES.

—

"THAT is a splendid likeness, by Heaven!" exclaimed Augustus, rapturously, as Mrs. Partington showed him a capital daguerreotype of her own venerable frontispiece.

"No, it is n't," said she, smiling; "no, it is n't by Heaven itself, but by its sun; is n't it beautifully done? All the cemetery of the features, and cap-strings, and specs, is brought out as nateral as if from a painter's palate. Any young lady, now," continued, she "who would like to have the liniments of her pretended husband to look at when he is away, could be made happy by this blessed and cheap contrivance of making pictures out of sunshine."

She clasped the cover of the picture, paused as if pursuing in her own mind the train of her admiration, and went out like an exploded rocket.

———

"MAN is born to work; and he must work while it is *day*."

"Have I not," said a great worker, "all eternity to work in?"

"Well," said Slug, who did n't love work, "if that's the case, what 'n time 's the use of putting in so? I 'd jist as lieves divide the work, and do part of mine when that cove 's resting."

PRECOCITY.

The elder Smith was somewhat astonished one evening at finding a berry pie for tea, — a rather remarkable thing in his gastronomical experience, for Mr. Smith indulged in few luxuries, for reasons which will be understood by people of limited means. It was an excellent pie, the *chef d'œuvre* of the culinary skill of Mrs. Smith, who prided herself upon what she could do if she only had the "grediences." Smith junior, numbering some three summers, sat opposite his sire.

"My son," said the old 'un, during a pause in the work of mastication, "did your mother make this pie to-day?"

"Certainly," said the precocious youth; "she did n't, of course, make it to-morrow!"

The elder Smith looked mournfully at the miniature edition of himself, then, wiping the crumbs from his mouth, and ejaculating "So young!" he left the house.

MR. THIMBLE'S MOUSE-TRAP.

THE old gentleman one morning discovered a mouse in his bed-chamber. A mouse or a rat was what he held in the utmost dread, and even the idea of getting his hand on one by any accident, always gave him a tremor. Seeing the little animal thus in his very bed-chamber was most provoking, and, reaching for an oaken cane always at the head of his bed. a defence against hostile invaders of this "inner shrine," he at once vowed the mouse's destruction, and, cane in hand, started upon its accomplishment.

"Ha !" said he, between his fixed teeth, as he closed the door and firmly grasped his stick ; "now, Mr. Mouse, I 've got you — I 'll fix your flint for you !" and the poor little timid thing running into a corner, the old gentleman levelled a furious blow at him, repeating his threat to fix his flint for him.

This offer to fix the flint of the mouse is hardly intelligible in this age of patent matches; but Mr. Thimble lived in tinder-box times, when flint and steel were inseparable, and he probably thought that an animal so inclined to steal must have a flint.

The blow was wrongly directed, and the mouse escaped to another corner.

Another blow, and another, resulted in the same manner; until at last the mouse finding cover beneath an antique bureau, the old gentleman was compelled to exert all his generalship to bring him out.

But in vain he got down on all-fours and looked beneath the bureau; in vain was the cane thrust in the direction of his eyes; the enemy was nowhere to be seen, and Mr. T. got up, flushed with the exercise, brushed his knees, and went down to breakfast, wondering where the little animal had gone.

After relating the incident, he was calmly engaged in cooling his coffee, when, dropping his cup, he darted from the table into the middle of the floor, dragged half the breakfast things after him, and practised antics very unbecoming in an elderly gentleman of sixty-two.

His family, astonished to see him thus, had incipient ideas of lunatic asylums and strait jackets dart across their minds — the old gentleman the while capering about the room like a mad dancing-master, shaking his right leg as if St. Vitus had selected this member for his particular favor, regardless of the rest, until, with a tremendous spasmodic kick, out fell the mouse from where he had secreted himself!

It was long before Mr. T. regained composure.

22

Some time after, speaking of his activity, Mrs. Thimble remarked, —

"My dear, I did n't think it was in you."

Mr. T. looked queerly at her, as she uttered this, but did n't say anything.

MRS. PARTINGTON *vs.* COOK-BOOKS.

"A BEEFSTEAK fried in water," said Mrs. Partington, "it seems to me, must taste very much as if it was biled. They do have *such* curious idees about cooking now-a-days! And people has to learn lots of outlandish names before they know what they 've got for dinner. Ah! the good old times was the best, when people seasoned their dishes with flag-root and such spices, and a poor man's fragile repast was eaten when he knew what he had to be thankful for."

What a cook she is, to be sure! And is n't it the cause of rejoicing for a week among the boys in the neighborhood when she fries up a batch of doughnuts, and Ike knows where they are kept? No wonder she thought, as she said, that he ate like Pharaoh's lean kind, that eat up the fat of the land of Egypt.

ON ELOCUTION.

"O, DOES N'T he disclaim fluidly!" exclaimed Mrs. Partington, delightedly, as she listened to the exercises of the Humtown Intellectual Mutual Improvement Society. Her admiration knew no bounds as a young declaimer, with inspiration truly Demosthenic, launched the flashing beams of his eloquence broadcast among his auditors, with thrilling, dazzling, burning force; anon soaring like a rocket into the "empyrean blue," dashing helter skelter amidst the stars, and harnessing the fiery comets to the car of his genius; anon scouring the land like a racer, the hot sparks, like young lightning marking his Phaetonish course; anon breaking through the terra-queous shell, and revelling in Hadean horrors in underground localities somewhere.

The voice of Mrs. Partington, whom we left standing on the threshold of her admiration some way back, recalls us to herself.

"How fluidly he talks! He ought to be a minister, I declare; and how well he would look with a surplus on, to be sure! He stands on the nostrum as if he was born and bred an oratorio all his life. I wish the President was here to-night; I know he 'd see he was an extr'ord'nary young man, and like as not appint him minister extr'ord'nary, instead of some that never preached any at all."

The old lady beat time with her fan to his gesticulations, nodding the black bonnet approvingly, and smiled as the young man told the world that Franklin had made it a present of the printing-press.

OUTRAGE.

DURING a concert one night, a reckless individual, in the upper gallery of the large hall in which it was held, whose name we did not ascertain, allowed his bill of the concert to slip through his fingers, which, falling below, by the rule of gravitation, fell suddenly upon the exposed head of one of our first young men ! The effect of the concussion upon an object so tender may be well imagined. Smelling-bottles were called for, and, none being at hand, one young lady applied her glove to the sufferer's nose, which, having been lately cleansed with turpentine, had the effect of bringing him to. The diabolical perpetrator of the act had the audacity to look over the edge of the gallery and grin at the injury he had done, but, before the officer could get to the gallery and arrest him, he had flown.

P. S. — We wish it to be distinctly understood that it was the *glove*, and not the *nose*, that had been cleaned with the turpentine.

IKE IN THE COUNTRY

IKE IN THE COUNTRY.

DURING the last winter Ike was sent to visit some of Mrs. Partington's relatives, who live on the borders of the Great Bay. Squid River, which empties into the bay, is a very beautiful stream in summer, but in winter it is dreary enough, with the tall trees, stripped of their foliage, standing, as it were, shivering upon its brink. But it is a rare skating course from Moose village to the river's junction with the bay.

Ike had used up all his resources for fun at the end of the third day. He had snowballed the cattle into a frenzy, caught all the hens in a box trap, tied the pigs together by the legs, sucked all the eggs he could find, and was looking round for something else to do, while the boys were at school. He was just calculating, as he poised a snowball, how near he could come to a tame pigeon on the window-sill without hitting it, when the glass was saved by the appearance of the house-cat outside the sacred precinct of the kitchen.

Ike had watched this cat wistfully ever since he had been there, and the cat had manifested a strange repugnance to him ever since he trod on her tail as she lay by the stove. He immediately seized upon her, and expedients, never wanting, soon suggested themselves to him.

There were plenty of clam-shells about the yard, and, selecting four of the smoothest, he, by the aid of some

22*

grafting wax at hand, soon had Tabby beautifully shod with clam-shells and on the way to the river. Ike's idea was to learn her to skate!

The river was smooth as glass, and a sharp wind blew along its surface towards the bay. "Now, Puss," said Ike, as he pushed her upon the ice, "go it!" An instinct of danger instantly seized upon her. Her claws, which Ike had found so sharp a short time before, were now useless to her, and, with a growl of spite, she swelled her caudal appendage to an enormous size which, taking the wind, impelled the poor feline like a clipper over the slippery path. The tail stood straight as a topmast, and grew bigger and bigger, and faster and faster flew the animal to which the tail belonged. Ike laughed till he cried to see the cat scudding before the wind. But now the bay lay before her, and far out over the smooth ice was the blue water of the sea.

The result can be guessed. The cat never came back, and everybody wondered what had become of her, and thought it augured ill luck for a cat to leave a house so suddenly. Ike thought so, especially for the cat.

Ike's conscience reproached him sadly, but he compromised the matter by leaving the tenants of the barn-yard in peace all the while he staid there, and came home with a pocket full of doughnuts and an enviable reputation for propriety.

THE NEW YEAR—AN ALLEGORY.

"WHAT are your intentions towards Miss New-Year?"
sternly asked the old Guardian of Years, as Time, in the
garb of youth, stepped forward to make his proposals.
The fair being to whom he aspired stood veiled before
him, in mystical beauty, beside the seer, whose dim eyes
had seen the birth and death of thousands of years, and
whose beard was white with the frost of centuries, and
whose voice creaked with the rust of many ages.

Time, buoyant with the hopes of youth, promised
much. Their union, he said, would be fruitful of great
events. Joy and prosperity would attend upon it. By
their union the arms of the weak would be strengthened;
the tyrant's power be shorn of its might; the poor and
down-trodden be exalted; the desponding be made to
sing for joy; abuse be banished from the earth; the
wrath of man be restrained; and the struggle for right
be crowned with success.

The old guardian shook his head incredulously, and a
tear fell upon his gray beard as he spoke:

"Alas! alas!" he said, "the same promises were
made by your sire to her fair mother, and broken, as
have been all the promises of Time since the world began.
Where is the fruition of the glorious hopes held out for
bygone years? They have found their end in gloom and

disappointment. How can I trust, then, this precious charge to your arms in view of olden failures? "

Then young Time, laying down his hour-glass and gayly swinging his scythe among the few weeds left of the herbage of the old year, made answer, with a firm tone and a cheerful air : —

" The violated promises of others should not be the criterion for judging of mine; nor their failure be urged as a presage of my own ill-success. Let me prove myself by my acts, and if endeavor may win the goal, my chance is good. Let me try."

The old guardian grasped Time by the hand approvingly; the hand of the virgin year was placed in his, and, as the clock struck the hour of twelve, the form of the old seer faded from view, and the mystical one, for better and worse, for joy and sorrow, became the wedded bride of Time.

———————

PERSONAL cleanliness is a virtue, but it is not pleasant to see a man cleaning his teeth with a questionable pocket-handkerchief; neither is it to see a man, however attentive he may be to the wants of his family, put a beef-steak in the crown of his hat, and fill his trousers' pockets with cucumbers. It don't look well.

THE ARCHITECTURAL BLACK EYE.

WE met old Guzzle one day, with a terrible black eye. "Ah!" said we to the interesting individual, "bad eye that."

"Yes, that 'ere 's a architectural eye."

We asked an explanation.

"I say this 'ere 's a architectural eye, because I got it from the Elizabethan architecture of our house."

We were in the dark as much as ever.

"T' other night," continued he, "I went home partially tight. I say partially, for, 'pon my honor, I had drank but seven times during the evening. I felt my way up by the wainscoting, because I did n't want to make a noise, and when I got to the top, I forgot what a deuced wide staircase it was, and when I turned to go towards my door, what does I do but walks right down stairs again, a good deal faster than I went up, and struck my head agin the corner-post, and be hanged to it! Bad eye, is n't it? And all from that infernal Elizabethan stairway."

We thought that the fault lay with the rum.

SEEKING A COMET.

IT was with an anxious feeling that Mrs. Partington, having smoked her specs, directed her gaze towards the western sky, in quest of the tailless comet of 1850.

"I can't see it," said she; and a shade of vexation was perceptible in the tone of her voice. "I don't think much of this explanatory system," continued she, "that they praise so, where the stars are mixed up so that *I* can't tell Jew Peter from Satan, nor the consternation of the Great Bear from the man in the moon. 'T is all dark to me. I don't believe there is any comet at all. Who ever heard of a comet without a tail, I should like to know? It is n't natural; but the printers will make a tale for it fast enough, for they are always getting up comical stories."

With a complaint about the falling dew, and a slight murmur of disappointment, the dame disappeared behind a deal door, like the moon behind a cloud.

———

AMONG the Roman priesthood was a class called *augurs*. There are many great *bores* among our modern priests.

BENEVOLENCE UNAPPRECIATED.

PHILANTHROPOS was at a public meeting one evening, where the heat was distressing, and, observing a lady on a seat in front of him who appeared to be suffering from excessive warmth, he went out and bought a large fan, which he delicately set in motion, as if fanning himself, while he made every effort to give her the benefit of the artificial breeze, becoming himself additionally heated from the exertion he made, losing all interest in the concert from his intentness in the benevolent action, and smiling to himself with the belief that his kindness was felt without its source being known. He was thus benevolently happy, until he heard the lady tell her husband to go and shut down that odious window behind her, for she had felt cold on her neck all the evening from the east wind. Philanthropos went out and sold the fan for seven cents that he had given a quarter for an hour before.

AN editor having stated in his paper that he had been presented with a number of varieties of *plumbs*, old Roger declared his preference for the perpendicular.

THE PARTING WORD.

IN telling a story about a Printer, I am not about detailing the mysteries and difficulties of his occupation, although a feeling and interesting sketch might be made of the business of his life, with its care and toil for the good of the world. I love the printers from association and long habit; am proud now of their companionship; and, when walking arm-and-arm with my friend, the President of the Franklin Typographical Society, I feel as well as if the individual in the hook of my arm were the President of the United States. My intention in this little tale is simply to give the incidents of a printer's life, wherein his heart was concerned, and not to meddle with his profession in any way, save to dignify my hero by the association.

The "Freeman's Star" was located in Patny, the shire town of Seaburn county, in *our* State, and it exerted a great influence upon the mind and manners of the people. Society took its tone from the printing-office. The magnates of the place owned its sway, perhaps through fear, and the humblest looked towards it with reverence, for they had heard of its power as the "defender of the people's rights," and never deemed how much of humbug there was in the profession. The editor was looked up to as a great man, and people would touch one another as he passed, and whisper, "That is the editor!" He had been foreman of a daily office in the city, and his importance was unbounded on the assumption of his new honors. In a proportionate degree all hands in the office were marked men. The single journeymen, the grown-up apprentice from the neighboring town, and the demon himself, were all marked individuals, and people treated them deferentially for their connection with the "mighty engine" that had such power. Their opinions, expressed at times about the weather, or the elections, or the crops, were listened to attentively, and everything that appeared in the Freeman's Star was imputed to one or the other of the "printers" by the particular friends of each. Let a piece of village poetry appear, or a good story culled from some city paper, and at once would be seen in it by the different parties traces of the mind of each of their favorites. They would have known it to be his if they had seen it in the moon, if they were by accident located in that planet and had met with it there.

It was in this office that I made the acquaintance of the hero of my story — the grown-up apprentice — who bore the uneuphonious name of Jabez Bee. He was a spirited fellow, very intelligent, and as full of mischief "as an egg is full of meat," to use an expressive modernism. He was a constant attendant upon the tavern, in

23

all his leisure moments, where, attracting a crowd of countrymen around him, he would astonish them by the keenness of his wit and the extent of his information, and many a marvellous story have his country friends carried home "as latest news," that originated in the teeming brain of Jabez. Steamboats were blown up and railroad accidents were as common then, in this way, as now, when the melancholy realities need no draught upon the fancy, for instances.

But he gained a character for wit at the expense of his moral reputation, which is too often the case; and at eighteen, though everybody liked him and laughed with him, he was set down as not likely "to turn out very well" — a great phrase in Patny. People cautioned their sons and daughters about going in his company, and "Evil communications corrupt good manners" was written as a copy in every girl's and boy's writing-book in town. But he laughed at them all, and the boys joined him; and the girls, who, somehow or other, always seem to set more by the wild and mischievous than by the staid and prudent, loved Jabez very sisterly. He was bold and generous — qualities which no true woman can see in a man without admiring them.

Far more discerning than older ones in matters of soul, they had discriminated long ago between the mischief and wildness of Jabez and his malice and wickedness, and a large balance was set down in their hearts in favor of his good qualities. They saw a sympathetic smile or tear where those who decried him saw but levity and heartlessness. They smiled upon him for striving to save the child's lamb from drowning in the well, and re-

joiced outright when he threw the bully over the fence,
who was maltreating the widow's son.

The most beautiful girl in Patny was Susan Bray.
She was a charming little creature, with an eye as blue
as a violet in spring, a voice as soft as the evening bird's,
a cheek like the blush of the apple blossom, and a breath
as sweet as its perfume breathed over the pearly purity
of her teeth. Her form was slight and graceful, and as
lithe as the bending corn or the wavy pliancy of the
yielding grass. I am not good at describing beauty in
ladies. 'T is not my forte; but I am determined here-
after to put myself under the hand of my friend Paul
Creyton, or some other master of art, and become better
versed in the science of drawing word-portraits. Enough
is it for my purpose to say that she was very beautiful,
and that over her beauty was thrown a fascination of
manner and a propriety that was peculiarly delightful.
She gained for herself from her admiring companions the
expressive soubriquet of "the lily of the vale," and her
modesty and grace justified the title.

She was the daughter of Mr. Bray, the village blacksmith, and having been educated in a distant town, her
return to Patny was like the rising of a new star or the
discovery of a new flower. The young men were delighted with her manners, and the young women —
pleasant creatures — gave her their hearts willingly, for
they feared rivalry from her no more than they would
from the new moon. She moved in a circle that the bold
printer boy did not enter. The blacksmith was a hard
man, and the reputation of Jabez was such that it did
not commend itself very favorably to the old man's mind,

and he had discouraged acquaintance with him. From
the time of her return, however, had Jabez Bee looked
upon the fair Susan admiringly, but at a distance. He
gazed upon her with a respectful feeling that had no
affinity with the lighter and laughing affection he felt
for the village girls of his acquaintance. He felt that
she was a superior being to the whole of them, and his
soul bowed with reverence at her shrine — hoping
nothing and asking nothing but to lay its silent offering
at her feet, as the simple votary brings garlands in the
still of the morning to hang upon the shrine of some
favorite saint. It was a beautiful feeling, and as pure
as beautiful. The love at first almost unconscious
became at length the absorbing feeling of his life. It
marked his conduct and conversation, and the unconfessed
passion he felt moulded the impetuous and the wild boy
into a dreamer and a visionary. He pored over books,
and the woods and glens and water-brooks were familiar
with his footsteps. He acted in short, dear reader, as
you, and I, and almost all others, have done, or might
have done, under like circumstances, made himself very
ridiculous, and the Freeman's Star literally groaned with
the efforts of his awakened muse; and well it might groan,
as everybody did that read what he wrote. The poetry
was more truthful than lovely, and its quantity, like
the Irishman's dance, compensated for its quality. The
change in his conduct was marked. Business was more
closely attended to, and the tavern frequented less. He
became a perfect marvel to his friends, who wondered
what had come over him, and as the spiritual knockings
had just come along, some, in levity, gave it as their

opinion that he had had an interview with the ghost of his grandmother, that had rebuked his gracelessness. But though he was less lively than formerly, he was none the less kind to all, and everybody loved him as well or better than ever.

But fate, so called — that officiates as a sort of junior Providence in the affairs of men — decided that a passion so fostered and concealed should be known, and that all the speculation with regard to Jabez Bee's mystery, grandmother's ghost and all, should be swallowed up by a knowledge of the fact.

There was to be a great picnic in Patny. The Freeman's Star had announced it for a month in big type, and in an editorial notice had apprized the people that it was to occur on such a day, weather permitting — the editor dwelling with great eloquence upon the happy combination of beauty and cold chicken, pancakes and poetry, crackers and conversation, cider and scenery, in making up the sum total of its enjoyment. The day came auspiciously; the sun was bright, and the air was balmy; the lads and lasses laughed lavishly, and the birds sang sweetly in the bushes. In a grove near, the company held high carnival to Pan, and the arches of the woods were vocal with the noise of mirth. Near by was a charming little lake, hemmed in by trees and bordered by sedges, dotted here and there by patches of lily pads, amid whose deep green the water flowers gleamed like stars, and this lake wooed many to its brink, to admire its beauty, to plash in its cool water, or sail upon its still bosom in a tiny boat that was at hand. Jabez and Susan were of the party, and through the

23*

atmosphere of her presence he saw a new and mystical
beauty in everything — the trees were greener, the berries were brighter, the air was balmier, and the music of
the pines had a new and sweeter melody.   Susan was
one of a few that had wandered towards the lake, and
Jabez had watched her at a distance, fondly drinking in
with every faculty of his being her charms as they
became revealed to him, in her playful movements among
the trees; and her smiles, though not for him, were sunshine to his heart.   And now his heart, that interesting
organ, throbs wildly, as he sees her with playful reck-
lessness step upon the tiny boat and push it from the
shore.   The treacherous twig to which the boat was tied
broke at the strain it received, and Susan Bray was afloat
and alone upon the waters of the lake.   Each effort she
made to gain the shore was fruitless, when, her paddle
having become entangled in the lily pads, she was
thrown, pale as one of her kindred lilies, into the water.
Confusion immediately ensued, and rash endeavor to
save her only threatened her more sure destruction, when
Jabez Bee rushed madly to the scene, and in a minute
was by her side.   The water was very deep, but, with
one arm grasping the boat and the other supporting his
fair burden, he held her above the current until assistance came, when, completely exhausted with the exertion used, he fainted as he reached the shore.

In such manner did the intimacy commence between Jabez, the printer, and the fair Susan Bray, an
intimacy that resulted in a mutual affection as pure and
exalted as ever burned in the breast of more noted heroes
or heroines of romance.   The heroic conduct and gener-

osity of her lover won her heart, as her beauty and innocence had won his, and they were mutually happy, of
course.

But the Freeman's Star waned in its brilliancy; its
four hundred subscribers did not pay; buckets and
apple-sauce, in which subscribers generally paid, had
ceased to be negotiable articles in the payment for paper
and ink; and the Star went down in darkness, leaving
poor Jabez minus employment, but with plus hope. Love
fed Hope, and Hope held out her candle, and Faith
grew strong within him that the future had great things
in store for him.

Lovers' partings have been so often described that the
parting of Jabez and Susan must be imagined; for, as
every one will at once perceive, it became necessary for
them to part. We will merely state with regard to it,
that it was tender and interesting to themselves, and also
to the miller's maiden sister, who watched the last kiss on
the door-step, when he tore himself away the night before
he went to Boston. But she did n't hear what he said.

"Dear Susan," said he, "keep up a good heart, and I
shall return to you, don't fear; and I will prove myself
worthy of you, too, God bless you, and when we meet
again we will love each other all the better. 'Absence
makes the heart grow fonder,' you know. So wipe your
eyes, Susan, dear, and give me some word that I may
remember when danger is nigh, and it will prove a love-
charm that evil and temptation cannot overcome."

He pressed her to his beating heart as he spoke, and
put the imprint of a kiss upon her brow.

"Jabez," said she, smiling through her tears, "your

ʳffections may be sorely tried in the great city, and ʲemptation will beset your path, but my prayers shall be ʲffered for you, and the word I would have you remem-ʲer above all others is FIDELITY. Let us be faithful to ·ach other. Remember, ' fidelity.' "

He kissed the lips that uttered the word and vowed to ʲemember.

Fidelity ! It is a strong word, and embraces in its ʲneaning the whole duty of man. All of love, truth, honesty, is comprised in its signification. Faithful ! Of course he would be faithful; and how could he be ʲtherwise ? In the ardor of his young love, it seemed ·he easiest thing in the world.

And now he is in the city, a wondering and admiring ʲtranger ; and, after considerable difficulty, a compositor ʲn a morning paper. Day by day, and night by night, ʲigh up under the eaves, is he toiling, breathing the ʲetid and smoky atmosphere of the printing-office. He ʲas become " the slave of the lamp — he and all the other slaves." Night, which brings rest to the world, brings no rest to him. The holy Sabbath, with its sweet influences, brings no solace — for him Christ has risen in vain. The click of types at midnight is heard, like a death-watch, denoting the flight of time. Telegraphs, steamboats and railroads, combine for his discomfort. The reckless and the unhappy are his companions, and grace struggles in vain to grow in an atmosphere impreg-nated with lamp-smoke and sin. It is a sacrifice of liberty and health, of body and soul, for money.

Jabez has a strong hope in him, which sustains him He hears the ribald jest, often aimed at what he regards most sacred; he sees the irreverence which bad men show for holy things. At first he is shocked; but the ingrain generosity of his associates leads him to think less unfavorably of their lack of morals, and he laughs at what at first gave him pain.

" FIDELITY ! " was it a voice at his side that uttered the cabalistic word in his ear, and that sunk down into his heart? That word saved him. It was a good angel enshrined in his memory that came to warn him of danger and exhort him to faithfulness, and his feelings became again pure and fresh as when he left their inspiration.

" Come, Jabez ! " said a brother typo, " 't is Saturday; for this day, at least, we are free; and now, my boy, what say you to having a good time? Let's go round and see the folks."

And with a laugh on his lip, and the fire of fun in his eye, and a sense of freedom in his mind, he went with his good-natured persuader — plunged with him into dens where rum flowed like water, and the hoarse shout of revelry smote his ear with the discordance of the bottomless pit. It needed no friendly warning to save him, for his spirit shrank instinctively at the sights he saw, and the sounds he heard. One after another of these places he visited, and each time with a dimming sense of their abominations ; the light of conscience became foggy in the dun of tobacco smoke, and sensibility was blunted in the frequency of the vile exhibitions that met his gaze.

FIDELITY ! That word came again to him, and the scales fell from his eyes. The demon had lost his power and the serpent was revealed in all his hideous-

From pleasure to pleasure, through temptation after temptation, in the dance, in the saloons, in the theatre, his secret monitor came to him like the voice of a fire-bell, and his spirit grew strong under its admonition. In seasons of quiet and peaceful enjoyment, too, the word came to him approvingly, and his soul received it as a beautiful token of unbroken love, and hope revived.

It must be confessed, I think, that never yet was printer attended by so faithful a monitor, or by one that was half so well heeded.

And now sickness pressed upon Jabez, and he thought he was going to die. I believe that it always happens that people in love, or homesick people, are more fearful of death than others. It is your jolly debtor, who, honest man, hopes, by paying the debt of nature, to pay all the rest he owes, that is ready to die. The poor printer was sad, and "Fidelity" was heard but faintly in his dread to go. He was delirious. His mind wandered amid early scenes again with Susan Bray. Her voice he heard in his dreams exhorting him to fidelity. Again they stood together upon the old door-step in Patny, and he was pouring into her listening ear the story of his temptations and his support, and received from her sweet lips the deserved approval of his faithfulness. The meeting-house came up in his dream of bliss, and within its walls, robed in white, stood Susan Bray, and by her side himself, arrayed in the bravery of a holiday suit, a happy bridegroom. A new Star arose in Patny, boasting innumerable subscribers, who all paid in money, and not in buckets and apple-sauce. himself its editor, and himself the most important man

in the village, and whispered about as he walked along
the street. Alas! 't was but the vagary of a diseased
mind, soon dispelled by the officious obtrusion of a spoon
with medicine beneath his nose. Day by day he was
watched almost hopelessly. At last, however, a youthful constitution triumphed over disease and medicine, a
fearful odds, and he became conscious. Bright eyes
were beaming over him; blue eyes, suffused with tears
and affection! Reader, can you guess whose eyes they
were? Right. You have guessed right the first time.
They *were* Susan Bray's, as bright and true as when,
two years before, he had left them at Patny, though they
had shed many tears over his prostrate form during his
unconsciousness, — as if he, or any printer that ever
lived, were worth such solicitude?

The first word they both pronounced was "Fidelity,"
and their eyes proclaimed the fidelity of their hearts.

It is now about four years since the foregoing scene
was enacted, and the other day I received No. 1 of a
new paper called the Freeman's Star, from Patny, edited
and printed by Jabez Bee. A letter accompanied the
paper, containing a request that I should visit him at
home, and that Susan, *his wife*, would be delighted to
see me. As soon as spring opens I shall go.

Success to the printers, say I; and when temptation is
besetting them, as it too often is, may they have a voice
to speak to their generous souls, exhorting them to
"Fidelity."

ON GHOSTS.

Do you believe in ghosts, Mrs. Partington?" it was asked of the old lady, somewhat timidly.

"To be sure I do," replied she, " as much as I believe that bright fulminary there will rise in the yeast to-morrow morning, if we live and nothing happens. Two apprehensions have sartinly appeared in our own family. Why, I saw my dear Paul, a fortnight before he died, with my own eyes, jest as plain as I see you now; and though it turned out arterwards to be a rosebush with a night-cap on it, I shall always think, to the day of my desolation, that it was a forerunner sent to me. 'T other one came in the night, when we were asleep, and carried away three candles and a pint of spirits that we kept in the house for an embarkation. Believe in ghosts, indeed! I guess I do, and he must be a dreadful styptic as does n't!" and she piously turned to the part of the Book relating to the witch of Endor.

STAGE COMPANIONSHIP.

SOME folks are always talking, and some, with provoking taciturnity, are always saying nothing, to use a left-handed expression. We like a good talker, intelligent, quick, ready, — whose happy conversational power tends to make the rough way of life pleasant; and we have a corresponding dread of one who drones, and hesitates, and speaks only by monosyllables, and then as if he took out each word and looked at it before he dared to utter it. It is amusing at times to observe two of these human opposites come in contact, — to hear the lively laugh and playful jest of the one, as he rattles on, like a fast horse over the paving-stones, striking a spark at every step, and the sombre glumness of the other, who, hardly deigning to smile, sits tongueless, brooding over his thoughts, like a hen at midnight. Put the two in a stage-coach or rail-car, to modernize a little, and see how the former will shine; while the latter, poor dummy, though perhaps morally and intellectually worth six of the former, sits unnoted, or regarded only as some cheap fellow of no consequence.

We were one of three who one day, long ago, occupied seats with the driver of a stage, during a fifty mile ride, and one of the company was the merriest fellow we ever saw. He told stories, sung songs, and laughed, till all rang again, with our accompaniment, by the "dim woods" that we passed, and over the hills that we

24

climbed. It was a jolly ride, surpassing that, we think, of the renowned Mr. Pickwick, where the very correct Bob Sawyer occupied an equally outside position with our illustrious selves. We were somewhat inclined to be merry in those days, may Heaven forgive us! and that ride was an event to be remembered life-long. The whole party enjoyed it, save one, and he was the most woebegone-looking customer we had ever seen. Joking would n't move him; he was impenetrable to any missile of that kind, and there he sat with a countenance fifty miles long, — 't is fair to reckon it by the length of the road, — gazing very sadly at the right ear of the nigh horse. Our funny companion at last bent his whole battery upon the silent man, and tried to draw him out. It was an entire failure, and the joker, a little chagrined at the other's imperturbability, asked him, in a somewhat hasty tone, why the (something) he did n't talk. Without moving his eyes from the contemplation of the horse's ear, he opened his head, and these words dropped out: *"What's—the—use—of—talking?"*

"MY son," said Mr. Smith to his little boy who· was devouring an egg, — it was Mr. Smith's desire to instruct his boy, — "My son, do you know that chickens come out of eggs?"

"Ah, do they, father?" said young Hopeful; "I thought that eggs came out of chickens!"

The elder Smith drew back from the table sadly, and gazed upon his son, then put on his hat and went to his work.

MR. SLOW UPON MORAL WORTH.

—

" 'BIMELECH, you must try and be a good man — I 've
always taught you that.   Never let your name be at a
discount on 'change; always mind and take up your
notes, 'cause credit 's everything in the world.   What 's
a man without credit ?   He a'n't nothing — he a'n't nowhere.   For a man to be without credit is about as bad
as poverty, and a man without money or credit is to be
despised.   Avoid such people as you would the small-
pox.   Look at your gran'ther. 'Bimelech; there 's a
sample for you to follow.   He always acted right.   He
never owed a dollar, and never lost one, 'cause he was
shrewd.   He never run round, lending his money to
folks — not he.   Morgidges did it ; and people used to
love to have him foreclose on 'em, 'cause he did it so
good-naturedly.   He was a *good* man.   His name was
always right on 'change.   *He* could always get money,
let it be ever so hard.   You never catched him squander-
ing his money on charitable humbugs, and encouraging
porpoises — not he ; and when he died he was worth two
hundred thousand dollars, and the ships' colors were
histed half-mast, 'cause a good man had fell in Israel ! "
'Bimelech must improve under such training, and is n't
it the world's teaching continually ?

MR. SLOW OFF SOUNDINGS.

"THE airth is round, my son," said Mr. Slow, impressively, taking an apple from Abimelech's hand, and holding it up between his thumb and finger, "like a napple, and revolves on its own axle-tree round the sun, jest as reg'lar as any machine you ever see. The airth is made up of land, and water, and rocks, besides vegetation and trees, and things growing. The mountings upon the service of the earth are very high, — more 'n a half a mile, I should think; some of 'em are called white mountings, because they a'n't black. The ocean is very deep, and some folks thinks it hasn't got no bottom. This is all gammon. Everything has got a bottom, my son. The reason they can't find it is 'cause the world is round. They throw their sinker overboard, and it goes right through one side, like this" — (thrusting his knife through the apple), — "and hangs down underneath, jest so. Of course they can't find a bottom."

Mr. Slow gave his boy the apple, and turned round, much satisfied with himself.

———

"WHAT is a waxed end?" asked one not posted in the vocabulary of Lynn.

"A waxed end," was the reply, "is the end that receives the whacks."

AN EDITOR A LITTLE HEATED.
—

Copy! quotha? copy!—with the thermometer at 96°.
What an unconscionable dog it is, to be sure, to worry
one so. Not one line, so help us Stebbings!—not one
line. Avaunt! quit our sight! for the heat of the day
is fused into our spirit, and,

> " By that sword which gleams above us,"

annihilation awaits you, if you dare provoke us with your
importunity. The idea of writing at such time is abominable, and no reasonable devil would insist on 't. A vile
knave thou art at best, with thy swart and lank jaws
there distended, bawling for copy. Grin away, you waif
from the lake of Tartarus, whose burning flood ne'er
yielded a more hideous whelp for our, or the world's,
torment. We tell thee, swart minion, vile Mercury of
inordinate jours, that copy thou canst not have. What!
write when the atmosphere, like hot lava, wreathes the
brow and sticks there with the tenacity of molten pitch,
and burns and burns upon the brain like the thirst for
revenge, or the seething scald of impending pecuniary
obligation? Away, caitiff! and " tell thy masters this,
and tell them, too," that we will see them hanged ere
we will write a line for them to-day. Vamose! mizzle!
scatter! or, by St. Paul, temper, outraged, shall take to
itself form, and launch its thunders on thy devoted head!
But, stay. This, the ebullition of our wrath, is copy,
poor at best, — give it 'em.

24*

DON'T CUT IT, MISS.

"Don't you think my dress much too long?" asked Seraphina, the youngest of the seven, of old Roger.

"Don't cut it, miss, even if it is. I beg of you as a friend not to cut it," said the old man seriously.

"Why not?" inquired she, timidly.

"Because, miss, I remember a difficulty of my own once, under like circumstances, which was a source of much shame to me. Overtaken by a severe shower far from home, I was terribly drenched, and a new pair of sheepskin inexpressibles that I wore, tied close at the knee, as was the fashion then, received the dripping streams from my body, and, distended like a bad case of the dropsy, fell below my calves; like your dress, they were too long, and I cut them off at the knee. But the warm sun came out, the sheepskin contracted; inch by inch I felt it creeping up my legs; and, by the time I got home, you may be sure I was a sight to behold. Don't cut it, miss, unless you feel perfectly sure it will not shrink more."

There was a smile at the old gentleman's delicacy in the matter, but there could be no fear of danger, and they did n't see how the cases were parallel at all.

TWENTY-NINE CATS.

"Scat!" screamed Mrs. Partington, from the head of the stairs, as the noise of an interesting quadruped of the cat species in the kitchen below met her ears. "Scat! I say!"

She listened to ascertain the result of her command; but the noise was resumed, and the little kitchen echoed again with the feline music, — spitting, and mewing, and growling with the concatenation of malignity in every note of it that reached her as she leaned over the banister.

"Gracious Heaven!" cried she, "I should think there was twenty of 'em; what *shall* I do? Scat!" she screamed again, and the noise redoubled; indeed, it appeared to her excited fancy that a reinforcement had arrived, and were all in full chorus, and now the crash of crockery added to her fear. She dared not go down, for, of all things in the world, she feared a spiteful cat. It became suddenly still in a moment or so, and she ventured down stairs. A broken plate was on the floor, with traces of molasses upon the fragments, and Ike very demurely sat behind the stove, counting his marbles.

"Has there been any cats in here, Isaac?" said the kind old lady, looking anxiously round the room.

"Twenty-seven, twenty-eight, twenty-nine"—

"Where, for goodness sake, did twenty-nine cats come

from?" asked she; "but I knowed there was a good many of 'em."

"And there's a twoser," continued Ike, still counting, "and a Chinese."

"Anything like the Maltees, Isaac?" inquired she.

"I mean marbles, aunt," said Ike.

"And I mean cats, Isaac," said Mrs. Partington, severely.

It was a scene for a painter, — Coffin should do it up, — her eyes alternated between the broken plate and the boy, as if pondering the mystery of the sounds she had heard, and Ike wiped the molasses from his mouth on his sleeve. Did n't the molasses on the plate explain it? He had to take a lecture, you may depend, on the certainty of roguish boys being awfully punished for plaguing the aged, and he had to read the story aloud, before he went to bed that night, of the boys who were eaten up by the she-bears.

A COACH containing a young man and woman with one trunk on behind, — behind the coach is meant, — is pleasingly suggestive of matrimony.

"Yes," says old Roger, sardonically, "but a half dozen young ones and seven bandboxes are much more suggestive, — there's no mistaking signs like those."

MRS. PARTINGTON ON TOBACCO.

"I KNOW that tobacco is very dilatorious," said Mrs. Partington, as Mr. Trask sat conversing with her upon the body and soul destroying nature of the weed. "I know that tobacco is dilatorious, especially to a white floor;" and, taking out her snuff-box, — the broad one with the picture of Napoleon on the cover, — she tapped it, and offered a pinch to her guest.

"Snuff is just as bad," said he, laying his finger gently on her arm and speaking earnestly — "snuff injures the intellect, affects the nerves, destroys the memory; it is *tobacco* in its most subtle form, and the poison appears as the devil did in Eden, under a pleasing exterior."

She gazed upon him a moment in silence.

"I know," said she, "it has a tenderness to the head; but I could n't do without it, it is so auxiliarating to me when I am down to the heel; and if it is a pizen, as you call it, I should have been killed by it forty years ago. Good snuff, like good tea, is a great blessing, and I don't see how folks who have no amusement can get along without it."

The box was dropped back to its receptacle, and her friend took his leave, sighing that she would persist in shortening her days by the use of snuff, and stopped a moment to lecture Ike, who was enjoying a sugar cigar upon the front door-step.

GUITAR IN THE HEAD.

—

Mrs. Partington's neighbor, Mrs. Sled, complained one morning of a ringing in her ears.

"It must be owing to the guitar in your head, dear," said the old lady. She knew every sort of human ailment, and, like the down-east doctor, was death on fits. "I know what ringing in the ears is," continued she; "for my ears used to ring so bad, sometimes, as to wake Paul out of his sleep, thinking it was an alarm of fire!"

There was no doubt she was telling what was true, but there were some that questioned it in a gentle cough. We have n't a doubt of its truth.

A SINGULAR FACT.

—

"Them are very fat critters," remarked Mrs. Partington, as she stood viewing a yoke of splendid steers.

"Yes 'm," replied the farmer, "and, would you believe it, mum, they were fattened on nothin' but oat straw, and it had n't been threshed, neither."

"You don't say so!" said she, and, for a moment, doubt of the probability of the story occupied her mind; it was but for a moment. "Well, I never!" continued she, and turned aside to admire the beauties of a new cider-press.

A HIT AT THE TIMES.

"Bred by steam-power!" screamed Mrs. Partington, as she heard Isaac commence a paragraph about making bread by steam. She laid down her work, placed her hands upon her lap, and looked broadly at the boy through her specs. "Bred by steam!" said she; "what will the world do next? I wonder if this is one of the labor-saving inventions, now. But I see what it will end in. People are fast enough now, in all conscience; but what will they do when they come to be bred by steam-power, if they act according to their bringing up? Ah, Isaac, people may be faster now, but they are no better than they used to be!"

Isaac explained that it was a new mode of making bread. She looked at him steadily for a moment, when, taking a thumb and finger full, she put the cover on the box, resumed her knitting, and told Isaac to go on, which he did.

THE POOR PRINTER.

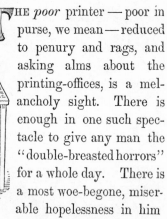

THE *poor* printer — poor in purse, we mean — reduced to penury and rags, and asking alms about the printing-offices, is a melancholy sight. There is enough in one such spectacle to give any man the "double-breasted horrors" for a whole day. There is a most woe-begone, miserable hopelessness in him as he asks your aid in the name of his profession, — of printing, — the noble art that he, perhaps, may have honored in his better days. Bad luck, or worse liquor, — often symptoms of the latter predominate, — combined with a want of self-respect, have reduced him to his present condition. He is no common beggar. There is a something in his tone, as he asks for your aid, that tells plainly it is not his true vocation; that he is forcing his nature into a most unnatural current in asking for assistance. He has none of the small lies that appear ready-framed on the lips of common beggars. No volcanoes have poured their burning lavas on his head or other property; no furious tornadoes have swept away his earthly hopes and homestead, and driven him forth a

wanderer; no overwhelming tide has pursued him relentlessly in other lands to give him a fortune here.   But he
stands before you, and his appearance pleads for him.
He looks like a low case, dusty and pied, or a form
picked for sorts and squabbling under the accumulation
of indulged dust.   There is persuasion in his seedy coat,
buttoned to the chin — a coat in which a dim gentility
struggles to overcome the poverty-clouds or cobwebs that
mar it; there is persuasion in the hat, that venerable tile,
whose form of three fashions past indicates certainly as
an almanac the date of the declension of his golden days;
there is persuasion·in his familiar look at things, and the
air that says, "This is nothing new to me — I 've seen
all this before;" there is persuasion much more in the
tone of the voice that asks the gift, as if it were a loan,
or the return of some money in your keeping for him.
There is no servility in his asking, and his story is a
direct recital of his troubles.   He is sick, has a disorder
in his head, his wife is dead, his hope has all fled, for days
has n't seen a bed, nor had one mouthful of bread, and is
quite famish-*ed*.   What a recital! and you cry, "Nuf
ced!"   and the quarter comes at once from your yielding
purse.   What a comfortable reflection it is, as we place
the coin in his extended hand! and it forces home a question of great moment, drawn from a contingency that grows,
some think, out of the nature of the art, "Whose turn
will come next?" and the *richest* of the journeymen feels
more humble as he ponders on what *may* happen.

25

MR. SLOW ON GRAVE TOPICS.

"'BIMELECH, my son," said Mr. Slow, shaking his
head with oracular and owl-like profundity, "it is n't
well to know too much, my boy; your father never did—
he know'd too much for that.   Thoughts is perplexin',
and the human mind, 'Bimelech, is too precious a thing
to be wore out with too much friction.   Don't abuse the
gifts of nater, my son, 'cause nater's one of 'em, she is.
Don't inwestigate anything new, my boy, 'cause there's
a thousand old things of more consekence to look arter—
the first of which is number one.   New notions perplexes
the mind, dear—there's full enough fools in the world
who like to look arter sich things, without your troublin'
your precious head about 'em—'t would n't be a cent of
benefit to you.   Call 'em all humbug and moonshine,
and them as believes 'em lunatics and scoundrels, and
that 'll save you a good many discussions, and give you
a character for dignity and prudence; and prudent folks
make money.   Phelosophy and scions, and them things,
is humbugs, and everything is humbug but money. Mind,
I tell ye."   Mr. Slow ceased, overcome by his own eloquence.

PAYING AN OLD DEBT.

WORKING out a debt is often called " working a dead horse," and we think not inaptly, the more especially when a man is poor, with a family depending upon him for support; then a pickaxe becomes a weary thing, and every shovel-full of dirt weighs four times as much as when the heart of the laborer is cheered by the hope of the dollar ahead. But it is well to pay one's debts; though it is far better not to owe anything, — a piece of advice that Saint Paul utters with great earnestness, as if he were practically sensible of the disadvantage of indebtedness.

A man who had run up a long score at a shop for liquor, cigars, and other creature comforts, found himself utterly unable to pay a stiver of it. In vain was he urged to pay the bill, and in vain was he threatened if he did n't; he had n't any money, — the true secret of his getting in debt in the first place, — and the creditor gave it up. At last he thought he would compromise the matter, and let the man work the debt out. The creditor had a large pile of wood in his barn, several cords of it, nicely sawed and split, and he forthwith set the debtor at work to throw the wood into the street and then pile it back again, at the rate of a shilling an hour, until the whole debt should be wiped out. The man took hold with a will, and, in a short time the wood was all in the street; then it went back with equal celerity, and then out again and then in; everybody wondering what it could mean. Some charitably intimated that he was crazy, and others, equally charitable, said he was drunk. He toiled on thus the whole day, throwing the wood back and forth, but every hour seemed full sixty minutes longer than its predecessor, as he watched the clock on the old church in the neighborhood. He was working a dead horse, and it was hard making him go. But the longest road must have an end, and the hour neared when the labor and debt would cease together, and, as the hammer of the clock told the hour of his release, the freed man threw the last stick of wood into the street with a shout of triumph. The shout brought the owner of the wood to the door, who found his late debtor putting on his coat to go away.

"Halloo!" said he, "you are not going away without putting the wood back again, are you?"

"I'll put it back again for a shilling an hour," said the man.

The proprietor of the wood saw that he had been done, but good-naturedly told his late debtor to go ahead and put it back. He went about it; but, strange to say, it took him just three times as long to put it back as it did to throw it out.

MRS. PARTINGTON having been asked what the consequences would be if an irresistible should come in contact with an immovable body, replied that she thought one or t' other of 'em would get hurt.

OPERATIC REBUKE.

"I CAN'T catch the malady!" said Mrs. Partington, at the opera, as she stood upon tiptoe, in the lobby of the Howard Athenæum, in vain attempting to look over the heads before her. She had received a ticket, but it secured nothing but an outside position, and she had gone wandering round like a jolly planet, without any particular orbit. Ike was in the gallery, eating a penny's worth of pea-nuts, and throwing the shells into the parquet below. "I can't catch the malady of the up-roar, and more 'n half the words are all Dutch to me. This is the first opiatic performance I ever went to, and if I can't get a seat, I can't stand it to come agin."

She said it very firmly. As she was going down the stairs, a young gentleman, with curly hair, reached over the banisters, and blandly informed her that he could furnish her with a seat. She turned her benevolent spectacles, and face attached, towards him, and told him it was rather late, after the evening had half gone, to think of politeness.

It was a picture! The young curly head bending over the banister, and the spectacles, and the black bonnet, and the widow of Corporal Paul, on the stairs looking up. It was sublime !

25*

"SMITH & ———."

It gives us a mournful feeling every time the above sign, on a business street, meets our eye. It is simply a white pine sign, with the letters upon it done in black. There is nothing peculiar in its construction; but the blank termination, with the ampersand, — once the connecting character of a prosperous firm, maybe, but now seeming to exist only with reference to some future contingency, — denotes separation, and thus, as indicating this, the sign becomes an important " sign of the times." The name that formerly graced it, though no longer needed there, is still to be traced through the white coat spread over it, as if yet asserting its claim to consideration. " Alas! poor ghost!" It is better to let Smith have it all to himself.

What caused the separation? Did the " Jones," whom we see dimly through the white lead, which covers him like a shroud, "shuffle off this mortal coil," and leave Smith there alone, like a boy tilting on one end of a plank? Had Jones a wife and children; and do they yet look up wistfully at the sign as they pass it by, as if with a sort of undefined hope in their minds that Jones may be in there somewhere now? Or do they weep as they gaze upon it at its suggestion of their own loneliness? Or has the widow forgotten, long ago, the man under the mould, and another Jones, with another name, taken his place in the domestic firm? Or does she yet stand, like the ampersand on the sign, beckoning some other Jones to write his name on the blank space in her heart, and begin anew?

It may have been a separation in strife, where uncongeniality of mind, temper, and habits, engendered bitterness, and the hours flew by freighted with mutual curses upon the ill-starred union of " Smith & Jones," and separation was the result. How happy were they, maybe, at the beginning, as they sat down to talk over their business schemes, while Hope held her candle for them as they ciphered out a path to fortune through the intricacies of trade, — talking as lovers talk; never dreaming, like lovers, that the elements might exist in themselves for the destruction of their hopes and happiness! We can fancy the bitter days, the reproaches, abuse, and violence, that ended in the painter's brush upon the sign, and the announcement in the Post, of " dissolution." But why is that ampersand left there? Does Smith, with his bitter experience, want another Jones to torment him?

Perhaps Smith & Jones were well-meaning men, who tried the firm on and found it unable to carry double, and then divided, good-naturedly, and are now carrying on trade, each by himself, and each happy in a knowledge of the good qualities of the other; each ready to endorse the other's note; each having for the other a cordial salutation when meeting, and " How are ye, Smith?" and " How are ye, Jones?" sounding heartily, as if they meant something more than the words usually imply, and inquiring about each other's business with as much earnestness as formerly, when together;

each referring to that time with satisfaction, and speaking of "my old partner *Smith*" or "*Jones*," with affection and respect. It is some comfort to conjure up a picture like this, and we regret that "Jones" should be "cut off" in his goodness.

"Smith & ———!" We don't like to see it, any how. If "Smith" should choose to let his name stand there forever, as now, he may do so if he can, — nobody can hinder him, or will want to. But Smith should not allow that ampersand to remain there, as if hinting at something it is afraid to say, — trembling upon the verge of it, and holding back without venturing upon it. The bond is broken that united the twain, and why should Mr. Smith offend our chaste eye by leaving that ampersand to drag along behind his name, now there is no use for it, like the end of a broken chain beneath a cart?

"Pull away, ma'am, pull away!" said old Roger, in the omnibus, as he saw a heavy lady dragging vigorously at the check-string; "another such a jerk as that and he must come through."

"Through where?" asked she sharply.

"Why, through the hole there, to be sure; you were trying to get him through it, wasn't you?"

"No, I wasn't; I was only stopping the horses, Mr. Impudence."

"O," said the old gentleman, "was that all? excuse me."

She got out, and the 'bus moved on.

A WOMAN THAT ONE COULD LOVE.

"Now, there is a woman that one could love," said old Roger, delightedly, as he saw a figure, arrayed in the full feather of fashion, in a window in Washington street. "A long life could be spent very quietly in such company; no quarrelling for precedence; no jealousy; no strife of any kind; no teasing for dress and follies, till one's purse-strings ache in sympathy with aching heart-strings, at unchecked extravagance. Even I could love such a woman as that."

"Perhaps you could," responded a sweet voice at his side; "but would it love you back again, think you? There would be no return for your investment of affection here in this heartless thing, this mere frame; you should turn your attention to something worthy of your love, where, for a small outlay of affection, a tenfold return would be made you in domestic joy."

"Alas!" said the old bachelor, "where shall I find this?"

But the beautiful eyes that met his proved how easily the question might be answered; and, with a melancholy step, he passed along. He was more a bachelor from habit than from choice, after all.

INTRODUCING THE WATER.

—

"BLESS me!" exclaimed Mrs. Partington, coming in out of breath, and dropping down into a chair, like a jolly old kedge anchor, at the same time fanning herself with an imaginary fan. She did not say "Bless me," because she was in want of any particular blessing at that time; it was merely an ejaculation of hers, expressive of deep emotion. "Bless me!" said she, "I don't see why the Water Commissionaries were so much worried and fretted about introducing the Cochituate water for; I think it is the easiest thing in the world to get acquainted with. Look at that bonnet, now," holding up the antiquated, but well-preserved bit o' crape, dripping with watery drops, like the umbrella of Aquarius; "look at that bonnet, now! ruined to all tents and porpoises by the pesky water-works. Introduce it, indeed!" continued she, ironically, looking severely at the wrecked article in her hand, "'ta'n't no use of introducing an acquaintance that makes so free with you at first sight."

She arose to hang up her bonnet, when Ike, who was hanging upon the back of her chair, fell heavily against the window, and thrust the rear portion of his person through four panes of glass.

" O, Isaac ! " said she, " you 'll be the ruination of me. If I was rich as Creosote I could n't stand it."

Isaac gathered himself from among the fragments of glass, and seemed quite tickled with an idea that he could sell the pieces, in conjunction with a reserve of old iron and half of the clothes-line and three junk bottles, to raise funds for the Fourth of July.

RATHER FUNNY.

OLD ROGER was standing in State street, and saw an Irishman rolling a keg of specie from his cart to the institution for which it was intended.

"There," said the old fellow to a foreign gentleman who was standing by him, "there you see the benefit of our free institutions; there is a man who came to this country six months ago, as poor as poor could be, and now, you see, he is actually rolling in riches!"

He said this, and turned round, very red in the face, and struck his cane several times violently on the sidewalk, and waited for his friend to explode. Hearing no sound of cachinnation, he turned and found the gentleman vainly endeavoring to decipher the emblems on the Merchants' Exchange. He evidently had n't understood the joke.

ON ONE STRING.

"THE Prayer of Moses executed on one string!" said Mrs. Partington. "Praying, I s'pose, to be cut down. Poor Moses!" sighed she; "executed on one string! Well, I don't know as ever I heard of anybody's being executed on two strings, unless the rope broke;" and she went on wondering how it could be.

SEEKING THE LIGHT.

—

" I DECLARE, I don't know what to think on it!" said Mrs. Partington, as she looked intently into the water-pail. The attitude was peculiar, and the iron-bowed specs were on duty, like a sentry on a bridge, keeping a bright look-out over the water.

" I can't see into it."

This was wrong if we take it literally, because the water was as pure and transparent as her own benevolence.

" I can't see into it, and the more I preponderate upon it, the more I'm in a bewilderness. How Mr. Paine can make light of water is more than I can see, — I can't throw no light on it. I know it's made of some sort of gin. My poor Paul's head used to be made light by gin and water, but it did n't burn, as they say this will."

Her listeners stood hatless, almost breathless, as her voice came up through her cap-border, like the steam from around the cover of a wash-boiler, while Ike put the experiment to a practical test by pouring a dipper of water into the stove.

26

JUDGING VIRTUE BY ITS SMELL.

—

"It smells virtuous," said Mrs. Partington, as she smelt of the hartshorn-bottle that had long lain away in an old-fashioned high closet, before which the old lady stood, on a tall chair, exploring the dark interior of the receptacle for "unconsidered trifles." "It smells virtuous." We had often heard of the peculiar *odor* of goodness, that rises like frankincense amid an atmosphere of vice; and here was a practical application that attested the justness of the term. It was sublime! and the figure standing there on the high chair, like Truth on a pedestal, with the specs, and the close cap, and the blue yarn stockings, formed a subject for a sculptor, poorer than which had immortalized hundreds.

———

ABUSES OF THE PRESS.

—

"The printing-press is a great steam-engine," said Mrs. Partington; "but I don't believe Dr. Franklin ever invented it to commit outrages on a poor female woman like me. It makes me say everything, Mrs. Sled; and some of the things I know must have been said when I was *out*, for I can't remember 'em;" and she dropped three stitches in her excitement. "They ought to think," continued she, "that them who makes sport of the aged don't never live to grow up."

MOUSE HUNTING.

MOUSE-HUNTING;

AN INCIDENT IN THE LIFE OF MRS. PARTINGTON.

IT was midnight, deep and still, in the mansion of Mrs. Partington, — as it was, very generally, about town, — on a cold night in March. So profound was the silence that it awakened Mrs. P., and she raised herself upon her elbow to listen. No sound greeted her ears, save the tick of the old wooden clock in the next room, which stood there in the dark, like an old chrone, whispering and gibbering to itself. Mrs. Partington relapsed beneath the folds of the blankets, and had one eye again well-coaxed towards the realm of dreams, while the other was holding by a very frail tenure upon the world of reality, when her ear was saluted by the nibble of a mouse, directly beneath her chamber window, and the mouse was evidently gnawing her chamber carpet.

Now, if there is an animal in the catalogue of creation that she dreads and detests, it is a mouse ; and she has a vague and indefinite idea that rats and mice were made with especial regard to her individual torment. As she heard the sound of the nibble by the window, she arose again upon her elbow, and cried " *Shoo ! Shoo !* " energetically, several times. The sound ceased, and she fondly fancied that her trouble was over. Again she laid herself away as carefully as she would have lain eggs at forty-five cents a dozen, when, — *nibble, nibble, nibble !* — she once more heard the odious sound by the window. " *Shoo!* " cried the old lady again, at the same time hurling her shoe at the spot from whence the sound proceeded, where the little midnight marauder was carrying on his depredations.

A light burned upon the hearth, — she could n't sleep without a light, — and she strained her eyes in vain to catch a glimpse of her tormentor playing about amid the shadows of the room. All again was silent, and the clock, giving an admonitory tremble, struck twelve. Midnight! and Mrs. Partington counted the tintinabulous knots as they ran off the reel of Time, with a saddened heart.

Nibble, nibble, nibble! — again that sound. The old lady sighed, as she hurled the other shoe at her invisible annoyance. It was all without avail, and "shooing" was bootless, for the sound came again to her wakeful ear. At this point her patience gave out, and, conquering her dread of the cold, she arose and opened the door of her room that led to a corridor, when, taking the light in one hand, and a shoe in the other, she made the circuit of the room, and explored every nook and cranny in which a mouse could ensconse himself. She looked under the bed, and under the old chest of drawers, and under the washstand, and "shooed" until she could "shoo" no more.

The reader's own imagination, if he has an imagination skilled in limning, must draw the picture of the old lady while upon this exploring expedition, "accoutred as she was," in search of the ridiculous mouse. We have our own opinion upon the subject, and must say, — with all due deference to the years and virtues of

Mrs. P., and with all regard for personal attractions very striking in one of her years, — we should judge that she cut a very queer figure, indeed.

Satisfying herself that the mouse must have left the room, she closed the door, deposited the light upon the hearth, and again sought repose. How gratefully a warm bed feels, when exposure to the night air has chilled us, as we crawl to its enfolding covert! How we nestle down, like an infant by its mother's breast, and own no joy superior to that we feel, — coveting no regal luxury while revelling in the elysium of feathers! So felt Mrs. P. as she again ensconced herself in bed. The clock in the next room struck one.

She was again near the attainment of the state when dreams are rife, when, close by her chamber-door, outside she heard that hateful nibble renewed which had marred her peace before. With a groan she arose, and, seizing her lamp, she opened the door, and had the satisfaction to hear the mouse drop, step by step, until he reached the floor below. Convinced that she was now rid of him for the night, she returned to bed, and addressed herself to sleep. The room grew dim, in the weariness of her spirit, the chest of drawers in the corner was fast losing its identity and becoming something else; in a moment more —— *nibble, nibble, nibble!* again outside of the chamber-door, as the clock in the next room struck two.

Anger, disappointment, desperation, fired her mind with a new determination. Once more she arose, but this time she put on a shoe! — her dexter shoe. Ominous movement! It is said that when a woman wets her

26*

finger fleas had better flee. The star of that mouse's destiny was setting, and was now near the horizon. She opened the door quickly, and, as she listened a moment, she heard him drop again from stair to stair, on a speedy passage down.

The entry below was closely secured, and no door was open to admit of his escape. This she knew, and a triumphant gleam shot athwart her features, revealed by the rays of the lamp. She went slowly down the stairs, until she arrived at the floor below, where, snugly in a corner, with his little bead-like black eyes looking up at her roguishly, was the gnawer of her carpet, and the annoyer of her comfort. She moved towards him, and he, not coveting the closer acquaintance, darted by her. She pursued him to the other end of the entry, and again he passed by her. Again and again she pursued him, with no better success. At last, when in most doubt as to which side would conquer, Fortune, perched upon the banister, turned the scale in favor of Mrs. P. The mouse, in an attempt to run by her, presumed too much upon former success. He came too near her upraised foot. It fell upon his musipilar beauties, like an avalanche of snow upon a new tile, and he was dead forever! Mrs. Partington gazed upon him as he lay before her. Though she was glad at the result, she could but sigh at the necessity which impelled the violence; but for which the mouse might have long continued a blessing to the society in which he moved.

> Slowly and sadly she marched up stairs,
>   With her shoe all sullied and gory ;
> And the watch, who saw 't through the front door squares,
>   Told us this part of the story.

That mouse did not trouble Mrs. Partington again that night, and the old clock in the next room struck three before sleep again visited the eyelids of the relict of Corporal Paul.

STAR-GAZING.

OUT beneath the starry heavings Mr. Slow took his son, Abimelech, to point out to him — to read to him from the broad page of nature — the wonders of

"The spacious *furnishment* on high,"

as he called it.

" All these 'ere stars, my son," said Mr. S., pointing up to the studded sky above them, "that you see up there, stationary and unmovable, marchin' along in sublime grande'r, and winking at the earth with their jolly yeller eyes, like gold eagles, them are called *fixed* stars ;' and " —

" But what 's that, father ? " said young Abimelech, as a meteor, like a racer, darted across the southerly sky.

Mr. Slow was prompt with his answer.

" That," said he, " I guess, is one of 'em that 's got *unfixed.*"

MRS. P. ON MOUNT VESUVIUS.

So there's been another rupture of Mount Vociferous!" said Mrs. Partington, as she put down the paper and put up her specs. "The paper tells all about the burning lather running down the mountain, but it don't tell us how it got afire. I wonder if it was set fire to. There are many people full wicked enough to do it, or, perhaps, it was caused by children playing with frictious matches. I wish they had sent for our firemen; they would soon have put a stop to the raging aliment; and I dare say Mr. Barnacle, and all of 'em, would have gone, for they are what I call real civil engineers."

There was a whole broadside of commendation of the fire department in the impressive gesture accompanying her words. "Time and space" for a moment became annihilated, and imagination figured the city engines pouring their subduing streams upon the flames of Vesuvius, and "Hold on, seving!" "Break her down, twelve!" rising above the vain roarings of the smothering crater.

THE PIC-NIC:

A GRAND DOMESTIC DRAMA,

IN MANY ACTS.

In which are detailed the Fun and Drawbacks attending a Pleasure Excursion in the town of Bozzleton.

PERSONS IN THE DRAMA.

Mr. Homespun — Who has something to say to all, and about everybody.
Jemima Short — A sweet little country rose.
Mr. Blisby — A gentleman from the city.
Miss Primrose — A refined lady of thirty-five, full of sentiment and some snuff.
Mr. Brindle — A bachelor of fifty-eight and a justice of the peace.
Miss Pidgin — A bird too tough for sentiment.
Auxiliaries, Horses, Pigeon Pie, &c., by the company.

The morn is bright in Bozzleton, and kindly beams the sun,
And spreads his choicest rays around as if he dreamt of fun ;
The girls are up and wide awake, the lads are spruce and gay,
For a pic-nic party is arranged for this bright summer day.

—

AND won't we have a time of it? Just see the bag of dough-nuts that Jemima Short has thrown out of the window into the wagon! And there go three chickens, and four pies, and a jug of cider. Goodness gracious. Jemima! You are an angel of a provider, you are! You don't mean to put us on a regiment to-day, do you? You look like an airthly goddess, too, in your new pink calico. I vow, it looks first-rate — I took it for chinchilli a rod off.

Jemima. —"I don't know — I don't think much of it, but folks tells me it's becoming. Miss Jeems, the milliner, got the pattern from the city, and ——"

How de do, Miss Short? Gwine to the pic-nic?

Mrs. S. (with a cold in her head.) — "No, guess not; don't feel smart, 'zactly, and the old man's got the romantic affection in his leg, and can't go nuther; but Mima is gwine; she has had her hair in papers a whole week to make her look pretty."

Jemima. — "Why, mother! how you do talk! But here they come — O, what a host of 'em! How proud Betsey Babb feels of her new dress! I guess some folks can look full as well as some folks; and there's that everlasting old maid, Miss Pidgin; how I hate her with her scraggy neck and long tongue! And there's Patty Sprigg's city beau — O, I wouldn't be *her* to be seen with such a fright!"

> The wagons packed with eatables go groaning o'er the road,
> The long carts filled with girls and beaus show an attractive load,
> And laughter rules the pleasant hour, and eyes shine gay and bright,
> The only kind of stars that show as well by day as night.

Laughter! guess you'd think so to hear it. Now the cart settles down into a rut. "Dear me," says Miss Tibbs, "we shall all be upsot, tipsy turvy; do hold on to me!" and then everybody thinks they must be held on to; and everybody else is trying to hold on to somebody. O, how frightened the city beauty is! "Do you apprehend any danger of a tergiversation?" "No," says Jo Hays, "the slack men look arter them things, and everybody's noclated for it."

Female Voice. — "Be still, won't you! O, you satan! see how you have tumbled my collar with your pesky nonsense; and my face burns like fire-coals. Right before a city gentleman too; O, for shame!"

City Gent. — " Upon my honor, miss, I was entirely oblivious to any impropriety."

" O, 't was n't very improper either, he, he, he; only such things should n't be done publicly, you know."

Miss Pidgin. — "If Susan Fry is n't setting on Sam Sled's knees, I a'n't a living sinner! Such conduct I must think improper. *I* never was guilty of such indiscretion, *I* never was!"

Boys singing —

> " There 's fun in a country cart,
>   And life on a dusty road,
> Where mirth warms every heart,
>   And pleasure finds abode :
> The town may boast of its joys,
>   Its racket and its din,
> But give a haunt away from its noise,
>   Some quiet nook within."

—

> Far from the busy din of town, in some secluded grove,
> The happy party sit them down, or unrestricted rove ;
> All austere rules that bind the world are here thrown far aside,
> And revelling in mirth's bright beam, how fleet the moments glide !

Arm-in-arm under the shady trees they now wander, picking posies or bright berries — and *such* fun ! Miss Primrose smiles languidly a sort of sky-blue benignity upon old Brindle, the bachelor.

Miss Primrose, (sentimentally.) — " How delightfully those pines sigh in the gentle breeze, like the soft music of love in the ear of youth ! "

Old Brindle. — " Yes'm, so it does."

Miss P. — " O, I do so love the pines ! "

Old B. — " They 're better in May, mum, when the sliver is thick and creamy. Come out here then, marm out with your jack-knife, throw away your tobacco, cut out a square, and sliver *up* the tree — allers sliver up, marm — some slivers down. Then's when you'd like the pines, mum."

Miss P. — " That's an entirely new aspect; I meant their romantic beauty."

Old B. — " Yes'm — beautiful wood, very; worth four dollars a cord in Boston."

Here come Patty Sprig and the musty-choked man from the city.

Cit. — " Miss Spwig, how delightfully ruwal it is here! Always thought I should like to live among the beauties of Nachure. It's a great pity we can't have any nachure in town, a great pity. I've heard of some *human* nachure round there, but never saw any of it."

Patty. — " I should think they might bring it in by pipes, as they did the Cochituate."

Cit. — " Are those gwound-nuts ? "

Patty. — " No, dear me, no; don't eat 'em; they 're toadstools."

> Thus we go on, chatting, walking,
> Voices ringing with the pines,
> Nothing our gay fancies balking,
> Doing all our heart inclines.

—

> Now on the green and beauteous sod the varied viands spread,
> And appetite shall wait on health, and wit its influence shed ;
> The social tongue with music rife blends with the platter's noise,
> As earth's rude jarring interferes with its harmonious joys.

" Here 's tongue, and ham, and sausages, and pumkin pie, and cheese. Mercy, what a bill of fare ! Miss Peewit shall I help you to a piece of tongue ? " — " No, thank you, I have enough of my own. But I 'll trouble you for a piece of the chicken." — " Chicken, did you say? From his toughness I should say he was a grandfather to thousands!"

" Pass the pigeon yonder, will you?"

" What, the old maid ? "

" No, no, the pie."

" There 's the plate — the pigeon is unavoidably detained."

Miss Pidgin. — " I 'd thank people who use my name to speak so that I can hear; I don't like to be backbitten."

" We were speaking of pigeon pie, mem"— *something more tender* (Aside).

" Say, Tom, what have you got in the dish there ? "

" Pickled grasshoppers, I should think. Will you have some ? "

" Miss Primrose, do allow me to help you; here 's some ham, delicate as your own nature, ma'am."

Miss P. — " I declare, you are quite complimentary! Comparing my nature with smoked hog ! "

" Will Mr. Blisby, the gentleman from the city, favor us with a song? Silence, ' ye gentlemen and ladies all that grace this famous' pic-nic; Mr. Blisby is going to sing."

Mr. B. — " I 'd rather be excused; but though I am not exactly in tune, I 'll endeavor for the occasion."

Mr. Blisby sings :

> " My love is fair, O, she is fair !
>   Her lips are red, her eyes like sloe,
>   A golden glory is her hair,
>   Falling o'er shoulders white as snow

27

> " And when her eyes upon me turn,
>   And burn with radiance divine,
>   My ardent gaze encounters hern,
>   The same as hern encounters mine."

Child, yelling. — "Mother, give me a nuther pieth ov pie!"

Mother. — "Hush, my darling, there a'n't any."

Boy. — "I thay there ith; I wanth a pieth ov pie!"

> " O, such a mingling,
>   Of talking and jingling,
>   The noise and glee
>   Sound merrily,
>   And set our ears a tingling."

—

A dance! a dance! and gleefully a set is forthwith planned,
A fiddle most mysteriously has happened here at hand;
And here beneath the dark tree's shade, with leaves and berries crowned,
Each happy lad and laughing maid whirl in the dance around.

"Go it, my top sawyer on the pussy-gut! Work your elbows lively, and we'll put her through by daylight!" "O, dear! I'm all of a perspiration with sweat. How slippery it is under foot!" "It a'n't slippery anywheres else." "I swow to man, there's Bill Nutter and Jemima Short both down! Up and try it again, clumsys!"

Miss Primrose. — "How these old woods echo with the music, Mr. Brindle, like the Arcadian groves, with the dulcet notes of the Satires!"

Mr. B. — "I never heerd of 'em; I guess they never was in these woods — they never was that I can remember."

"I declare, there's Mr. Blisby dancing like an animated bean-pole. Ha! ha! ha! he's on all-fours Now all he wants is a tail."

Then moving to the tuning of the fiddle and the bow,
How sparkles every eye with mirth as round and round we go !
No ball-room artistes now are here to circumscribe our sport,
And Nature smiles approvingly, for here she holds her court

—

A lake romantic lying near tempts to its cooling vale,
And tiny boats in swift career across its bosom sail ;
And waving handkerchiefs respond in answer to the song
That, rising from the venturers, is borne the breeze along.

" Jump into the boat, Patty; not the least danger in the world of its tipping over." — " O, my ! I 've got my shoe all satiated with water. I shall get my death a cold." — " You 've got your foot in it this time, that 's a fact."

Mr. Blisby. — " Is there any danger of sea-sickness ? "

" Now just see that boat — how she scoots it! I vow if Patty Sprig has n't got hold of the bow oar, and pulls away like a little satan. If I thought that spindle-shank from the city was going to have that gal, I 'd cut his eternal — acquaintance, I would. I e'enamost said throat, but that would be manslaughter; and I don't see how it could be, neither, for killing such a thing as he is."

A Voice. — " Some love to roam
O 'er the dark sea's foam,
Where the shrill winds whistle free."

" Well, they do. Hallo ! here 's Jim Sly. What have you got in that bottle, old fellow ? Have n't seen you to-day afore."

Jim Sly (drunk). — " I 've got some c-c-cough-
drops to c-c-cure the sea-sickness with — a little rum
t-t-t-tea with s-s-some sperrit in it to k-k-keep it."

Sally Twist, his sweetheart. — " You Jim Sly, you
drunken, miserable fellow, you — you sot — you brute —
you individual — you — you — you Jim Sly" ——

Jim. — " Go it, S-S-Sal, and I 'll hold yer b-b-bonnet !
What yer goin' to d-d-do 'bout it ? "

Sally. — " You 'll see when we get home, you sot —
you brute — you vagabone ! "

Sam. — " Let her lean, elder —

> ' Wine cures the gout, boys,
> The colic, and the ' ——

sea-sickness.	Who cares for S-S- Sall ? "

" Can you tell me, Jemima, why Miss Pidgin yonder
is like forty-nine big apples ? " — " No, I 'm sure I can't,
unless it 's 'cause she 's sour." — " No, 't a'n't it ; it 's
'cause she 's a vergin' nigh fifty."

—

> But gracious ! what an awful cloud has risen in the west !
> And what a frightful lightning flash then swept across its breast !
> I feel a drop upon my hand — the pine trees rock and roar —
> The waves like blacks, with nightcaps on, rush madly to the shore !

" O, what *shall* we do ? where *shall* we go ? what
will become of us ? " screams everybody. " Do, dear
Mr. Wiggin," says Miss Pidgin, " tell us *what* we shall
do ? "

Mr. Wiggin. — " Why, 't a'n't no use to run 's I
see, for the rain is here, and there a'n't a house within a
mile ; and my 'pinion is that we get in the woods and
make ourselves comfortable."

" But don't the lightnin' always strike trees ? "

" There 's more danger from your eyes, Jemima. Lightnin's attracted by anything bright; you 'd better shut 'em up."

Jemima. — " Your wit is n't bright enough to attract it, any how, Mr. Impudence ! How does that strike ye ? "

Old Mrs. Fog. — " O, that folks should joke and trifle so, when there 's so much to make 'em solemn ! A'n't you afraid the thunder 'll kill you ? And where would you go if you died a laughing ? "

—

The rain pours down in torrent force among the forest shades,
And timid men the closer cling to timid, shrinking maids ;
The whitened cheek and blenching eye denote the force of fear,
And many a head bows low with dread the thunder loud to hear.

" Well, this is a comfort ! See where Miss Primrose has cornered old Brindle — cheek-by-jowl. That 's right. Go it, old gall ! My eyes ! how it rains ! If Pan is the presiding genius of these woods, in my opinion he 's a dripping Pan."

Old Brindle — " Young man, I 'm a justice of the peace in this 'ere jurisdiction, and if you commit that agin, I shall commit you for contempt of court."

" Here comes Jim Sly through the wet, pitching like a mackerel-catcher in a chop sea. Hallo, Jim, here 's Polly, like a widowed hen, refusing to be comforted."

Jim (sobered). — " Sally, will ye forgive me ? "

Sally. — " No, you disreputable individual. To think that you should go away, and — and — leave me to — boo — hoo — hoo " ——

27*

Jim. — " There, don't cry, and I'll go and take the totetal pledge, Maine liquor law and all, and become a useful membrane of society, and if I drink any more, I hope I may never — starve ! "

" See, Mr. Blisby, while we are soaking, how the horses outside are smoking."

Mr. B. — " Do horses in the country smoke ? "

" Yes, and we've got a filly at home who throws all that choose to back her."

" You don't say so ! "

> Thus, while the rain is pouring so,
>   Fun may mingle with our fear :
> And, while the wind is roaring so,
>   Still may waken words of cheer.

—

The rain clears up, the burnished sun comes out with scorching ray,
Dispelling from the sky and heart all shapes of gloom away,
And laughter now bursts forth once more in cheerful, merry peal,
And " Home Again " is sung with glee as o'er the road we wheel.

" Are you all comfortable ?   Sit close as possible. Here we go !   And now, on the road for home, let us be merry as we can be.   Miss Pidgin, did you enjoy your duck ? " — " You are a goose, sir, to talk so." — " Miss Primrose, you look refreshed since your sprinkling from nature's water-pot.   Mr. Blisby, this is fine — a subject for a letter, Mr. Blisby.   Jemima, my dear, you look as blooming as the rose in June, and twice as sweet.   There's the Bozzleton factory rising above the trees, and the old vane, like vanity, pluming itself in the sunshine.   Hurrah for home !   Old lady with the mob-cap, take your head in doors.   Urchins in corduroys, scatter.   Young maiden with the milking-pail, *who* are you looking at ? "

Mr. Blisby (rising). — "Before we part, I should like to say that the pleasure I have experienced has far exceeded my expectations, and that I shall always entertain a pleasing recollection of the delightful moments spent in this — in this — hay-cart ! "

"Three cheers for Blisby ! Ladies and gentlemen, if it is your opinion that we have enjoyed ourselves (a great way over the sinister), you will please to manifest it. Yes ! Then we 'll adjourn with the chorus —

> Some seek for glee by the heaving sea,
> Some rush on a railroad train,
> But give us a part on a country cart,
> And a pic-nic out in the rain ! "

Exeunt Omnibus, R. U. E.

AN EXCELLENT TEST OF AFFECTION.

"THE summer is no time to try the strength of affection," said Mrs. Partington; "though it's pretty well to sing love songs beneath a window at midnight, in a rain-storm, or stand billing and cooling on the door-step till two o'clock in the morning. The winter season is the one. Many's the time my poor Paul has rid five miles to see me, the coldest weather ; and often, the dear cretur has been found in the morning fast asleep in the middle of the cow-yard, with the saddle on his own shoulders, from fatigue with courting me, and riding a hard-trotting horse There *was* devotion ! I never see a cow without thinking of poor Paul ;" and, saying which, the good old lady went to bed.

HIGH-DUTCH *vs.* POLITENESS.

AS the Washington street train gone by here?" asked Mrs. Partington of a gentleman with a huge mustache, who stood picking his teeth on the steps of the Revere House. The old lady meant the Washington street omnibus that runs between the Lowell depot and Dover street. The gentleman still picked his teeth, and looked gravely at her, but said not a word. " Has the Washington street train passed by here?" she asked again, thinking the gentleman had n't heard her. He still stood, and stood still, and looked and picked, but said nothing. " Well!" said the old dame, half musing and half addressing the man with the' mustache; " it was only a civil question, and I did n't think there was anything harmonious in asking it; but *some* people thinks 'it a great hardship to do any one a favor. It would n't have required much effort, I should think, to have answered me, nor took a great deal of anybody's time, nor interfered with anybody's occupancy. If anybody has got focal organs I should think they might use 'em."

" Nein ferstan," responded the man with the mustache, as he put his hands beneath his coat-tails, and walked up the steps, leaving Mrs. Partington standing like a note of interrogation at the end of her speech, while the omnibus, which had passed while she was speaking, was seen far in the distance.

GOOD TASTE.

'I CAN'T bear children," said Miss Prim, disdainfully.

Mrs. Partington looked at her over her spectacles mildly before she replied.

" Perhaps if you could you would like them better," she at last said ; " but why is it that unmarried old maids and single bachelors are always railing at children ? It seems as if they had never read the command given to our forefathers to ' increase and multiply and punish the earth.' For my part, I love the little dears, and I had rather hear a child cry any day than hear the Brass Band."

And she went right to work covering a ball for Ike.

OLD ROGER MUCH EXCITED.

—

"MRS. TIMMS," said old Roger, one morning to his landlady at the breakfast-table ; he was an old bachelor was Roger, and, as such, was an object of considerable interest, both with the landlady and three antiquated spinsters who boarded with her. "Mrs. Timms, what sort of a house *do* you keep ? What sort of a neighborhood *is* this that you live in? and *why* is it that you have such a bad character round town, ma'am ? "

The landlady was astonished, and well she might be, for he looked excited — incensed.

"I 've boarded here, ma'am," continued he, "just seven weeks, and every week we have had a tract left here, and each tract is against some cardinal sin, ma'am. that you, nor me, nor the *young* ladies here, I *hope* ever committed. Here 's drunkenness, and gambling, and swearing, and lying, and stealing, and adultery, and bearing false witness, — almost all the sins in the church calendar, ma'am, and what 'll come next I can't guess. *I* can't stand it, ma'am. Why, the devil himself could n't stand it."

And his brow looked hot and steamy, and he bore the look of a man injured by an implied reflection on a heretofore bright reputation.

RARE DUN.

One morning old Sledge got capsized out of his wherry, halibut and all, at the Spring Market, in P* * * * *, under the old dynastiness of that institution, and was nearly drowned when they got him out. He was so near death that the ones who caught him could n't see any signs of life in him. But they rolled him and rubbed him and shook him, and sent off among the neighbors for warm blankets to put him in. Old Mrs. Twist, who lived on Church Hill, in the kindness of her heart, stripped her beds at once, and left her work all hanging, as she said, by "sixes and sevens," to go and help bring the man to. She warmed the blankets, and rubbed away vigorously at the inanimate Sledge, working as if her heart was in the operation, as undoubtedly it was. After a while, the rubbing took effect, or, as some suggested, his ugly nature refused to die, and he revived — slowly — slowly — first a gape and then a groan — then he opened his eyes, and the first person he looked upon was Mrs. Twist, busily engaged in her benevolent manipulations. He looked at her a moment, and consciousness returned.

" Ah ! " said he, as he spit the salt water out of his codlike mouth, "glad to see ye; been looking arter ye for a long time; would like to have ye pay me the two shillings ye owe me ! "

Mrs. Twist assured us it was the most unthankfulest thing she ever heard of, and we think so too.

THE BEAR-SKINS.

"HERE come the sogers, aunt!" cried Ike, at the door, "here they come in their bear skins!"

"In their bare skins!" said Mrs. Partington, glancing out of the window into the cold, towards the weathercock that had looked obstinately east for three days, much to the danger of a return of her rheumatism that an east wind always induced, — so much so that she had declared her determination to move in the vicinity of some Catholic church, whose vane always points one way, — "in their bare skins such a day as this! Highlanders, I guess."

She hastened to the door, and a company, with huge and hideous caps, were then marching by. She saw that she was sold.

"Ah!" said she, "this is one of the horrors of war, to go looking so; and s'pose one of them poor creaturs should fall down, — he's so top-heavy his heels would go up in the air, like a cornstalk witch, and all his brains would run down into his head. I can't bear to look at 'em."

She closed the door carefully, but she stood in the entry and beat time to the music till it had got far past the house.

AWFUL DEWY.

OLD ROGER stood looking from the window out upon the solitary tiger lily, — the only one that could be coaxed to grow for the summer, in the meagre atmosphere of the boarding-house yard. The sickly lily held its head up stoutly beneath the refreshing dew that had fallen upon it during the night, and the shed-top, and the ashes-barrel in the yard, and the few blades of grass that sturdily struggled against difficulty and managed to grow in spite of circumstances, were all wet. Old Roger turned around, and all knew by his looks that something was coming, and were prepared for it.

"Why," said he, in a cheerful tone, "was this last night that has just passed like a certain very eminent clergyman?"

All guessed it at once except the deaf milliner, who had n't heard a word of it; but they did n't say so, and gave it up.

"It is because it was awful dewy!"

What a laugh greeted the answer! in the midst of which the jolly old brick put on his hat, and went off, like a rocket, in a blaze of glory.

28

A SLIGHT MISAPPREHENSION.

—

" How do you like the bustle and confusion of Boston ? " asked the shop-keeper, as Mrs. Partington stood by the counter.

" It gives me confusion to see 'em," said the old lady; " folks did n't do so when I was a girl; and, besides, what an awful sight of bran and cotton it takes, to say nothing of their awkwardness when they get slipped on one side " —

" I mean," broke in the shopkeeper, " the bustle and confusion of the streets."

" O," said Mrs. P., " that is quite *another thing !* " and immediately left the store.

———

THE steak was terrible tough one morning, and Old Roger worked away at it in silence. At length his patience and masticators gave out; turning to the landlady, " Madam," said he, " your boarders should all have been umpires at horse-races."

" Why so ? " said she, coloring highly.

" Because, being accustomed to ' *tender stakes,*' they would have none of the difficulty that I experience ; they could obviate it."

It was an unpardonable thing in him, thus to expose her before all the boarders, and she thought the outrage more than offset the tough meat.

PEPPERCASE REBUKED.

"Stop your noise in there!" roared Mr. Peppercase, as he heard the sound of a juvenile riot in the kitchen. "If I come to you I'll give you something that you will remember for a fortnight! I'll knock your heads off! I never saw such children in my life; always yelling and fighting."

"I declare, that's queer!" said Mrs. Partington, who was there to tea; "that *is* queer, when they have such a very mild man for a father; I should think they would be as gentle as doves. Some fathers are like the frightful porcupine, and of course their children will be fractious; — as the old hog squeals the young ones learn, you know."

She stirred her tea gently, and smiled as she spoke; and Mr. Peppercase, after a vain effort to detect malice in her looks, changed the subject to the best mode of raising cucumbers, which cooled him down in a short time.

A REMEMBERED MISTAKE.

"It is all very true, Mr. Knickerbottom," said Mrs. Partington, as she read in the Knickerbocker something concerning brevity and simplicity of expression; "it's true, as you say; and how many mistakes there does happen when folks don't understand each other! Why, last summer I told a dressmaker to make me a long visite, to wear, and, would you believe it, she came and staid a fortnight with me? Since then I've made it a pint always to speak just what I say."

Her mouth grew down to a determined pucker at the end of the sentence, and the snuff-box was tapped energetically, as if the fortnight of unrequited bread and butter was laying heavy on her memory.

"Faith is a great thing, and confidence in the cook, and the trust that what you have before you is the true representative of the name it bears," said old Roger, in his lecture over the bread pudding; and he peered intently into his plate, as at some mysterious thing which had there arisen to perplex him. "But," he continued, "can I be expected to swallow everything, always in blind credulity, or go so far as to construe pork-skins and cheese-rinds to mean bread crumbs?"

And he gently pushed his plate away and took a piece of the pie.

MRS. PARTINGTON AND JENNY LIND.

"I NEVER liked the Swedenvirgins," said Mrs. Partington. She was orthodox, and always sat in the Asylum pew in the north-east corner of the gallery, and had charge of the children in sermon time. Her raised finger was an admonition that brought young refractories to their obedience at once. Every Sunday was she there, and people expected to see the faded black bonnet above the railings, in prayer-time, as much as they did the parson. "I never liked the Swedenvirgins; but I a'n't one that believes nothing good can come out of Lazarus, for all that. Now, there 's Jenny Lind, — may Heaven shower bags of dollars on her head ! — that is so very good to everybody, and who sings so sweet that everybody 's falling in love with her, tipsy turvy, and gives away so much to poor, indignant people. They call her an angel, and who knows but she may be a syrup in disguise, for the papers say her singing is like the music of the spears. How I should love to hear her ! "

She grasped hastily at the long bead purse in her reticule, but an unsatisfactory response came back from it to her hopes, and she laid it back again with a sigh.

28*

THE USE OF THE AZTECS.

—

" WE are fearfully and wonderfully made ! " said Mrs. Partington, after she had stood for a long time contemplating the Aztec children. Her hands were resting upon the back of a chair as she said this, and she made the remark so loud that a tall gentleman, who stood near her, stooped down to get a look under her black bonnet. He thought she had spoken to him. " We are fearfully and wonderfully made," continued she, " 'specially some of us. The ways of Providence is past finding out, and we don't know what these Haystack children are made for, no more 'n we do why the mermaids were made, or the man in the moon. Perhaps they are made a purpose for curiosities, and nothing but Providence could make anything more so, unless Mr. Barnum should try. Human natur never come done up in so queer a wrapper before. They say they are distended from the Haystacks long ago gone to grass. And Isaac," said she, turning to Ike, who was teasing one of them with a stick, " Isaac, look upon 'em, and pray you may never be born so."

The people had gathered around, and were listening to the words as they fell, like the notes of a hand-organ, from her lips ; and when she ceased, they turned with renewed eagerness to inspect the objects that her remarks had rendered classic.

THE MYSTERY OF THE BRAZEN NOSE;

OR, THE MAIDEN'S REVENGE.

CHAPTER I

THE HERO OF THE STORY.

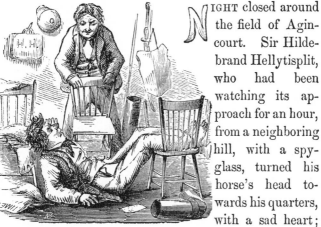

NIGHT closed around the field of Agincourt. Sir Hildebrand Hellytisplit, who had been watching its approach for an hour, from a neighboring hill, with a spyglass, turned his horse's head towards his quarters, with a sad heart; for the day had been destructive to horse-flesh, and thousands of the French and Norman chivalry bit the mud (not dust) of Agincourt. He sought his tent. His brow was dark and gloomy, as could be plainly seen through his iron helmet; and an unevenness of gait, as he strode along, betrayed great agitation of the nervous system.

"Walter de Coursey Stubbs," said he, hoarsely, to his squire in attendance, "hang up my horse, and give my casque some oats and water. And, hark ye! disturb me not until the Connecticut wooden horologe in the vestibule striketh the hour of seving. Now, away."

Sir Hildebrand Hellytisplit slowly divested himself of his armor, which clanged upon the stillness of the night like a tin kitchen, and then taking a match from his vest pocket, he lighted a three-cent regalia, and puffed away at it in moody silence. He stretched himself upon three chairs, with a bundle of old newspapers under his head, and dropped asleep, and then caught a nap. But his sleep was troubled. Anon he started, and shouted, "St. Dennis for France! give 'em fits!" Again a clammy sweat covered his brow, and he muttered, " Ha! thrice to-day hath the brazen nose gleamed upon me in the battle-field. Down, old copper-head, down!"

But soon his slumbers grew calm, and not a sound disturbed the silence, save the man-at-arms, who sat whetting his jackknife on a brick in the entry, and indulging in whistling some old familiar psalm-tunes, as if his mind were elsewhere; for *that* man-at-arms had a heart, *he* had.

———

CHAPTER II.

THE BRAZEN NOSE.

It was midnight, within about ten minutes, and Sir Hildebrand Hellytisplit still slept. At this moment a slight noise was heard at the door, and, bearing in his hand a tin lantern, a knight of gigantic size, — some five feet six in height, — in complete armor, strode into the tent. He gazed in*tent*ly upon the sleeper, and then, in a suppressed voice, of great anguish, sighed out, "Ah! oh! um!" and sank into a seat, like a cooking-stove. His face could not be seen, but there was a dignity about the strange knight that betokened a genteel bringing-up, which had won the respect of the man-at-arms, who had been bribed by a ninepence to admit him to the tent, on the plea of "special business."

His armor was of complete black, with no distinguishing mark, save a huge nose of brass, borne upon the casque, which gleamed in the light of the lantern like a quart pot. Taking a pencil from one pocket, and a card from another, he wrote a few hurried lines; when, whispering to the man-at-arms for an envelope and a wafer, he sealed the missive, and deposited it by the side of the sleeping Sir Hildebrand, saying to the admiring attendant, "No trouble, sirrah, about mailing letters here; we can mail them with our own *mailed* hands, eh!" It were better he had not uttered this; for the man, who hoped for further *largess*, laughed loudly at the pleasantry.

The light in the lantern disappeared, as Sir Hildebrand Hellytisplit awoke, and, starting upon his elbow, he cried aloud, "What, ho! without there? What 'n thunder 's all that noise about?" The men-at-arms and squires came rushing in, rubbing their eyes. None had heard the noise, and, at the suggestion of Walter de Coursey Stubbs, that he had been awakened by his own snoring, Sir Hildebrand turned over and went to sleep again.

"Keep shady," was the parting word of the stranger knight, as he placed a quarter in the hand of Walter, and strode forth from the tent. Mystery crowned the hour.

CHAPTER III.

THE GAME IS UP!

SCARCELY had the wooden clock done striking the hour of seven, the next morning, when Walter de Coursey Stubbs stood by his master's side to awake him from his slumbers, which he accomplished by pulling one of the chairs from beneath him. Sir Hildebrand Hellytisplit wiped his eyes with his hand, and combed his hair with his fingers, and then, as was his wont, commenced pommelling his attendant by way of gentle exercise, after which he proceeded to dress himself in the panoply of war. Stooping to pick up one of the stove-pipes that encased his legs, Sir Hildebrand espied the letter left by the stranger, lying upon the ground. He gazed upon the writing, and a mortal paleness covered his face. His limbs trembled in every joint and rivet, and his teeth, which were not metallic, shook like a set of props. He read —

" Perfigis retch : — your our is cum. . . Mete me to-morrar outside the Inglish lines, and Ile giv yu Jessy. Yours respectively,   NOSEY."

Sir Hildebrand Hellytisplit drank his coffee in silence; after which, arming himself with two spears, a battle-axe, a sword, mace and shield, besides filling his belt with bowie knives, revolvers, and slung shot, he walked forth into the fields, in the rear of the English camp, where he soon discovered the Knight of the Brazen Nose sitting on a rock, reading a newspaper, who sprang to his feet and pulled out his sword.

The contest was speedily begun and quicker ended; for Sir Hildebrand had " too many irons in the fire," and he could n't " come in " well.   One blow from the powerful arm of him of the Nose, and the head of Sir Hildebrand Hellytisplit, like an iron pot, rolled at the feet of the victor.

Uttering a fearful cry of agony at this consummation, the strange knight tore off his helmet, revealing beneath a head of hair like a pound of flax, the fair but hard countenance of Judy O'Brien, the washer-woman. " Gentlemen," said she, " he was a perjured man, and I have avenged myself upon him.   He owed me a bill for washing, but, alas! in wiping out that score, I've flummoxed myself.   Tell this to my countrywomen; never seek for vengeance; 't is better to forgive a little, if they lose a shilling on the pound.   Farewell." Saying which, she disappeared up a tall tree that was near by, and they never saw her more.

Coroner de Smythe, under the circumstances, did not think it advisable to summon a jury, and informed Sir Hildebrand's friends, by telegraph, that they had better come on and look after his effects, as ne was n't exactly in a condition to do it for himself.   A Flemish Jew bought Sir Hildebrand Hellytisplit's *war*drobe, after a few keepsakes had been taken by friends, for about the price of old iron.

GOING TO CALIFORNIA.

" DEAR me ! " exclaimed Mrs. Partington sorrowfully,
" how much a man will bear, and how far he will go, to
get the soddered dross, as Parson Martin called it when
he refused the beggar a sixpence, for fear it might lead
him into extravagance ! Everybody is going to California
and Chagrin arter gold. Cousin Jones and the three
Smiths have gone ; and Mr. Chip, the carpenter, has left
his wife and seven children and a blessed old mother-in-
law, to seek his fortin, too. This is the strangest yet,
and I don't see how he could have done it; it looks so
ongrateful to treat Heaven's blessings so lightly. But
there, we are told that the love of money is the root of
all evil, and how true it is ! for they are now rooting
arter it, like pigs arter groundnuts. Why, it is a perfect
money mania among everybody !"

And she shook her head doubtingly, as she pensively
watched a small mug of cider, with an apple in it, sim-
mering by the winter fire. She was somewhat fond of
drink made in this way.

A TOUGH CUSTOMER.

"WILL you help me to a piece of chicken?" asked
Miss Seraphina of old Roger, on Thanksgiving day.
The old man was engaged elbow-deep in the intricate
task of carving; the perspiration stood upon his brow,
from his exertions, — truly herculean efforts, — in dis-
secting a large fowl.

"Chicken!" muttered he; "do you call this a
chicken? Why, it has been the father of thousands,
miss."

He had n't a very thankful spirit that day, and the
older boarders, with bad teeth, joined with him in ques-
tioning the propriety of being thankful.

OLD ROGER'S boarding-house having failed, and the
furniture being taken to be sold on *mean* process, as he
called it, he asked one of the chambermaids, who always
had been saucy to him, if she was to be sold with the
rest of the furniture. She answered him "No!" as
sharp as vinegar.

"O," said he, coolly buttoning up his coat, "I supposed you were, for the advertisement reads that the
house is to be sold with all the impertinences thereto
belonging."

He very cruelly laughed at the indignant look she
gave him, and stepped out.

29

FUNERAL OBSTACLES.

"How solemn these funeral obstacles is!" said Mrs. Partington, as she looked down from an upper chamber window, on the day of a mock funeral of one of the presidents. She took off her specs to wipe the moisture from their discs, tapped her box mournfully to the measured time of the distant drum, and looked anxiously down the street, to catch the first glimpse of the funeral train. "Here it comes at last," quoth she, "with the soldiers all playing with muzzled drums, and their flags flying at half-mast. Is that the catastrophe?" whispered she of a gentleman near her.

"That is the catafalque, madam," replied he.

"Well, well," said she, "no matter; I knowed there was a cat about it, and I didn't know but it might be a cataplasm. Will you tell me when the artillery flies over, that come on here to tend the funeral?"

"Good gracious, madam!" cried he testily, "they don't fly. They are artillery men on horseback, merely."

"Dear me!" replied she, "I thought it was one of the wings of the army, and flew. How easy it is to get mistaken!"

She pensively gazed upon the pageant that slowly passed before her.

"What a pity it is," said she, "that we don't vally people till arter they are dead; but then what paragorics we pour upon them!"

She here paused; a silence pervaded the chamber; the procession had passed, the company had departed, and two hours after the old lady was found still sitting by the open window fast asleep.   So powerful is grief!

EXCELLENT ADVICE.

"NEVER get in debt, Isaac," said Mrs. Partington; and she raised her tea-spoon with an oracular air, and held it thus, as if from it were suspended the threads of a fine argument on economy, discernible to her eye alone, and she was watching an opportunity to make it tangible.   "Never get in debt, no matter whether you are creditable or not; it is better to live on a crust of bread and water and a herring or two, than cows and oxen cut up into rump steaks, and owe for it.   Think of our neighbor; what a failing he had, and had all his goods and impertinences took away on a mean procession and sold, and his poor wife reduced to a calico gound, starvation, and shushon tea, and he in Californy!"

"Some tea, please," said Ike, as he handed over his tin dipper.   The tea, like her own reflections, trickled out musically; and she passed along the caution, with the cream and sugar, never to get in debt.

TIMELY REFLECTION.

—

" DEAR me ! " exclaimed Mrs. Partington; and her hands were raised above a basket of potatoes, in a provision store, as if she were asking a blessing upon it. It was in response to the shopkeeper, who had told her, in sepulchral tones, that the potatoes were all rotting. " O, dear me ! " said she, " if the potatoes is all rotting, what upon airth will poor people do for bread ? What will the poor Paddygonians do that don't eat nothing else ? And flour is very high, too. They tell us every now and then of an improvement in the market ; but flour is always just as dear after it, and we have to pay full as much for a half dollar's worth. It takes almost a remissness of Californy gold every week to get along now-a-days. Heaven help the poor ! "

What a heartiness there was in that simple prayer ! The provision-dealer was affected. He dropped the long red, he had been holding, pensively into the basket again, and wiped his eyes on the sleeve of his white frock. That stern man, who had unrelentingly cut up tons of beef, nor shed one tear over the struggles of expiring lambkins, showing no quarter while quartering them, — that stern man wiped his eyes on his frock-sleeve, and murmured " *Yes'm !* " It was touching ! Everything was sixteen ounces to the pound with him for that day.

PREPARING TO SEE THE PRESIDENT.

MOTHER wants to know if you'll lend her a little merlasses to starch a cap, to go and see the President," said a little girl, coming into Mrs. Partington's kitchen, bearing in her hand a tin cup.

"Certainly, dear," said the good dame, pleasantly.

She never thought of the unreasonableness of the request; she never dreamed of guile. The treacle depository was brought out, the golden liquid filled the tin receptacle, and the child departed.

"Well!" said the old lady, "everybody is going to see the President. But what is a president, or a king, or a justice of the peace, but a man, arter all, with flesh and blood, and bones and hair, like any of us? And thousands will come further to see him than they would to see Saint Paul, or Hebrews, or Revelations, or any of 'em. Sich man-worship! sich man-worship!"

"The President's coming, aunt!" said Ike, bursting in; "and he is going by our door;" and the little fellow was half crazy with delight, and threw his cap in a pan of milk upon the table in his enthusiasm.

"How do I look, Isaac?" said the dame, with anima-

29*

tion; " is my hair combed, and my handkerchief digested right on my neck, and my cap border even?" and she took her place by the window, when these questions were answered, as eager as any one to " see the President," and Ike stepped out. But her eyes were strangely dim, and those hitherto faithful specs gave indications now of failing her. She took them off to wipe them, and both glasses were gone! An hour before, Ike had borrowed them for a telescopic experiment. But it did n't make any odds, for the procession had turned down another street, and did n't go by her door at all.

A CHURCH INCIDENT.

THE bell had tolled for some minutes after the time of meeting, and some signs of impatience were manifest. A stranger, touching the occupant of a pew in front of him, asked, " Is your preacher often as late as this?"

" O, yes, sir," replied the interrogated; " it often happens that he don't get here till the sermon is half through!"

The stranger looked at him intently a little while, and then made a memorandum of this fact in his note-book.

A DRY-GOOD LESSON.

"HAVE you any stout, dark marines?" said Mrs. Partington to the shopkeeper. He was one of those good-humored young men, whose hair, nicely-curled, betokens an elegant taste, and he stood swaying back and forth, leaning on his yardstick, and smiled amiably as the old lady spoke. "Have you any dark marines, suitable for thick ladies' outside under garments?"

"We have dark *mo*reens, ma'am," replied he, and cast his eyes towards a brother clerk, and winked archly. She gazed upon him a moment before she spoke again. "Well, well, young man, it was only a slip of the tongue; and if you never make a greater slip in measuring cloth, you will be much more honest than many clerks I know."

The clerk colored and stammered out an apology, but it was needless. There was no unkindness in her looks. The spectacles bent their bows upon him steadily from the cavernous gloom of the big bonnet, but his perturbed fancy alone made them terrible. She made the purchase she intended, and in measure it proved full half a quarter over what she had bargained for.

A GLANCE AT POVERTY.

—

"It must be very inconvenient to be poor;" said Mrs. Partington, as she glanced with honest pride at her high-backed chairs and old-fashioned chest of drawers, and continued her eye on to the open cupboard in the corner. "How people can contrive to get along with so little I don't see. There is our poor neighbor down the yard, now, is so pinched for room that she has to have a bed in the very room where she sleeps!"

Kind old lady! her benevolence walked ahead of her grammar; but a trifling error in speech is as pardonable in Mrs. Partington as in Henry Clay.

SLANDERERS.

—

"If there is anybody under the canister of heaven that I have in utter excrescence," said Mrs. Partington, "it is a tale-bearer and slanderer, going about, like a vile boa-constructor, circulating his calomel about honest folks. I always know one by his phismahogany. It seems as if Belzebub had stamped him with his private signal, and everything he looks at appears to turn yaller."

And, having uttered this somewhat elaborate speech, she was seized with a fit of coughing, and took some demulcent drops.

A STORMY SEASON.

"Cease, rude Bolus, blustering railer!" said Mrs. Partington, as she reached out into the storm to secure a refractory shutter, and the wind rushed in and extinguished her light, and slammed to the door, and fanned the fire in the grate, and rustled the calico flounce upon the quilt, and peeped into the closet, and under the bed, and contemptuously shook Mrs. Partington's night-jacket, as it hung airing on the chair by the fire, and flirted with her cap-border, as she looked out upon the night. It was a saucy gust. "How it blows!" said she, as she shut down the window. "I hope Heaven will keep the poor sailors safe that go down on the sea in vessels! This must be the obnoxious storm," continued she, "when the sun crosses the Penobscot."

She donned her specs, and sat down to consult her almanac, — next to her Bible in importance, — and she found she was right, while the wind howled around the house most dismally, and yelled wildly down the old chimney.

DIETETICAL COUNSEL.

" You must n't be too greedy, Isaac," said Mrs. Partington, as, with an anxious expression, she marked a strong effort that young gentleman was making to achieve the last quarter of a mince-pie. " You should n't be so glutinous, dear. You must be careful, or you will get something in your elementary canal or sarcophagus one of these days, that will kill you, Isaac (she had been to hear a course of physiological lectures), and then you will have to be buried in the cold ground, and nobody won't never see you no more ; and what will I do, Isaac, when you are cut down in your priming, like a lovely jelly-flower ? "

Much affected by the picture her own prolific fancy had conjured up, she pensively sweetened her tea for the fourth time, and looked earnestly upon Isaac, who, unheeding all she was saying, sat gazing at the street door, revolving in his mind the practicability of ringing the door-bell unperceived, without going outside.

DOMESTIC peace can never be preserved in family jars.

MRS. P. CONFERS WITH PAUL.

—

" AND do you believe in the spirituous knockings ? " asked Mrs. Partington, as she leaned forward over the table, and bent her eyes on a queer individual who had related some wonderful things he had seen. " O, I would so like to have poor Paul come back ! "

A gentle rapping upon the old chest in the corner attracted their attention, and the whole of them immediately surrounded it.

" If it 's Paul's apprehension," said Mrs. Partington, " I know he 'll answer me. Paul, is that you ? "

Knock.

" Just like him," said she, smiling, " when he was living ; he was always tapping when we had anything in the house to tap, did n't you, Paul ? "

Knock.

" Can't you speak to me ? "

Knock.

" Does that mean yes or no ? "

Knock.

" Which does it mean ? "

Knock.

Some of the party suggested that the alphabet should be called, which was done.

" Are you in want of anything ? " said she.

Knock.

" What is it ? "

And the anxious spectators, through the medium of the alphabet, spelled out "S-i-d-u-r."

"It is Paul!" cried the old lady, delightedly; "that's the way he always spelled it. Do you want me to come to you, Paul?"

The answer came back, "No, I'm in better company!"

The old lady turned away mournfully. There was sorrow in the wavy lock of gray that straggled beneath her cap border, — there was a quaver of grief in the tone that inquired for the scissors, — there was a misty vapor upon her specs, like the dew upon the leaves after a rain, — the cap-border, like a flag at half-mast, trailed in woe over the ruin of disappointed affection. At that instant the cover of the chest opened, and the head of Ike, protruding, disclosed the secret of the knockings.

"Ah, you rogue!" said she, a smile dispelling all evidence of disorder, "Ah, you rogue! was it you? You'll never be a good spirit as long as you live, I'm afraid, if you go on so. But I knowed it wasn't Paul!"

There was triumph in her tone, and it seemed as if a whole basket full of sunshine had been upset in that room, it was so pleasant all the rest of the evening.

MRS. PARTINGTON AT THE PLAY.

"THE play-house is the '*way to the pit!*'" said Mrs. Partington, solemnly, and pointing significantly downward.

"But," remonstrated a friend, who had asked her to visit the Museum with him, "there is no pit in this theatre, and the *way* to the pit is removed."

She looked earnestly at him a moment, and then said she would go. The play was the "Stranger," and she was much interested in it.

"Why don't he make it up with her?" she inquired. "What's the sense of being ugly when she's so contricious for what she had done, I should like to know? I think it shows a bad temper in him; and the dear children, too, coming in like little cherubs, to make 'em forget all old troubles and follies! We had n't ought to dwell so upon old grievousness, because we are all liable creturs. How I do pity her!"

And the old lady wept copiously. She would n't leave the house till she ascertained from the policeman whether old Tobias got back his son that had 'listed, for he looked but feeble, she said, when he went away, and the great grief and the long pole the old gentleman carried for a cane must have broken him down.

30

BREACHES OF FAITH.

"BREECHES of faith!" screamed Mrs. Partington, as she heard that term applied to Mexican violations of an armistice. "Well, I wonder what they will have next. I have hearn tell of cloaks of hypocrisy, and robes of purity, but I never heard of breeches of faith before. I hope they're made of something that won't change and wear out, as old Deacon Gudgins' faith did, for his was always changing. He went from believing that nobody would be saved, to believing that all would be, and at last turned out a phrenologer, and did n't believe in nothing! I wonder if it 's as strong as cassimere?"

And she bit off her thread and prepared a new needle-full.

A QUEER CONCEIT.

"WHY don't they make these tragedies turn out different?" said Mrs. Partington, after seeing *Virginius* performed. "I think they might end them with a dance; and all that are killed should take a part in it, just to show folks that they're alive. This, now, was too savage; and when Mr. Virginius got the other gentleman by the throat, I looked round for the police, to see if he would part them, and there he was enjoying it as well as the rest of 'em. I should like to know what he is there for, if it a'n't to keep the peace."

And the old lady was tucked up for the night.

MRS. PARTINGTON ON COLPORTERS.

"So, they've took our minister and made a *coal-porter* of him," said Mrs. Partington to her neighbor, Mrs. Sled. "I suppose they're going to set him to work carrying all the coal in the parish, and so take the bread out of the pockets of the foreigners and Irishmen, poor creturs, that do it now. He preached last Sunday on mortifying the flesh; but when he gets to carrying the baskets, I think he will look like one mortified all over."

She smiled at the conceit, and then turned to see what David said on the subject, and what analogy there was between "hewing of wood, and drawing of water," and coal-portering; but dropped the search on a summons to tea.

"No matter," said she, "it won't hurt him any, and my dear Paul used to say that everything honest was honorable, and that black coat of his'n won't show the coal-dust at all."

FOURTH OF JULY.

saac!" said Mrs. Partington, rapping on the window, as she saw the boy in the act of putting half a bunch of crackers into the pocket of a countryman who stood viewing the procession. The caution came too late, and the individual was astonished! Isaac had stepped inside the door to await the explosion, and the old lady met him in the entry. "O, you spirit of mischief!" cried she, "what will become of you if you go on in this way? Is this all your idees of liberty and regeneration, that you must fill that poor man's pockets with your crackers? Do you suppose this was all that the days of 7 by 6 was made for? I should think you would be ashamed to look upon your Uncle Paul's picter there, and hide your face in conclusion, arter behaving so! Ah!" she mused, "how different boys are now from what they used to be! — so wild, so rakeless and tricky" — (crack!) — "what's that? I should like to know who fired that. It was a great piece of impudence" — (crack!) — "goodness gracious! somebody must be throwin' 'em into the windows." She ran to look out. Not a soul was near that could have done it. Crack! another explosion at her feet, and she looked round. Isaac sat demurely eating some gingerbread by the table, but said nothing. There was an expression about his mouth which looked torpedoish, and for a moment she mistrusted him; but *he* could n't have done it, he was so quiet, and she shut the window that opened upon the street, to prevent their throwing in any more.

SEEING THE FIREWORKS.

"O, DEAR!" said Mrs. Partington, stretching herself on her toes to get a better look at the fireworks. "I always wish I was seven foot tall at times like this."

"And I wish I was *nine* foot," said the little woman before her, spitefully.

"How I hate to see people so selfish! don't you, Mrs. Brown?" whispered Mrs. Partington to her neighbor. "There — there — they are touching off the volcano, I vow!" said Mrs. P.; "now look and see if the burning lather runs down the hill this way!"

And the old lady looked anxiously toward the Park.

30*

THE TELEGRAPH.

—

MRS. PARTINGTON is much prejudiced against the magnetic telegraph, and takes an entirely new ground in her opposition to it.

" *You* may send *your* letters on it," said she to the philosopher, " if you 're a mind to; but I shan't trust one of mine on it while people can cut it off before it gets there, and let the whole world into family secrets. And how presumptuous it is, too, for men to draw heaven's blessed lightning down and set it a dancing on a tight wire, like a very circuit-rider ! It 's absolute blasphemy, and outrage on the highway, and agin all natur and scriptur."

And she turned to the books to find an appropriate text, but changed the subject by commencing a discussion with her niece on the relative merits of ball yarn and skein, and, taking her *sides*, she went on like a jolly old wheelbarrow.

———

LET none be vain of imagined superiority over their brother men; for whatever advantage may be fancied in one respect, in another there may be a deficiency. The man who has law and divinity at his fingers' ends, in the lore of horse-flesh may be instructed by his stable-boy ; and she who speaks Italian and embroiders, can, perhaps, take lessons in yarn-stockings from Mrs. Partington. Franklin, who could draw the lightning from heaven, made a poor hand at tending a baby.

A CHRISTMAS STORY

A STORY FOR CHRISTMAS.

IT was with a clouded brow and an angry eye that young Frank Harlowe stood looking upon his father's face, and hearkening to his words, as he violently rebuked him. The flush upon the old man's cheek betokened the tempest that raged within his breast, and his raised and clenched hand descended in fearful emphasis as he uttered the words — "Obey me, or, by Heaven, you leave my house forever!"

Mr. Harlowe, the father of Frank, was one of those unfortunate men, whose impulses are stronger than their powers of resistance. His passion once aroused, reason, affection, common kindness were forgotten in the storm that held him in mastery. The hasty and severe word that conveys such bitterness in its utterance, in his moods of temper was always ready, and the hasty blow fell upon his children with cruel violence, at the least provocation. Correction they never received. It was the vindictive visitation of an avenger of wrong rather than the chastisement of a parent.

At heart Mr. Harlowe was a kind man, and oftentimes and bitterly, when the storm had blown by, and his mind was calm again, did he repent with a sincere repentance the evil he had done, of which he was fully sensible. Benevolent, intelligent, noble-spirited, self-sacrificing, as occasion called for action, he had won himself a name for probity and usefulness that was enviable, and, but for the turbulence of temper above described, few finer men could be found. This weakness was his besetting sin, his temptation, and his will was insufficient to resist it.

Frank Harlowe, his youngest son and favorite, was his counterpart in body and mind. Handsome, intelligent and witty, at seventeen he was the favorite of all in the village in which he lived. His generosity was unbounded, and the tendrils of his youthful nature shot forth and strengthened in the fertile soil of congeniality. At social gatherings he was the crowning spirit. His voice rang merriest at the harvest home, his story elicited the warmest plaudits at the husking-frolic, and in the old woods his song echoed through its sombre arches with the joyousness of unrestricted freedom. No jealous rivalry stood in the way of his supremacy; young and old admitted his claim to the distinction, and the smile of beauty — the rustic rose of rural artlessness — beamed for him with constant and kindly glow.

Such was Frank Harlowe in his social intercourse, petted and happy in the genial flow of his unembittered enjoyment; but at home he was a different being. The contrast between the sphere of home and that of neighborhood was too marked. The reverence due parental authority was too little excited by parental love. Disobedience to imperious command was followed by violence of invective or blows, and his high spirit revolted at the irksomeness of domestic oppression. His two elder brothers had no sympathy with him. They were plodding and matter-of-fact men. Taking from their mother a more passive and quiescent nature than his own, they grubbed along the way of life, like the oxen they drove, that knew no joy beyond the herbage they cropped, having no aspiration beyond the bound of their enclosure. Content with old routines, no new hope obtruded upon their ruminations. They frowned upon the bold boy, whose spirit and brilliancy cast a reproach upon their lethargy, and they rejoiced when tne reproof came to curb his ambition. Home was no longer home to him; the ties of consanguinity were to him iron bonds from whose release he would pray to be freed; his mother's love alone sanctified the existence he led, — it was the one solitary star in his night of domestic gloom.

His affections, thus turned from the home circle, had concentrated upon one, the fairest of the village, but whose coquettish predilections had rendered her obnoxious to censure, and her fame having reached his father, the knowledge of Frank's attachment for her had provoked a discussion, the result of which was the imperative command with which my story commences, a command that he must renounce her forever.

The boy stood gazing upon his father, with a flashing eye and a swelling breast, as he spoke. Feelings too powerful for utterance were depicted in the look he gave, and he left the room with an expression of bitter rage.

The next morning there was confusion in Mr. Harlowe's house. Frank had fled, no one knew whither, and the circle, whose union was so illy cemented, was broken. A letter in the village post-office explained the reason. It read as follows : —

" Dear Mother, — It grieves me to bid you farewell, but longer sufferance from father's tyrannical usage is impossible. I go to seek my fortune, and when we meet again may it be when he and I shall have learned a lesson from our separation, and the alienation of father and child may be forgotten in the renewed intercourse of man and man. Farewell, mother, and may you be more happy than I should have been able to make you had I lived with you a thousand years. Farewell. Remember sometimes your poor boy,   FRANK."

The letter fell like a thunderbolt upon that household, so unprepared for such an event, and deep contrition wrung the erring father's heart, who saw too late the evil he had wrought. The spirited boy had been his favorite, so like him was he in form and mind. He remembered that no word spoken to him in kindness had been unheeded. He heard his praise in every mouth, admitted the justness of the meed that was awarded him, and every word and every thought was a dagger to his soul in view of the ruin he had caused. Then, for the first time, he felt the weight of the responsibility that rested upon him as a parent, and trembled as he reflected how far he might be instrumental in his son's eternal doom. Too late came penitence for the past, but he vowed reform for the future, and prayed for strength to fulfil his vow.

A change came over the man and his home. The mould of years and care mingled with the raven hues of youth, for years had passed and no line of remembrance

had come from the absent boy. The brothers had married, and had children, and the old homestead was glad
with the music of childish laughter, and a sad happiness
smiled upon the lives of Mr. and Mrs. Harlowe. The
mother had mourned for her child, and his remembrance
often came to her in the voices of her grandchildren, and
in the sweet reminiscences which solitude brought. The
hope of seeing him had long died out in her breast; for
twelve weary years had elapsed since he went away.

The village had changed. The young and joyous
companions of Frank had turned into grave family men,
or had moved to strange cities, and become the devotees
of the money-god, or worshipped Fame in high places.
The maids with whom he had sported had lost their
smiles in the matronly cares of life, or had transferred
them to their children, upon whom they bloomed again.
The coquette of Frank's old idolatry had years before given
place to younger rivals, and mourned her faded charms
in singleness of state. The village had become populous,
and new steeples gleamed above the trees in the sunlight,
and new streets and houses marked the steps of progress.
A railroad whistle greeted the morning sun instead of the
song of birds as of old, and the quiet of village life had
been usurped by the confusion of city habits.

Frank was forgotten in the march of present excitement, or only remembered as a pleasant dream.

It was Christmas night in the year of grace '50, and
a pleasant party had met in the house of Mr. Harlowe,
to celebrate the birthday anniversary of his eldest grand-
son. The wind howled around the old mansion-house,
and growled down the spacious chimney, as if threaten-

ing the elements of geniality, that reigned below, with a submerging visit. The snow rattled against the windows, red with indoor light, and piled itself in little heaps upon the sills. But all was unheeded by the party within, and the wind and snow were unheard amid the music of mirth. The song was trilled from pretty lips, and manly voices joined in a chorus of praise to the festive season, when a loud knock of the ancient brazen lion upon the door arrested every attention. The sound reverberated along the old entry, and up the broad stairway, and through the large and airy rooms, with remarkable freedom for such an intruder, at such a time. The timid shrunk at the sound, as from a boding of evil, and anxiety marked every face. The door was opened, and a female form was ushered in, in whose scant and ragged habiliments poverty was but too plainly read, and in the bronzed and wrinkled face, revealed by the removal of a red hood, were seen the traces of want and exposure. Her keen, black eye, as she entered, surveyed the scene, and her bronzed complexion glowed ruddily in the firelight.

"Good people," she said, in a cracked and tuneless voice, that made the flesh of her hearers creep at its sound, "I am weary and hungry, — give me of your bounty, in the name of Him who upon this day took upon himself the condition of man. I am weary, — I am hungry."

An appeal thus made could not be resisted, and the best the house afforded was provided for the poor stranger. The voracity with which she ate attracted the attention of the circle, fully attesting her famished condition; and a glance at her apparel confirmed the impression of want and distress, and mercy conquered the disgust which her presence had at first occasioned. Her feet protruded through her travel-worn shoes, and the snow melted from their soles and ran down upon the sanded floor.

As soon as her hunger was appeased, she turned to depart, but the voice of Mr. Harlowe asked her to remain, and, in sympathetic tones, reminded her of the inclemency of the night.

The woman expressed her thanks gracefully, and seated herself by the fireside. The sport went on, noisily and happily, when it became whispered that the old dame was one of those weird people who tell fortunes by the stars, or more ignoble means, and open to view the destinies of men that lay concealed in the future.

" Can you tell fortunes, good woman?" asked one of the youngest and boldest.

" I have travelled far," replied the beldame; " and I have learned strange arts in my wanderings. The heavens are open to my gaze, and the stars, where the mysteries of fate are hid, are as the printed page. The human palm is to me a key to character. Who will test my power?"

One by one did the company pass before her, and the prescience she displayed was most marvellous. The lines of the hand seemed pregnant with meaning, and the past life of each individual was read with an accuracy that gave importance to her predictions for the future. Scenes were recalled to many that had long been forgotten, — loves that had been disappointed, hopes that had been destroyed, prospects that had been blasted, and many a tear was shed at the recollection of some old grief revealed by the power of that singular woman.

At length Mr. Harlowe presented his hand for examination. Gazing upon it a moment intently, with a voice choked by emotion, she said, — "Here is violence and strife; the line of life is crossed by threads of bitterness and woe, and the whole of its deep course is marked by traces of grief. Tears, tears are here, and the lines of penitence and anguish of soul are strangely interwoven with the strong lines of resolution. I see that a deep sorrow is yours, — the result of fierce passion, repented of and subdued. Is it not so?"

She fixed her eyes suddenly upon Mr. Harlowe's face. It was pallid as death, and the tears stood in his eye. "Yes," answered he, and trembled as he spoke; "God knows my sin, and God knows my repentance. Secret tears have been my portion for years; and, O, what would I not give if the memory of my wrong might be wiped away!"

He bowed his head upon his hands, and sobbed in the anguish of his spirit, and Mrs. Harlowe wept in sympathy with her husband, whose deep grief she had thus discovered, which had long been concealed beneath the calm exterior of philosophical resignation.

"Woman!" he cried at last, "what is the future of this picture? Is there no balm in store for my wounded spirit?" He grasped her hand forcibly, as if he would have wrung from it an answer to his question.

"Yes," said she, with deep emotion, "there is a future of peace and happiness in store for you, and the sun of your declining years shall be radiant with serene splendor, and, — thank God, who has given me power to verify my prophecy, — " Father ! mother ! behold your son ! "

He threw off his ragged habiliments as he spoke, removed the gray and matted hair from his brow, and the patches from his cheeks, and stood before the company in the noble form — matured in manly strength and beauty — of Frank Harlowe.

There was a new joy in the house that night at the wanderer's return, and tears and smiles mingled at the recital of his story. The wide world he had travelled, and he had learned and profited by the lessons it had taught him. He had returned home rich in gold, but he was richer in the spirit he had gained. It had become softened by the trials it had suffered, until it had brought him back to his father's house, and to his mother's feet.

His letters home had failed to reach their destination, and, deeming himself an outcast, he had at length refused to write at all. He had married a lady of wealth, and had become a denizen of a far-away city. But the thoughts of home pressed upon him, and the smile of his mother haunted his sleep with fond persistence, and he longed to see once more the " old, familiar faces " that were his companions in childhood. He had thus come back to revisit the home of his early life. Stopping at the hotel he had made such inquiries concerning his old friends as led him into the secret of their past lives. Then, assuming his disguise, he went to his father's house in the manner above stated. The secret of his soothsaying ability was thus revealed. The whole of

Christmas night was occupied with the story of Frank's adventures, and in thanksgivings for the reünion.

The next summer a splendid mansion graced the hill opposite the old homestead, which soon became and is now the residence of Frank Harlowe, Esq., who, retired from business, has here settled down to enjoy himself amid the never-forgotten scenes of his boyhood, and to endeavor to make up by attention to his parents for the long years he had failed in his duty to them.

Mr. Harlowe is a happy old man, and instils it as a sacred lesson into the minds of his grandchildren to beware of cultivating a hasty temper, which had been so full of misery to himself.

MRS. P. AMONG THE ANIMALS.

ou call this a carryvan, don't you?" said Mrs. Partington at the menagerie. "May be it is; but I should like to know where the silks and other costive things are that we read of, which the carryvans carry over the deserts of Sarah, in the eastern country."

" The elephant has them in his trunk, marm," replied the keeper.

"Then that is the reason, I s'pose, why he always carries it before him, so he can have an eye on it. But what is this animal with a large wart on his nose?"

" That is the gnu, marm."

" Mercy on me!" exclaimed Mrs. P., " this must be one of them foreign news that the steamer brings over. They feed 'em, I dare say, on potatoes and vegetables, and that is why breadstuffs and flour are so awful dear most always after they arrive!" and the old lady left soon after, full of new light, and admiration for the monkeys.

31*

A LEAF FROM MEMORY.

—

As Mrs. Partington stepped from the steamboat, she perused the signboard which requested passengers not to leave till the boat was secured to the drop.

"How different from my poor Paul!" murmured she, as memory awakened something long forgotten. "How different from my poor Paul! for he never would leave till the 'drop' was secured to him. Dear, dear! it seems as if I could see him now, holding to his lovely lips the big quart tumbler, which he used to call his 'horn of plenty;' and plenty it was, to be sure, and often too much for him. How much better off he'd have been if he had n't taken such deep importations!"

And she passed up the steamboat wharf, her mind still pondering on the inscription that had so vividly recalled the past, and did n't even recognize the minister as he bowed his sedate neck to her.

———

It is often shocking to perceive, in "thrilling tales of the seas," the indifference with which authors tell us of the winds "whistling through the shrouds!" as if such wanton levity did n't deserve a rebuke.

PEACEFUL COGITATIONS.

—

"When will distention and strife cease among our foreign relations ? " said Mrs. Partington with a sigh, as she looked abstractedly at the black profile on the wall, as if she thought it could answer the question.   " When will distention cease ?   The peace congress did n't do no good 's I see, for the Rushins and Austriches are a carryin' on jest as bad as ever they did, committin' all sorts of outridges and wrongs on the Hung'ry.   Heaven never smiles on them that distresses the poor.   We ought to hold the Rushers and all that belongs to 'em in excrescence, — I don't know about hating the Rushy Salve, though, because that ha'n't done us no harm, — and the Austriches, too, that lives on nails and gimblets, that the wild-beast man told us about — the onnateral heathen !   Then the Frenchmen are all in a commotion, and I should think they would be, eatin' frogs and sich things, and the English ministers are quarrelin' like ' dog's delight.'   Where it will end I can't see."

She laid down the Times as she said "I can't see," and Ike, who had been burning off the outside pages of Leavitt's Almanac while she was speaking, here poked the light out, leaving the room and the subject equally in the dark.

HOME MISSIONS.

"So Mrs. Brattle has become a member of the Home Missions," said Mrs. Partington. "Well, I am rejoiced to hear it, for her poor husband's sake; for, though I think it a husband's duty to help about house some, he should n't be left to wash and cook for himself and children, and mend his own clothes, as poor Brattle has had to while she was running round. I hope the *home* missions will keep her at home now;" and the old lady stirred her souchong with animation, as she made the comment, and did n't see that Ike was making tremendous havoc with the pound-cake.

IT is astonishing what opposite effects will be produced by the same cause. As, for instance, suppose a blacking, whose principal component is alcohol; its effect, when applied to boots, is apparent in the cracking of the leather, and in the opening of fissures admitting the free passage of water; when applied to man, in quantity, the same fluid has the effect of making him " tight."

OLD ROGER AND THE BOARDERS.

OLD ROGER attempted the following upon the boarders one morning. They were all sitting quietly at breakfast, when, with a most provoking smile around the corners of his mouth, as if he himself fully appreciated what he was going to say, he asked if any of them could tell him why a man deeply impressed with reverence was like a very hungry one. The idea of hunger associated with the bountiful board at which they were seated, caused the blood to rush through every vein of the landlady's body, to her face, for she felt hurt. The boarders all said they did n't know, — they could n't see the least resemblance.

"Why," said he, chuckling, "it is because he inwardly feels a gnaw."

They could n't understand that he meant "an awe," and he said it was no use talking to men whose stomachs were full of the bounties of life. This he said to propitiate the landlady, who was all smiles again, as bright and sparkling as the coffee in his cup, which, catching the rays of the sun, danced and shimmered on the wall overhead.

BAD TEMPERS.

"How these shopkeepers will fib it!" said Mrs. Partington, with an expression of pain on her venerable features; "that young man I bought these needles of said they were good-tempered; — only see how spitefully this one has masecrated my finger."

She held up the wounded member, a small red spot denoting the injury. The sewing-circle sympathized with her.

"It will feel better, I dare say, after it has done aching," continued she, as she took the last stitch in a "thick little boy's jacket," and rolled up her work for the day. Many a pair of razeēd trousers has the world seen added to its wealth, and the world never knew where they came from — perhaps did n't care.

GIVING THANKS.

"May the Lord make us thankful for the critter comforts spread out before us!" said Deacon Haze, over the hard-boiled beef on the table.

"Well, perhaps he will," says Mrs. Partington to herself; "but it seems to me it would be easier to be thankful if the meat was tenderer;" and then, like a barefooted boy, she went cautiously among the muscles.

A GOOD DEAL OF TRUTH.

"Poor Girls' Fair!" said Mrs. Partington, as she spelled out the inscription upon a flag that swung across Washington street, her eyes dimming with the vapors that arose from her warm heart; "Poor girls' fare! indeed they do, and fare hard, too, God help 'em, many of 'em, — fare hard with them that should treat 'em better, trying to rise till all their risible powers is gone, and they are shipracked and cast away and driv to making trowsis and shirts for a living, and die on it. I do pity 'em."

A melancholy tone pervaded her speech and thoughts the rest of the day; her snuff, the choicest maccaboy, bore a taint of wormwood and rue; her tea was salt, as if tears were an ingredient in its composition; her specs revealed red eyes in every visitor, and the faces of the "poor girls" looked out at her from the teapot and the sugar-bowl, the lamp, and the little scrap-box on the work-table. Bless her kind heart!

———

There is a wide difference between the throes of an expiring Titan and the throws of a straggling tight un.

POLITICAL EXTRAVAGANCE RE-BUKED.

"I DON'T blame people for complaining about the extravagance and costiveness of government," said Mrs. Partington, as she was reading an ardent appeal to the people in a political newspaper. She always took an interest in politics after Paul was defeated one year as a candidate for inspector. "I don't blame 'em a mite. Here they are now, going to canvassing the state, as if the airth was n't good enough for 'em to walk on. I wonder why they don't get ile-cloth or Kidminister, and done with it."

" And I heard yesterday," said Ike, putting his small oar in, " that some of 'em was going to scour the country to get voters."

" Well," continued she, " that would be better than throwing dust in the people's eyes, as they say some of 'em do. Canvassing the state, indeed ! "

She fell into an abstraction on the schemes of politicians, and took seven pinches of snuff, in rapid succession, to aid her deliberations.

SLEIGH-RIDING.

s the last paving-stone hides itself beneath the descending snow, the jingle of the bells informs us that sleighing's come, and from that minute riding on runners becomes a mania. Every young head, and some pretty old heads, are full of expedients for fun. Boys hunt up their sleds and dash out of doors, to the terror of nervous mammas, who prophesy disaster dire for their progeny. The old sleighs and new sleighs, the big sleighs and little sleighs, are put in requisition, and the streets are full of the "music of the bells, bells, bells!" All the day long their silvery notes are sounding in our ears, and late o' nights staid citizens who are staying at home are disturbed by the frantic yells of returning sleigh-parties, mingling with the noise of bells, making the hour hideous; or the sound of voices in cheerful song making melody with the tintinabulous accompaniment. We like to hear this last; we gladly

listen to its approach as we snuggle beneath the blankets
in the watches of the night, and distinguish the chord of
male and female 'voices in some familiar strain, and are
almost sorry to hear it melt away upon the midnight air,
in distance, like voices heard in dreams.

There used to be great sport to us in sleighing,
though we never were sanguinary; but time has tempered us by matters of graver import. We can indulge
now in little beside our daily omnibus rides, and can
hardly realize in these the buoyancy of old enthusiasm.
We watch for the appearance of our domicil, coming to
meet us, and pull the check-string at our door, careful
not to go a step beyond, so little do we feel now about
riding. But in the old time—Jehu! how our heart
leaped to the music of the bells! how quickly our pulse
throbbed to the maddening impulse of the moment as we
— quiet and sedate though we now are — flew over the
slippery road. Hi-yah! hi-yah! hi-yah!—how we
dashed on our course, leaving house and tree and mile-
stone behind us! We knew no greater speed than this,
for it was ante-railroad time, and the "iron-horse"—
we think some one has given it this name before — had
not then "annihilated space," as we believe somebody
has said. We loved to feel the cool air revel upon our
cheek and whistle among our hair, and, as it came up
from over the smoothly frozen ponds, with stinging force,
we laughed at its violence in the glow of excitement.
The hoar-frost gleamed upon hair, and eyelash, and fur
collar, and our breath streamed away behind us on the
cold air, like steam. Hi-yah! hi-yah! hi-yah! we

cried. The old pine-woods echoed the eldritch scream,
and people in distant cottages caught the sound, and
listened to the unusual strain, and the wood-choppers
ceased from their labors to catch a glimpse of the fleeting
fiends that awakened such strange echoes. Then a stop
at " mine inn," and the old-fashioned " suthin' hot "—
we took mulled cider, of course — made all right for the
return, and a ride by starlight closed the day's joy. It
was joy then. It was long before we knew Mrs. Partington and Ike, and the perplexity of types.

Ghosts of big sleighs come up before us, brimfull of
happy people nestled beneath the buffaloes, and hats
and hoods occupy alternate positions throughout the
party. Pleasant voices come back to us, and the " old
familiar faces" renew themselves to us. Delightful!
But as memory recalls the happy scene, the thought of a
fair form and face, the brightest of the group, flits like a
spirit across our mind, leaving behind a shadow of sorrow
and gloom. Ah, Maria! The sweet eye and voice that
animated and blessed us are now blessing other spheres
— the music of that glad tongue is now attuned to the
music of celestial harmonies. There is no memory of
joy that we may recall, however bright, but has some
woe connected intimately with it, and twinned smiles and
tears make up the sum of the past.

" Hi-yah! hi-yah! hi-yah! " comes up to our domicil
and startles us as we write ; and, dashing along the nearly
deserted street — alarming ponderous watchmen on their
walk — a sleigh comes furiously by, and another, and
another, and the music of the bells chimes gratefully

upon our ear. Here is a sleigh-ride song, that may
do to sing some time, if any one can find a tune to
fit it : —

> Over the snow, over the snow,
> Away we go, away we go !
> The earth gleams white
> 'Neath the stars to-night,
> And all is bright
> Above and below.
>
> Old Care good-by, old Care good-by,
> From you we fly, from you we fly —
> As if on wings,
> Our fleet steed springs,
> And the welkin rings
> With our joyous cry.
>
> Gay Mirth is here, gay Mirth is here,
> Our hearts to cheer, our hearts to cheer :
> While on we glide,
> There 's one by our side
> To cheer or to chide,
> Who is always dear.
>
> Over the snow, over the snow,
> Away we go, away we go !
> There 's freedom rare
> Abroad in the air,
> Everywhere,
> Above and below.

HUNK FOR THE UNION.

" THE Union dissolved ! " said Mrs. Partington, with her specs upon her forehead, and her finger raised, as if admonishing the universe. " Dissolve the Union ! and who would dare assassinate such a thing as that, — such an outrage on the body's politics ? I thought it would come to this. And if they dissolve the Union, which on 'em will have the children ? or will they let 'em grow up without nobody to look arter their moral training, poor things ? Never think of dissolving it, nor breaking it. ' What God has joined together let not man put us under,' and that's gospel truth; and they can't do it, if we stick by each other."

With what an emphatic, *italic* jerk the snuff-box came out, as she concluded speaking ! The remembrance of her felicitous union with Paul crossed her mind, and the remembered pain of its dissolution mingled with her patriotic emotion, and she dropped a tear as she uttered, " What would our foreign relations think of it ? " The union was safe from that day, thenceforth and forever.

MRS. PARTINGTON says it seems to her a queer provision of natur that eggs should be " skeerce " when they are so dear.

32*

LEAF FROM PHILANTHROPOS' JOURNAL.

—

MONDAY morning, 7 A. M. — Summoned to the door when shaving. A boy after cold victuals. Sorry we had none. Ours were all hot. These evils come not as single spies, but in battalions. Seven beggar boys in succession for *cold* victuals. Strange that they should be so anxious to have it *cold*. It shows a corrupt taste. Probably the vitiating effect of poverty.

8 A. M. — Woman and child asking alms. Heart bled for them. Strong smell of gin. Persuaded that it was a gentle soporific for child, nothing more. Subject to colic. Husband in California — been there three years. Seven children dependent on her exertions. Did n't seem to exert herself much. Promised to call and see her.

9 A. M. — Foreigner with a certificate. Fine-looking man. Certificate reads right. Signed "John Smith." Honest-sounding name! Think I 've heard it before. Horrible volcano in Italy. Swallowed up his vineyard, and threw him and a large family upon the world. Heaven help him! Can't speak a word of English. Told me so himself. Felt strongly inclined to aid him. Will hand his name to the Wandering Samaritan Society.

10 A. M. — Dressed to go out. Gentleman, a stranger, asked me if I had a ninepence in my pocket, and if I would loan it to him to procure a letter from the post-office. Sorry I had n't the precise amount, but gave him

a dime. Was surprised to see him go into a drinking-house. Suppose it must be one of the new sub-offices.

11 A. M. — Asked by a little barefoot boy for a cent. Implored me, for his mother's sake, to give him one. Knew the deceptions of this kind of beggars, and refused. The urchin called me a most scandalous name, and followed behind me, repeating it, though several of my friends were in hearing. Gave him a quarter to get rid of him. Shall never forget the horrid leer he gave me. Great depravity.

TRAINING DAYS.

"I DON'T object to training-days altogether," said Mrs. Partington to the Major, as the Ancient and Honorables passed her door; "the dress looks well, and the children likes the music; and I know this is moral training, because the Governor is there and his suet, with his chateau on his head and his sword by his side. How finely he does look! So bold and portable! I declare, he looks too good to be a malicious officer!"

She here leaned out of the door to catch a last view of the "corpse" as it turned a near corner, and a portly-looking gentleman under a cocked hat waved his hand to her as the pageant swept from her view. Mrs. Partington resumed her knitting, that had been disturbed by the music.

LIFE—LIFE—HOW CURIOUS IT IS.

—

"Curious" is the word — we would n't have any other, for it expresses the very thing. How curious it is, from the cradle to the grave! The hopes of the young are curious — reaching forward into the future, and building castles in perspective for their possessors, that will crumble before them ere they arrive at that spot in time where their fabrics are located.

How curious it is, the first dawning of love, where the young heart surrenders itself to its dreams of bliss, illumined with stars and garnished with moonshine! How curious it is, when matrimony crowns the wishes, and cares, fancied to be surmounted by ardent hearts, are found to be but just commenced! How curious it is! says the young mother, as she spreads upon hers the tiny hand of her babe, and endeavors to read in its dim lines the fortunes of her child. Curious indeed would such revealings be, could she there read them.

How curious it is, the greed for gain that marks and mars the life of man, leading him away after strange gods, forgetting all the object and good of life in a heartless chase for a phantom light, that leaves him at last in three-fold Egyptian darkness! How curious it is, the love of life that clings to the old, and draws them back imploringly to the scenes of earth — begging for a longer look at time and its frivolities, with eternity and its joys within their reach! How curious it is, when at last the great end draws nigh — the glazing eye, the struggle, the groan, proclaiming dissolution, and the still clay that denotes the extinguishment of the spark known as life ! How curious it is, that the realities of the immortal world should be based upon the crumbling ashes of this, and that the path to infinite light should lie through the dark shadow of the grave ! How curious it is, in its business and pleasures, its joys and sorrows, its hopes and fears, its temptations and triumphs ! And as we contemplate life in all its phases we must exclaim —" How curious it is ! "

AN INTERESTING FACT.

DR. DIGG and Old Roger were conversing upon wonders in nature, and the doctor had given a long account of discoveries he had made, during his travels in the East, of intelligence in different kinds of animals — the elephant, the ichneumon, and Oxford County bear, being particularly mentioned for their sagacity. With regard to the last-named description of animals, he relied principally upon the testimony of his friend Fitzwhistler, who had given him some wonderful particulars concerning their habits, Mr. F. having stated to him, during a conversation, that the Oxford County bear has been known to be at times devotedly attached to New England rum, and to make no great scruples about using, now and then, tobacco in its various forms, which he considered a degree of intelligence very nearly approximating to the refinement of human civilization, and surpassing that of all other animals.

Roger admitted the truth in the main of what the doctor submitted, but said that however much he was disposed to yield to Fitzwhistler and the doctor in most matters, in this one particular of superiority he must differ from them, for there were animals in his own State, New Hampshire, that excelled them all. The doctor had not claimed for either class he had named any knowledge in mathematics; but, from a long residence in the Granite State, he had found it generally known that among the serpent family there were frequently found great adders.

The doctor, with that greatness of mind so characteristic of the individual, immediately tendered his hat to Roger, who magnanimously placed it again upon the pundit's head.

NEW PATENTS.

We often read, in Patent-office reports, of patents being granted for improvement in "governors." We don't care how much governors are improved, and all efforts in this direction will receive the full "consent of the governed." We have seen, too, not long since, that a patent has been given for an improvement in "railing." This invention must be of vast utility in quarrelsome neighborhoods, where the quality of the railing has long needed improvement.

SHILLABER'S POEMS

NOW READY, THE THIRD EDITION

OF

Rhymes with Reason and without.

By BEN. P. SHILLABER

ONE ELEGANT 12mo. VOLUME. 336 pp., AND A PORTRAIT OF THE AUTHOR, ON
STEEL.   PRICE $1 00

NOTICES OF THE PRESS.

Our pen sheds ink very cheerfully, in announcing that Mrs. Partington makes her appearance among the poets and poetesses, in elegant party dress. That is to say, Mr. Benjamin P. Shillaber, who has been the amanuensis. or "writing medium," of the benevolent and venerable lady, has given the public a volume of verses, entitled "Rhymes with Reason and without." Many of them have appeared in the *Post* and the *Carpet Bag*. If a tenth part of the people, to whom these pieces have given pleasure purchase the volume, the author will be properly complimented and rewarded. We cannot doubt that Mrs. Partington's wit and wisdom will be *bound* to have a place on every centre table.—*Boston Transcript.*

Mr. Shillaber ranks as one of the finest writers of the present time. As a poet, editor, gentleman, and scholar, we will endorse him to any amount. it will be a "card" for the publisher.—*Lynn News.*

The work, we have no doubt, will be sought after with great avidity by the lovers of choice and elegant poetry. Mr. Shillaber, besides being a witty and racy prose writer, is a poet of much excellence, and, more than all, a whole-hearted and estimable gentleman.—*Boston Times.*

We confess to a liking of the poetry and the man, whom we knew before the world knew his writings. A retiring man, and of singular modesty, Mr. S. would never have made his advent with a book, save through the solicitations of friends. The poems are of undoubted merit, and have received favorable notices from the first writers in the country. Mr. Bryant, of the *New-York Evening Post*, himself perhaps the first poet of America, accords unqualified praise to the "Rhymes."—*Kennebec Journal.*

Mr. S. is a favorite with the public, the whole reading public; and when the cold effusions of poets of greater pretensions lie on the booksellers' shelves, the varied and genuine humor which marks his productions will find their way to the heart of the public, and win for him a fame such as he deserves.—*Olive Branch.*

A collection of the fugitive pieces of an excellent-hearted and intelligent man, who is almost world-wide known as the veritable Mrs. Partington *herself*, who has created almost as many broad grins as Hood, in his time, and whose wit and humor have always a genial character, which never wounds of itself, but rather disarms sarcasm in others. These Rhymes are modestly put forth by the author, who lays no claim to be considered either a Milton or a Beranger ; and yet in their homely modesty their lies more real merit than in many a pretending volume, which is lauded in proportion, apparently, as it lacks merit. and requires puffing to keep it from tumbling by its dead weight to the dull earth There are many pieces of genuine merit. which no one can read without pleasure, and none which will sink to mediocrity. Throughout the volum· there are displays of wit, hum·r, and pathos ; and the pieces are of such convenient length. and so various, that no one will ever lay down the volume from fatigue, as he would an epic, but be sure to find something agreeable to wile away pleasantly some leisure moments.—*Providence Post.*

Mr. Shillaber is now best known as the originator of that most glorious myth, Mrs. Partington ; but, as we predicted months ago, the publication of these poems will place his title to fame on even a surer footing. He lays no claim to that finished e'egance of style that comes from the careful study and elaborate imitation of classic models; but he is a poet such as Horace speaks of,—one who "was born. not made." The printing-office has been his o ly college,—the various phases of human nature, as seen in real life, his favorite text-book. One of the most marked characteristics of his writings is the indomitable good humor that pervades them Although he has all his life earned his bread by the sweat of his brow, working early and late to secure a bare competence, neither in his prose nor in his verse is there the slightest trace of the cynicism and moroseness that a continual struggle with poverty is apt to beget. He carries a brave, generous, trusting heart in his bosom, and you recognize its throb in every line he writes.—*Portland Eclectic.*

We are glad Mr. Shillaber has concluded to collect his fugitive pieces in book form. Some of the sweetest and most pathetic, as well as many of the humorous poetic productions which have been "going the rounds" of the newspaper press for the last five years, without the name of the modest author attached, are from his pen. We know of no writer who puts more heart and soul—more genuine good feeling, and genial, glowing humor—into his compositions. His poems, in a handsome volume, must be popular, appealing, as they do, directly to the sympathies of the great brotherhood of humanity.—*Yankee Blade.*

In truth we know of few political compositions of the day so well worthy of preservation as Mr. Shillaber's They are not often highly imaginative; they are not mystified by artistic polish ; there is no straining for effect in them ; but as simple, natural, spontaneous expressions of a fine poetic soul they have not been surpassed by any modern writer. They are at times exquisit ly touching ; at others, they glow and sparkle with the humor, wit and fun, which have given the author of Mrs. Partington's sayings so wide a reputation. Rhymes and measures gush forth from his heart. like crystal rills from pebbly springs ; his fancies laugh and babble between grassy banks, refreshing every lip that tastes them. His poems are vital ; they give us new glimpses of life ; they make us happier and better.—*True Flag.*

Mr Shillaber is exceedingly successful in comic verse. and especially so, if not so broadly, in a certain sly and pleasant mingling of the grave and gay, the satiric and the kindly. He writes earnestly and feelingly, also, in the pathetic. Very many of the "Wideswarth" sonnets give the best idea of his peculiar powers, which consist, for the most part, in a quick and thorough perception of the real significance, and of the ludicrous and serious aspect of things, a lively wit and a ready command of language—the whole being toned off with a generally philosophical idea of human life, with its joys and sorrows. —*Boston Post.*

We do not know when we have read a volume of poems with so much pleasure as this. It contains not "Rhymes" merely, but much true, living poetry, pathos, sentiment, vivid description, original thought, enlivened by the most gen al humor. The creation of Mrs. Partington was enough to prove the author a man of rea' wit and origina' genius, but we were hardly prepared for the varied powers which this book exhibits. and especially for the depth and tenderness of feeling displayed in many of the pieces For fine genial humor, rarely or never degenerating into coarseness, and often intermingled and adorned with true and sincere sentiment, we know of no American writer that equals Mr. Shillaber. His wit, we think, fully equals that of our celebrated Dr. Holmes; and in facility and ease of versification he is in no respect inferior.— *New Hampshire Gazette.*

SHILLABER'S POEMS

Can be ordered through any Bookseller in the United States, or by remitting the Price to the Publisher. It will be sent by Mail, Post-paid.

J. C. DERBY, Pub'isher,

8 PARK PLACE, N. Y.